DEAD RINGER

Dead Ringer

Judith Cook

Severn House Large Print
London & New York

This first large print edition published in Great Britain 2004 by
SEVERN HOUSE LARGE PRINT BOOKS LTD of
9-15 High Street, Sutton, Surrey, SM1 1DF.
First world regular print edition published 2003 by
Severn House Publishers, London and New York.
This first large print edition published in the USA 2004 by
SEVERN HOUSE PUBLISHERS INC., of
595 Madison Avenue, New York, NY 10022.

British Library Cataloguing in Publication Data

Cook, Judith, 1933 -
    Dead ringer - Large print ed.
    1. Ex-police officers - England - Cornwall - Fiction
    2. Fisheries - England - Cornwall - Fiction
    3. Environmentalists - England - Cornwall - Fiction
    4. Detective and mystery stories
    5. Large type books
    I. Title
    823.9'14 [F]

ISBN 0-7278-7378-4

Except where actual historical events and characters are being
described for the storyline of this novel, all situations in this
publication are fictitious and any resemblance to living persons is
purely coincidental.

Printed and bound in Great Britain by
MPG Books Ltd, Bodmin, Cornwall.

Prologue

The death had gone very smoothly, without the slightest hitch. The man in the anonymous grey van considered he had organized it most efficiently. That was to be expected. It was what he did. The victim had made it easy for him, arriving where they had arranged to meet already half drunk and in a foul mood after a shouting match with his wife. The quarrel had been accompanied by the Capercaille CD *Delirium* played at full blast and the music was now going round and round in his head.

The public bar of the small hotel on the corner of the road down to the quay was as crowded as usual on a Saturday night, but mostly with local drinkers. The barman had already remarked how few visitors were about for August, putting this down to the poor summer and cheap package promotions. The three men had come in towards the end of the evening and, from the state of at least one of them, they'd obviously been drinking elsewhere beforehand. The victim

5

was recognized and greeted by several of those present, but his two companions were strangers and he made no effort to introduce them.

At some time in the past, the bar had been enlarged by knocking through a wall into a tiny room behind, now partly screened by large potted plants, a popular spot for young men bent on plying girls with Bacardi before taking them down along the river bank. It was empty, however, when the three men arrived and they immediately made their way to it, sat down and were soon in close conversation.

An elderly man, who owned a holiday home next door to the hotel, looked across at them as he ordered a gin and tonic. 'The guy in the middle looks as if he's had enough already, Joe,' he remarked to the barman.

The barman followed his gaze. 'That's not unusual. At least, it isn't when he comes in here, which isn't all that often. He works on the boats. They must have had a good catch and he's been paid off well.' The drunk was now holding forth to his companions, who appeared to be listening with interest, but the general noise in the bar, coupled with the sound of the jukebox, made it impossible to hear what was being said. At this point the older of the two strangers came down to the bar and ordered drinks.

'Can't drink myself, I'm on a course of antibiotics,' he explained to the barman, as he asked for two pints of heavy with whisky chasers for his companions, and a tonic water with ice and lemon for himself.

'On holiday?' enquired the barman.

'Something like that,' replied the other but did not elaborate further.

Afterwards, when questions came to be asked about the two strangers, no one could clearly recall the appearance of either of them. They'd both been 'average looking', 'neither tall nor short', with 'ordinary' features: nothing memorable about them at all. One was a good bit older than the other, probably in his forties, his companion about ten or fifteen years his junior. They'd been civil enough, but had shown no desire to join in general conversation in the bar and no, they were definitely not local men. The only thing remarked on was that the older man was footing the bill for all the drinks, coming over to the bar again to buy at least two more rounds.

Closing time in the hotel bar tended to be a moveable feast, especially at weekends, but by twenty past eleven on this particular Saturday the bar staff were firmly persuading people to be on their way. There'd been a wedding in the afternoon, making it a long day and even the small noisy group at the end of the bar optimistically hoping for a

7

lock-in finally realized they were going to be out of luck. The three latecomers started making their way out of the bar with the rest, the buyer of drinks thanking the landlord for his hospitality, but as they reached the outside door, the drunk stumbled. His companions caught him by the arms as he almost sagged to the floor.

The older man made a tutting noise. 'Oh dear, I suppose I should have called a halt earlier. I didn't realize quite how far gone he was.'

'D'you want me to call a taxi for him?' enquired the barman. 'I don't know where you're going, but I know he lives quite a way from here.'

'Don't worry,' replied the second man, 'we've transport. We know where he lives and we'll see him safely dropped off.'

Once outside, they made their way down to a dark corner close to the quay, where they had left their van. By the time they reached it, they were virtually carrying their companion, and were both out of breath. The older man unlocked the back of the vehicle. 'Don't just stand there like an idiot, Mike. Help me shove him in.' Together they did so, looking round to see if they were observed but there was no one about. The drunk groaned a little as he was dumped unceremoniously on to the van floor.

'Is he likely to wake?' enquired Mike.

'No chance.' His companion threw him the keys. 'Here – you drive. I'll keep an eye on him.'

'Where now?'

'Right out of the car park, then along the front and over the bridge.'

Mike followed the instructions, turning first into the High Street, then crossing the water. 'Now take the first left': the man in charge, whose name he did not know and who had not volunteered it. 'I'll tell you when to stop.' The road was narrow and winding and while Mike had paced himself fairly carefully during the evening and was more sober than he appeared (a proportion of his drink having been poured into the plant pots), he was aware that he had drunk more than he should in view of what they had to do. After driving for several miles between stone walls and through clumps of trees, without sight of a house or another vehicle, the road suddenly dipped before him and began to run alongside a wide bay, the far end of which was thickly wooded.

The man beside him peered ahead. 'This is it. Pull over into the trees there, well out of sight.' It was a clear but almost moonless night, dark and silent. Across the water, almost opposite to them, they could see the lights of the small town they had just left. The older man looked over his shoulder at the recumbent figure on the van floor. 'We'll get him out now.'

They parked among the trees and opened the back of the van. The figure on the floor lay face down, breathing heavily. They heaved him out and carried him several yards on to the short grass above a narrow expanse of beach. He stirred slightly as they put him down before relapsing again into a stupor.

'Great stuff, Rohypnol,' remarked the nameless man, 'it's tasteless, doesn't smell of anything, is easy to spike drinks with, and within a couple of hours there's virtually no trace of it. After which it clears the system completely. And when you come round from it you can't remember a thing. No wonder they call it the date rape drug. Stay with him while I get my bag, I won't be a minute.'

Mike looked across the dark water, wondering, while he was alone, what the outcome of all this might be. It was so quiet that he could hear the sound made by small waves slapping against the sand. Up in the trees an owl hooted. He shivered. The man beside him stirred again, he seemed to be trying to say something. Mike bent over to hear what it was. It didn't make sense and he said nothing more.

The older man returned carrying a small box, from which he took a hypodermic syringe. 'Get his jacket off. Quickly now.' They did so. 'Now, roll up his sleeve.'

10

'Which arm?'

'Either. Oh, make it the left.' He stretched the arm out and peered at the inside of the man's elbow. 'Sod it, I need more light. There's a torch in the pocket on my side of the van. Fetch it.' Mike did as he was told and brought it over. 'Now hold it steady so that I can see what I'm doing.' He felt for the vein, plunged the needle in and pressed the syringe mechanism down.

'But it's got nothing in it!' exclaimed Mike, his voice raised in amazement.

'Shut up,' the other retorted, 'are you trying to draw attention to us?' He withdrew the needle and there was an immediate spurt of dark blood. He pressed his thumb to the puncture. 'And switch that bloody torch off!' The man on the ground writhed a little, grunted, began to gasp for air, then, after a few laboured breaths, was still. For several minutes neither of the other two moved, then his killer leaned over him and felt for a pulse in the neck. 'OK – he's gone!'

He looked across at the lights of the little town over the water. There were now other lights to be seen, those of two or three fishing boats making their way towards the sea on the top of the tide. The sight seemed to give him pause for thought for he nodded as if a sudden idea had come to him.

'Change of plan,' he said. 'We'll put him back in the van.'

Mike was now completely mystified. Beyond where they were parked the land ran out into a sharp point and even from where they were he could see that the tide was running out fast, helped by the waters of a river swollen by the rains of a wet summer. 'But you said we were bringing him here because it was such a good and convenient place to put him in the water as he'd be carried out to sea by the tide and current,' he objected. 'Surely to God we should get rid of him now as quickly as possible. This place is ideal.'

'So I've changed my mind,' grunted the other. 'Do as you're told. Then change the number plates. The others are wrapped in sacking behind the seats. Come on then. Move!'

They lugged the victim across the grass and once again loaded him into the back of the van. Mike unscrewed the plates which were on the van and swapped them for the others. It took him a little while to fumble with them, as he found his hands were shaking, but his companion did not offer to help, continuing to stare out across the water, before walking a little way away and talking on his mobile. Finally Mike stowed the old plates in the back of the van beside the dead man and made for the driving seat, but the killer motioned him away. 'I'll drive now. I've not been drinking.'

12

Mike shook his head. 'I don't understand any of it.'

'There's no need that you should,' replied the other.

'Will you explain one thing at least. There was nothing in the syringe, yet he died almost straightaway.'

'But there *was* something in the syringe. It's called air. If you inject air into a vein, it acts like an embolism. Your heart stops. There's nothing to show for it and to all intents and purposes you've died of a heart attack. Now, let's head back towards the town, then park up near the old railway line. I've a call to make.'

'Are you really telling me after all this that we're not going to put him in the sea after all? I thought that was the whole point of the exercise!'

'Oh yes, he's going into the sea, all right.'

'He said something while you were away getting the syringe.'

'What was that?'

'I'm none too sure. It sounded like "delirium".'

The man beside him shrugged, then relaxed for the first time that evening. He smiled to himself. The death had gone very smoothly, without the slightest hitch.

One

www.fisherking.com. This website has been set up to reveal important health information which is being kept from the public. Details below. Click on 'seaweed' for a specialist assessment. We welcome your views and any information. Visit us again for further news and leave your own comments.

In the run-down church hall the lecturer hired by Becketts Literary Tours was coming to the end of her second session In front of her sat thirty-one Americans signed up for ten days of cultural sightseeing. Becketts were noted for their concentrated itineraries. After a day in Oxford ('Dreaming Spires and Morse'), another in Stratford-upon-Avon ('The World of Shakespeare'), the party had continued on relentlessly through 'Hardy's Wessex' to 'Lorna Doone's Exmoor', followed by Tintagel, and had now reached what the local tourist office deemed to be 'Du Maurier country'.

Lecturer Liz Symons noted that, as usual,

at least two of the more elderly members of her audience had nodded off while she spoke, though the rest had remained sufficiently awake to listen to her. 'Now, are there any questions you would like to ask?' she concluded.

There were always a few and she answered them to the best of her ability, keeping an eye on the time, for the party was to be off again tomorrow, bound for the far west of Cornwall ('Land of Legend'). At this point John Latymer, the tour manager, arrived with details of the programme for the next day. After visits to Falmouth and Frenchman's Creek, they would be taken to the Duchy Hotel in Penzance. As the following day was August Bank Holiday, they were free to spend it as they wished.

The question of what to do with the bonus of free time had arisen the previous evening when Liz and Latymer were having dinner with the party.

'Say,' said the woman from Wisconsin with the iron-grey hair, 'is there lots to do in Penzance? Shopping malls, theatres and suchlike?'

'Er, not exactly, Myra,' Liz had to admit.

'There's this St Michael's Mount though, isn't there?' queried her companion. 'They say you can get there on foot.'

Liz agreed. 'You can if the tide's out. Otherwise you take a boat.'

16

'If you want to go over there and visit the castle, and so on, I can arrange taxis for you,' added Latymer.

'And they can drive us over if the tide's out?'

'I'm afraid the causeway isn't suitable for cars,' replied Liz. 'It's very rough.'

'So there'll be cars waiting over there, will there, to take us up to the castle?' persisted Myra.

Again Liz had to disappoint her. 'The only way up is on foot, and I have to warn you the path's very steep.'

It was in the nature of things that most of those making up the Becketts Literary Tour parties were middle-aged to elderly, but even so Liz had been surprised at first to discover how few of the book-lovers disliked walking anywhere at all. Myra shook her head. 'Well, I don't know.' She turned to Latymer. 'So, John, what are we supposed to do all day on Monday if there's nothing laid on?'

Liz was about to come up with a suggestion, when one of the men sitting at the table broke in with a question directed at Latymer. 'Tell me, sir, is it true you used to be a law enforcement officer?'

This proved an immediate conversation-stopper. Latymer was used to it. It arose on almost every tour. 'I was in the West Midlands police force for thirty years. When I

17

left, I was a chief superintendent in the CID – that is, our Criminal Investigation Department.'

'Heck – fancy that!' commented Myra. 'So why did you leave?'

Latymer paused for a fraction. Why indeed? There'd been so many reasons. He made his usual reply. 'I was fifty and had come to think thirty years was enough. Also, I'd recently remarried. It's a hard life being the wife of a policeman – I'd already lost one marriage that way.'

'So how come you end up managing tours?' enquired the original questioner.

This part was easy. 'When I first left the Force I thought I'd be happy playing lots of golf and getting away whenever we felt like it without constantly having to cancel everything. Living a regular life, going to bed and getting up when it suited me. But after about six months, I woke up one morning and realized I was bored out of my mind. My wife noticed an advertisement for a tour manager for Becketts and I thought, Why not? So ... this is my third tour of duty and it suits me fine. I'm very busy in the summer but have the winter off.'

It was obvious that his interrogator would have been only too happy to talk about policing and crime all night, but when Liz finally managed to get a word in edgeways she suggested how the group might spend their day. 'It's the Newlyn Fish Festival on Monday. It's like a kind of carnival day. Stalls all round the harbour and on the quays, stages for folk and rock groups and so on, entertainment for the kids and usually a tall ship or two. If the weather's good, you should enjoy it.'

Inevitably this drew from Myra the doom-laden query as to how far she would have to walk. 'Hardly any distance,' Liz reassured her, 'about ten minutes along the prom from your hotel.'

Coffee finished, the party began to break up and Latymer thought that with a bit of luck he could make a pub before closing time.

'I must say, John,' commented Myra as she said goodnight to him, 'you don't look like a cop to me. I'd never have guessed. I reckoned British policemen were different.'

He laughed. 'What's a policeman supposed to look like?'

'Sort of big and burly, I guess, and you're kinda tall and thin. I'd've taken you for a lecturer or teacher or something.'

He looked at his watch. Half an hour to go. 'We come in all shapes and sizes.'

'You should know that, Myra,' broke in the woman's companion, 'think of that Morse.'

Before setting off the next morning to

Falmouth, Latymer informed the party that the Fish Festival might well prove an attractive option for Monday and that he trusted that they would find the local poet, hired to talk to them in Penzance on 'Myths and Legends of the Far West', very interesting.

'That is if you can keep him sober,' Liz whispered to Latymer, as she made for her own car.

'Will I see you again?' he asked her.

'Why don't we meet at the first entrance to the Fair tomorrow morning? Say at eleven?' He gave her a salute and the book-lovers departed into the west.

Latymer greeted the bright sunshine the following morning with relief. The idea of finding himself faced with pouring rain and a party of thirty-plus with no ideas as to how to spend their free day was little short of a nightmare. After listening patiently to the usual list of complaints made to him after the first night in every hotel on the tour, and arranging for the woman who had left her luggage at the previous stop to have it sent on (there was usually one), he told them he hoped they'd have a good day. He would see them again in the lounge bar at six thirty, when he would introduce them (over free sherry) to the poet who was to give the talk the following morning. He then set off briskly to meet Liz.

He apologized for arriving late. 'You know how it is, some people are never satisfied.'

'I couldn't do your job,' she admitted. 'You need the patience of a saint.'

'Then, just as I was leaving, there was a call from Becketts to say that another couple from a Scottish Borders tour, who are Agatha Christie fans, want to join us in Torquay. It's as well we've a couple of spare seats in the coach.'

Together they joined the slow-moving queue buying tickets to get into the Fair. The fine weather had brought the crowds out in force and the smaller quays with their stalls were so crowded it was almost impossible to force a way through. 'Let's make for the harbour proper,' suggested Liz. 'Hopefully by the time we've done that the crowd will have thinned out a bit.'

Living inland as he did, Latymer always found harbours fascinating. Possibly because of the Festival, the main harbour was crowded with boats of all sizes, including many from other parts as well as its own still considerable fleet. He noted half a dozen trawlers from various ports in Brittany, a beamer, *Star of the Sea*, from Newry, and two brightly coloured vessels, *Tam o' Shanter* and *Lizzie May*, both registered at Kirkcudbright on the far-off Solway coast of Dumfries and Galloway. He stared down at them, puzzling over the complex tangle of chains on the decks.

A man on the deck of the *Tam o' Shanter* looked up and caught his eye. 'We're scallopers,' he called up. 'That's what the gear's for.'

'You've come a long way,' returned Latymer. 'Here for the Festival?'

The other laughed. 'No way. Didn't know about it. There's algae in the sea off our coast and we're prohibited from fishing there for now, so we decided to come west since we've a living to earn.' He motioned to the small trawler tied up behind them. 'Don't know why *Lady of Annan* is here, though. She must have come in overnight.'

Tied up alongside the middle quay was a two-masted tall ship flying the skull-and-crossbones, offering children between the ages of nine and fourteen a chance 'to be a pirate for a day'. It was picture-postcard Cornwall. As the crowds thinned out, Latymer looked for a souvenir to take home to his wife from the many stalls offering 'handmade crafts', some genuinely made locally, all too many 'hand-crafted' by nimble fingers in Taiwan or southern China. He finally settled on a pottery jug and hoped Tess would like it. The smell of cooking reminded him that he'd had little time for breakfast. 'Can I buy you lunch?' he asked Liz.

'It's kind of you,' she replied, 'but I

promised the children I'd go back for them. Josh's desperate to be a pirate and the afternoon session starts at two.'

'You should have brought them with you this morning.'

'Not a good idea! All three would've careered off in different directions and I'd have spent all my time making sure they hadn't fallen into the harbour. Pete's away trying for a job again. We've given up thinking we can stay here, there just isn't enough work. It's sad, but we'll have to move. Thanks for the invitation though. You'll find there's plenty of places to eat – if you can get into them.'

Latymer set off in search of lunch. A quick stroll round the town's half dozen pubs showed the impossibility of even trying to get inside even if they were serving food, as every one was packed to the doors, the crowds spilling out on to the road and pavements. It would be easier to go back to Penzance. The drinkers outside the pubs seemed good-humoured and well-behaved, if raucous, but the policeman in him wondered what it would be like by the evening, when many revellers had been drinking all day in the hot sun. Happily it was no longer his concern, but he didn't envy the task of the local police. Turning his back on the busy scene, he decided to set off back along the promenade in search of either a café or a quiet pub – but first he had to find a Gents.

The nearest was at the entrance to the harbour, put there presumably for the convenience of fishermen. Inside, let into the wall opposite the stalls, was a slot with a notice above it. He peered at it in the gloom and was chilled to discover it exhorted drug addicts to drop in their dirty, used needles pointing out that clean ones could be collected from several chemists.

He mused on his unpleasant discovery for some time after he had eaten, sitting on the promenade in the sun watching the crowds drifting down to the harbour or on to the beach. At least he was away from telephone calls and had deliberately switched off his own mobile. He must remember to call Tess before half past six. Only four more days, two here, one in Torquay, then back to London and the end of his responsibilities. Until next time. He walked slowly back to the Duchy, still nursing his purchase from the Festival, and went up to his room to tackle some of his rapidly mounting paperwork.

He came down to the lounge bar just before six thirty to find the poet there before him. Luke Rain was a consciously colourful character, his hair in a pony tail, which Latymer considered deeply unsuitable for a man who was at least in his mid-forties. It was also obvious that the small glass of dry sherry he clutched in his hand was hardly his first drink of the day. However, he seemed courteous enough to the Becketts tour as its members straggled in, eager to tell Latymer of their day. Some had made the trip to St Michael's Mount, of which a handful had actually managed the climb to the top. Others had taken his advice and gone to the Festival, which they described variously as 'quaint', 'olde worlde' and 'kinda unusual'. They had been particularly impressed at the elaborate displays of different kinds of fish in the market building, and even more with the demonstration of how to cook it by a television celebrity chef.

At dinner Latymer was careful to sit next to Luke Rain just in case the poet should say something out of turn, which, as the meal progressed, seemed quite likely as by the time they reached the second course, he'd demolished most of a bottle of claret and was pressing for a second. He became more and more talkative. Cornwall was not what it was. In the good old days there were *real* artists and poets around, though he had to admit when pressed, that he hadn't been one of them. Nor was he a local.

'It's not all that long ago since people down here called anyone who came from across the Tamar in Devon "a foreigner". The locals are a rum lot. Nowadays, though, it's all well-off Birmingham greengrocers and City financial analysts with second homes. And then there's drugs.'

'Drugs?' chorused half a dozen voices.

'Yes, drugs.' He waved his glass in the air. 'Ladies and Gentlemen, you are now in the drugs capital of the west of England.'

Oh God, thought Latymer, and hastily intervened to change the subject, praying Rain could be contained until the end of the meal. It seemed to take an age before coffee was served, signalling the end of the meal and getting him off the hook. He never had got used to the fact that the Becketts parties always insisted on having dinner by seven, not because they were eager to get out and make a night of it but because all they seemed to want to do was retire to their rooms, watch television and go to bed early. Finally, to Latymer's relief, the poet (after two large brandies) rolled off in to the town in search of something more interesting, promising faithfully that he'd be back at the hotel in exactly twelve hours and Latymer was left alone in the lounge bar except for the remains of a wedding party.

He looked out of the window. A bright day had been followed by a fine, mild night and he went out. The Fish Festival would be over by now but he felt drawn to the harbour and began making his way towards it. The sun had just set behind the nearby hills, leaving behind an eerie, greenish glow. It was dead water and the tide at its lowest, leaving a wide expanse of shingle beach, on which a few people were still strolling. It was very peaceful.

The noise from the pubs hit him as he crossed the small stone bridge between the baker's shop and the Seamen's Mission. As he'd anticipated, scores of people had been drinking all day and were still at it. The fish-and-chip shop and the Chinese takeaway were also doing a roaring trade, crowds gathered so thickly on the pavements that he was nearly run over stepping into the road to avoid them. He walked on to the far side of the harbour and down to the lighthouse at the end of it, then turned back again determined to get himself a drink. Even so, the first two pubs he peered into looked impossible and he walked on until he came to several, grouped together opposite the fish market almost next door to each other.

As he reached the door of the first, a sudden rush of people coming out into the street enabled him to get inside and buy himself a pint. The ceilings were low and the air so thick with cigarette smoke that it made his eyes smart. One or two of those standing near to him attempted to make polite conversation, but it was an unequal struggle against the loud beat of the jukebox and the drinkers shouting across it. He

27

pushed his way back to the door and joined the crowd on the pavement.

There was an interesting mix of accents, the obviously local holidaymakers from upcountry, French fishermen from Brittany, northern and southern Irish and a handful of Scots, one of whom was the man he had spoken to on the scalloper that morning. He saw Latymer and came over to him. 'This is all very well,' he commented, waving his glass, 'but I'll be glad to get off back to sea. Not that we could now even if we wanted to. Where we're tied up, we'll have to wait on the tide.'

He was about to elaborate on this when there was a sudden interruption. A man had appeared from the direction of the quays almost running, pushing his way blindly through the crowd and shouting incoherently. His face was white. He seemed to be looking for someone and was almost on top of Latymer when he saw the object of his search and grabbed hold of him, elbowing Latymer out of the way.

'Yer sick bastard!' he roared.

'What the hell d'ye mean?' enquired the other, struggling to pull his assailant's hands of him.

The pursuer prodded him in the chest. 'Yer know full well what I mean, Harry.'

The nearest bystanders fell silent, waiting on events. The man addressed as Harry finally managed to wrench himself free then dragged the other man away, telling him to shut up and behave himself.

'I'm afraid our lads tend to hit the drink when they're away from home,' commented Latymer's companion, 'and not only when they're away.'

'Never fret,' intervened one of the local men, 'we can drink with the best here, especially after a good catch – though that's getting bloody rare these days. Don't worry, it's quite usual on a Friday or Saturday night to see a couple of guys given the heave-ho through a pub door or a bit of a fight outside.' A sudden noise made him stop. 'Looks like your lot are the same.'

The two men had now come to blows. Most of those watching were laughing, enjoying the entertainment and prepared to let them get on with it, until both men fell to the floor and matters took a more serious turn. Harry, who had managed to get on top of his attacker, suddenly cried out, clutched his chest, then twisted the other's hand with all his strength. A knife dropped to the ground. Suddenly everything went quiet.

'Ye've stabbed me! Ye've bloody stabbed me,' he shouted and smashed the other's head down hard on to the road. There was a brief pause, then he staggered to his feet clutching his chest, where a red stain was spreading rapidly over his shirt front.

Behind him a girl screamed.

Without even thinking Latymer pushed his way to the front of the crowd. 'Someone call an ambulance,' he shouted. 'Quickly. You,' he said to the injured man, 'find somewhere to sit. Anywhere. And keep your thumb and fingers pressed on that wound while I see to your friend.' He knelt down and felt the unconscious man's pulse, then pulled up an eyelid. 'Well, that's something. He's out for the count and he's had a nasty crack on the head but he's not dead.'

'You a doctor or something?' enquired one of the bystanders.

'No, but I know what I'm doing. Now we'd better get the police.' He pulled out his mobile.

There was a guffaw from behind him. 'Good luck to you, mate. Police station's only open nine till five weekdays. It's like a frigging coffee shop. You're lucky if you even see a policeman here come weekends.'

'Last time I dialled 999,' broke in another voice, 'I was put through to Newcastle. *Newcastle!* I ask you. A fellow was getting his head kicked in in a local park. They didn't even know where Penzance was let alone the park and by the time the local cops arrived from God alone knows where, it was all over and everyone'd gone!'

But to Latymer's relief an ambulance arrived within ten minutes, its crew immediately taking charge and after a brief examination, both combatants were loaded into it.

'How serious is it?' he asked one of the paramedics.

'One nasty flesh wound,' she replied. 'Can't tell exactly how much damage's been done but I don't reckon the knife hit anything vital, though he might need some blood. The other's still out for the count, he'll need a scan.'

'Has anyone got the knife?' asked Latymer. Several people immediately started looking on the ground.

'Reckon this is it,' a lad called out. 'Must be, it's got blood on it.'

'Don't pick it up,' ordered Latymer. 'Here, let me.' He took his handkerchief out, carefully slipped it under the knife, then folded the cloth around it.

The lad gave him a surly look. 'Think you're on TV or something, do you?' Latymer was about to reply when a police car finally rounded the bend and screeched to a halt. A sergeant and a constable jumped out and made straight for the ambulance. After a brief exchange they waved it away, its siren blaring, towards the local hospital before turning to the now rapidly diminishing crowd demanding to know what had been going on. A dozen voices immediately attempted to give their version of events.

'One at a time, please,' shouted the sergeant then turned to Latymer. 'Is that your blood on your jacket or were you part of the fight?'

'No, sergeant, it's from one of the wounded men. I took a look at the damage while we were waiting for the ambulance.'

'First aider?' enquired the constable.

'No. Ex-police.'

The sergeant raised an eyebrow. 'I see. Perhaps *you* can tell us what happened then.'

'I didn't see all of it. I was standing talking to this gentleman here–' Latymer motioned towards the Scot – 'when one of the men involved came running up, grabbed hold of the other and called him a bastard. He tried to hustle him away and a few minutes later they were fighting. One stabbed the other with this knife–' he produced the handkerchief, stained with blood – 'after which, the man who was stabbed forced his attacker to drop it, then thumped his head on the ground. That's about it.'

'I see,' responded the sergeant. 'Anyone here know these fellows?'

'I do,' replied the Scot. 'They're both from the trawler *Lady of Annan*, sailing out of the Solway. My name's Sean Elliot, skipper of the *Tam o' Shanter*.'

'Are there only two of you to a boat?'

Elliot shook his head. 'No, we scallopers usually carry a crew of four. *Lady of Annan*'s nothing like the size of your beamers, but could have had four or five. The guy who was stabbed's the skipper, Harry Douglas, him with the dunt on the head's Andy Mc-Kinley.' He looked around. 'The other lads could be anywhere.'

The sergeant made a note. 'Well, thanks for your help, Mr Elliot. Can you come into the station in the morning to make a formal statement? Ask for me, Sergeant Willis. And if you come across the other crew members, ask them if they know what it was all about.'

'Aye, I'll do my best. But I doubt it was about anything other than too much drink and fighting talk. Those two have worked the boats together now for some time and there's been no trouble between them back home.'

'Right then,' said Willis, looking at his watch. 'Off you go the rest of you. Show's over. And it'll soon be closing time.' Then he turned to Latymer. 'And you, Mr...'

'Latymer. John Latymer.'

'I'd like you to come in and make a statement too.'

'No problem. But it'll have to be after half nine. I'm a tour manager you see, down with a party. I'll have to see them all safely settled with their speaker. Then I'll come up to the station. I presume it's not far away.'

Willis gave him a thoughtful look. 'Must seem a bit odd for you, doing your job after being in the Force. How long were you in?'

'Thirty years.'

The constable whistled. 'Why'd you leave? Passed over too often for promotion?'

'No,' responded Latymer, somewhat nettled. 'When I left I was a chief superintendent, CID. West Midlands.'

'Well, thanks anyway,' said Willis, tactfully. 'See you in the morning.'

Latymer walked back over the bridge to the promenade. His jacket was damp with the man's blood. It was almost dark and the streets had emptied. Cornwall no longer looked like a picture postcard. He thought again about the slot for used needles in the Gents.

Two

www.fisherking.com. 'To Fisherking (whoever or what you are). I've been following
the information on your site with interest as
I've been looking into this myself and am
now convinced you are right. Therefore I
will start putting my own information on to
your site. I cannot, however, identify myself as I do not want to put my family at
risk. Kinmont Willie.'

The middle-aged woman manning the
Duchy reception desk regarded Latymer
with suspicion when he asked her whether
they could clean his coat and launder his
shirt for him. She peered across at him.
'That looks like blood.'

'I'm afraid it is. There was a fight when I
was in Newlyn, a man was stabbed and I got
blood on me when I went to help.'

'They drink themselves stupid. Don't
know when to stop. You'd have best kept out
of it,' she advised.

'It just looked to me like a disagreement
that got out of hand between two men

who'd been drinking hard all day. Though Luke Rain, who came for dinner with us this evening, said there was something of a drug problem down here.'

'Isn't there everywhere these days?' She sniffed. 'Luke Rain! Problems is it? He should know. Drinks like a fish. Left his wife and two kids high and dry because he says domestic life stifles his talent! Give me your coat now, then bring your shirt down and I'll see what can be done.' She paused. 'They say they bring drugs in on the boats, but I don't know.'

He said nothing of the night's adventure the next morning but as soon as he had settled his charges in front of a bleary-eyed Luke Rain for an hour and a half, he walked up the road to the police station where he found Sean Elliot there before him.

'Won't keep you waiting long,' the clerk at the desk told him as he gave his name.

Latymer sat down beside Elliot. 'The receptionist at the Duchy gave me a funny look when I arrived back with blood on my coat and shirt.'

'I don't suppose they're used to it in a pricey place like that. What do they rush you – eighty plus a night? More?'

'It's less for a party booking and anyway I don't have to pay it.' He paused. 'I wonder-ed if the fight might have been to do with drugs. She said there are rumours that the stuff comes in on the boats, but it was only rumours. If it did, then obviously it would get dealt down here.'

Elliot nodded. 'Wouldn't surprise me. We've a terrible problem back home in some of the ports, especially Aberdeen and Peterhead. But somehow I don't think this was to do with drugs though I can't be certain. There aren't that many of us fishing out of the Solway these days and word gets around. Mostly you know who the users are and I haven't heard that Andy or the skipper of *Lady of Annan* are involved.' He thought for a moment. 'I suppose if someone had drugs stowed away on the boat and Andy found out and thought Harry was in on it, it might explain what happened. But I doubt it.'

At this point Sergeant Willis appeared and ushered them to an interview room. 'Must feel strange,' he remarked to Latymer, 'you being on the other side of the table, as it were. But we'll start with you, Mr Elliot.'

Elliot confirmed that he'd been present at the events leading up to the fight, which were exactly as Mr Latymer had described to the police the previous evening. No, he had no idea what it was all about. But as all of them had been drinking most of the day, it would take very little to start a quarrel and McKinley was known to have a short fuse. Later he'd found the other two crew members, one asleep on board, the other returning from a club in the small hours after taking a girl back to her home. They were as baffled as he was as to the cause of it all. 'But have you any news of how they are?'

'According to the hospital, Captain Douglas will be discharged later today. It seems he was lucky the blade didn't hit anything vital. He's been stitched up and told to take it as easy as possible and take it easy when he gets home. As for McKinley, he's come round now and seems OK but they'll be keeping him in a little while longer, just in case.'

'Then surely you can ask them what started it all,' declared Elliot.

Willis shook his head. 'We already have. They claim neither of them can remember. Say "it was just one of those things". And both have made it clear they don't want to press charges. Now, Mr Latymer, can we have your version?'

He repeated what he had said the previous night including his own intervention. 'Most of the crowd were well away,' he explained, 'which was why I took matters into my own hands. Got the captain to sit still and put pressure on the wound, made sure McKinley was alive and wouldn't choke, then got someone to send for the ambulance while I rang you.'

38

'I think you said last night you heard what McKinley said when he pushed past you?'

Latymer considered for a moment. 'I believe he said something like "you sick bastard" and Douglas replied that he didn't know what he was talking about and hauled him to one side, presumably to try and quieten him down. Next thing they were beating the daylights out of each other.' He paused. 'When I got back to the Duchy last night and I told the receptionist, she thought it was most likely to be too much drink but she also mentioned drugs. I see you've a needle disposal box in the Gents on the harbour, so you obviously have a problem.'

'Drugs are always a possibility, unfortunately, these days,' agreed Willis, 'but the casualty people automatically check for that. Nothing showed up in their blood samples except a large amount of alcohol and there were no signs of needle marks. Nor were there any traces of anything in or on their clothing when we examined it. Two of my men went down to the boat early this morning – the other two lads needed a fair bit of waking – and had a good look round, so far as was possible without a sniffer dog. It didn't seem to bother them. They even asked if we'd like to go through the ice down below before they take on any more.'

'Are you going to charge them?' enquired

Latymer.

'Shouldn't think we'll bother with anything but a caution since neither of them want to take it any further. Could be charged with breaching the peace, but it hardly seems worth it. Captain Douglas says he's planning to sail back home tomorrow, fishing for scallops on the way although the doctors don't advise it.' He grinned. 'It's Virgin trains all the way up to Scotland for McKinley. That'll teach him to come down here and start fights.'

Elliot and Latymer signed their statements, shook hands and left. 'When will you be going?' asked Latymer as they walked back towards the promenade.

'Just as soon as I've taken on supplies from the co-op and kicked the crew up their backsides. And you?'

'On to Torquay tomorrow. For "Crime Night". After that, thank God, home.'

Elliot smiled. 'D'ye ever get to Scotland?'

'Occasionally. Becketts run a tour which goes through Brontë country, then crosses the Borders for Walter Scott and Burns.'

Elliot felt in his pocket, brought out a grubby diary and tore a page out. 'I'll give you my address and phone number then. If you ever do, perhaps we can meet up and I'll show you a couple of good pubs in Kirkcudbright. Hopefully without a fight.' Latymer thanked him, put the note in his pocket and gave Elliot his own card.

He woke very early the following morning, so early that he had time to walk down to the harbour again before breakfast. It was almost empty of boats, and the quays had returned to normal, piled up with green, orange and dun-coloured ropes, heaps of old tyres and stacks of yellow oil drums. From the slipway opposite, where a trawler was being repaired, came the clang of heavy hammers on metal. As he looked on, two of the remaining French vessels sailed out of the harbour mouth. Elliot's boat and its sister vessel had already left and only *Lady of Annan* remained tied up alongside the inner quay. He returned to the hotel, had his breakfast, and rounded up his charges. The coach was already waiting outside. It would soon be over.

A couple of weeks later the morning's post brought him two letters, both enclosing newspapers. One was from Elliot. All the Scots vessels had eventually reached home safely, he wrote. Douglas was getting over his stabbing and McKinley had arrived back more vocal about the rigours of the journey (which had taken sixteen hours as the train had broken down twice) than his cracked head. However the story had appeared in the local morning paper and he thought it might amuse Latymer. The item was headed: 'LOCAL MEN IN BRAWL IN CORNWALL'.

Captain Harry Douglas of the Kirk-cudbright-registered trawler, *Lady of Annan,* is recovering at home from a stab wound suffered while the boat was in harbour at Newlyn in Cornwall. It is understood it was inflicted by a member of the crew after an argument led to a fight in which the assailant also suffered a head injury. Both men admit to having been drinking heavily at the time. A spokesman for Devon and Cornwall Police told the paper: 'Since neither of the men wished to press charges, no one else was involved, and both have expressed their regret for the trouble they have caused, it was decided on this occasion to let them go with a caution. But it has been made clear to them that if any such breach of the peace arises again when they are in a local port, it will be a very different matter.'

There was also a brief comment from a local councillor to the effect that once again, a couple of Scotsmen, who didn't know when they'd had enough, had dragged the country's reputation through the mud.

The other cuttings were from Liz Symons.

'It's been pretty quiet since you left,' she wrote, 'no more fights. I understand you played a part in mopping up the remains of one when you were down here. However, we've had a real mystery since then, as you will see. Can you confirm the dates of your next tour? Mine differ from those in the new brochure. Best wishes – Liz.' The story she sent him was dated four days after he left Newlyn and was headed: 'BODY FOUND OFF NEWLYN HARBOUR'.

Boys fishing off the end of the pier at Newlyn alerted the harbour master to a body floating in the sea off the harbour mouth. He immediately organized its being brought ashore and sent for the police, who have now issued a statement. The body is that of a white male, aged between twenty-five and thirty-five. He appeared to be in good health. Preliminary examinations suggest that he had not been in the water very long. So far there have been no reports locally of any missing person and it is understood that there is no clue to his identity.

The second cutting was from the following week.

There is still no clue as to the identity

of the dead man found off Newlyn harbour last week. A police spokesman told the *Cornishman* that the post-mortem, carried out by pathologist Dr Mervyn Jones, had failed to establish a definite cause of death, although drowning could not be ruled out. Examination of the stomach contents revealed that he had been drinking fairly heavily in the few hours before he died, but there was no suggestion that violence had been involved and foul play was not suspected. It is estimated that the death is likely to have occurred some time within the previous twenty-four hours. No one has yet come forward to claim the body. The body is that of a man about five foot ten inches tall, weighing around eleven stone, with dark hair and grey eyes. He was dressed in jeans, a dark shirt and navy jersey.

Underneath was a picture, which Latymer recognized as one of those where the corpse had been made presentable enough to be photographed before the post-mortem, the result then 'enhanced' to make it look as if it had been taken in life.

Chief Inspector Paul Treglown, the man put in charge of the case, had immediately put all the usual enquiries in place, praying that someone would come along soon and identify the body, thus relieving his overstretched police force. Two constables were sent to Newlyn with the dead man's photograph to do the rounds of the pubs, shops, second homes and holiday lets, to see if anyone knew the man or had seen him about. The landlord of the White Lion spoke for all of them when, after shaking his head and commenting that the picture didn't ring any bells, he pointed out that as there was still at least a week to go before the schools went back, the town was still heaving with summer visitors. It was quite possible the dead man had been in the pub, but if he'd come in with a group and sat in a corner while someone else bought a round, then it was unlikely he'd have noticed him.

Next, as the consensus view was that the man had not been in the water long, all the visiting fishing boats in both Newlyn and Penzance harbours were checked out, along with a number of yachts and a Polish sail training ship on a courtesy visit. A further round of visits to hotels and boarding houses in Penzance also drew a blank, as did the circulation of the corpse's picture to police stations throughout Cornwall and Devon.

As a last resort, and in spite of Treglown's objections, the photograph was then shown on local television. This prompted the flood of confusing calls Treglown had dreaded. The dead man had been seen in St Ives, on St Michael's Mount, in half a dozen pubs and boarding houses, 'acting strangely' in a red van in Truro, with a group of vagrants outside Exeter Cathedral, in a golf club in Dorset. Every one had to be followed up and every one drew a blank. Slightly more hopeful were several reports from Porthleven, a small fishing harbour along the coast, that he had been seen in the local pub at about the relevant time but these proved just as vague. The inquest took place shortly afterwards, Chief Inspector Treglown giving evidence regarding the finding of the body, pointing out that it had still not been identified. However foul play, he told the coroner, was not suspected. It was then adjourned to a later date.

At the end of three weeks Treglown stood the inquiry down. There seemed no point in continuing to waste precious manpower on what appeared to be an increasingly fruitless quest. All that had been established was that he was not known locally. Cornwall at least trebled its usual population in summer. There was no way men could be spared to question the thousands of tourists, many of them in rented holiday cottages in out-of-the-way places or on camp sites, licensed and unlicensed. It would be like looking for a needle in a haystack. A suggestion that he might have been an unlucky surfer had immediately been ruled out as he was fully clothed. So the body stayed where it was in a drawer in the local mortuary.

Then, at the very end of September, a bored police constable staring down from the first floor of Penzance police station saw a dark blue BMW pull into the forecourt and park in the visitors' section of the car park. The driver got out, reached behind for a briefcase, and made his way to the entrance. The desk clerk, asking him the purpose of his visit, saw a well-dressed man, probably in his early forties. He had a decided air of authority. The visitor opened his briefcase, took out a crumpled piece of newsprint bearing the picture of the dead man then came straight to the point. 'I'd to see someone in authority at once. I think I might be able to identify this young man.'

The clerk looked startled. 'I see. If you'll just wait here a minute, sir, I'll fetch someone straightaway. You are...?'

'David Bentley.'

The clerk disappeared and Bentley looked around the small waiting room. On one of the walls, now almost covered with other notices, was the same picture he had in his hand. He regarded it thoughtfully. Within a couple of minutes a police constable appeared. 'Come this way, would you, sir?

Sergeant Willis will see you.'

He was ushered into an interview room, where Willis was waiting. 'Do sit down, Mr – er – Bentley. Would you like a coffee? Milk? Sugar? Bring us some, will you, Dawson. It's hardly special,' he added, 'but at least it's not out of a machine.' He sat back in his chair as the constable departed. 'So you think you might know the identity of our unknown young man, sir?'

'I'm almost certain I do and I'd obviously have come sooner had I known. But I'm based in Brussels, and it was only two days ago that I'd a letter from a friend who'd been on holiday in the West Country, enclosing this cutting and remarking on the likeness to Graham. My brother Graham, that is.'

'I see. So you think this man might be your brother?'

'As certain as I can be without actually seeing the body.'

'Then when we've had our coffee, I'll run you up to the mortuary and you can make a formal identification. Perhaps you can give me a few more details in the meantime.'

Fifteen minutes later they were greeted by a green-suited mortuary attendant. The drawer containing the body had been pulled out and the corpse decently covered with a sheet. He pulled it back to chest level. Bentley looked at the waxen face. 'Yes,' he said.

48

'Yes, I'm afraid that is Graham.' The attendant pushed the drawer back.

Willis thanked him. Then, to Bentley: 'We'll go back to the station and you can sign confirmation of identification. Obviously there are questions I now need to ask.'

'Obviously.'

'Have you any idea why your brother was visiting Cornwall?' asked Willis as soon as they were back at the station.

Bentley sighed. 'I don't. Graham was a law unto himself and, being so much younger than I am, our paths didn't cross all that often. To be blunt, he was what you might call a drop-out. Never finished his degree at university, tried this and that, but was always pretty idle. I can't count the times I've bailed him out of debt. He has, or had, a small flat in Lambeth and I can only assume he'd come down here for a break. But then, I suppose...' He paused.

'What?'

'Well, the last time I heard from him – and, mind you, this was weeks ago – he was in something of a state. He'd fallen madly in love with some girl and then she'd dumped him. He was full of it, saying life wasn't worth living, and all that kind of stuff. I must admit I didn't take it in the least seriously, it's happened so many times before. A few days later I'd a card from him apologizing for his maudlin state. He blamed it

49

on too much whisky. Possibly he was drunk when he went into the water.'

'The post-mortem did show a fair amount of alcohol.'

'That figures. But what I can't understand is why he had no means of indentification on him. There surely should have been a wallet, credit cards. And he certainly had a driving licence.'

'We think they might've been in his jacket and that he left it somewhere.'

'I assume this photograph was widely circulated?'

'Oh yes,' Willis assured him. 'It even went out on television, resulting in a lot of useless calls leading nowhere. There were a couple from a little place down the coast—'

'Where was that?' Bentley broke in.

'Porthleven. We were told he'd been seen in the local pub close to the harbour, but we couldn't firm it up.'

'Porthleven?' mused Bentley. 'That does ring a bell. I'll check when I get back to London and see if I can find out anything more back in town. This place, Porthleven – would it have been possible for him to fall into the sea there but end up near here?'

'Extremely unlikely,' stated Willis. 'If that had been the case he would almost certainly have fetched up further south on the Loe Bar. The currents are all wrong. And if he had somehow been swept from Porthleven to Newlyn, the body would have been in a far worse condition than it was. It would also have taken too long. Our pathologist is pretty certain death occurred within the previous twenty-four hours.'

Bentley accepted this. 'Well, Sergeant, you seem to have done everything possible. Will I be able to make the necessary funeral arrangements?'

'I see no reason why not. I'll have to clear it with Inspector Treglown, but I don't imagine he'll have any objections. He'll be only too relieved to have the matter settled. The inquest was opened and adjourned, as is usual in such cases, but as the coroner was informed that foul play was not suspected, there shouldn't be a problem now the body's been identified. You'll have to get the necessary death certificate, of course, and I can tell you who to go to for that. Will you be wanting to take the body back to London?'

Bentley shook his head. 'I see little point. Graham was a rolling stone with few roots and both our parents are dead. And if you can give me the name of a funeral director, I can see to it before going back to London tonight. I have to get back as I've unfinished business to attend to, though obviously I'll be back in good time for the funeral. I'll also call my wife in Brussels. She might well wish to come down for it with me. There may even be a friend or two of Graham's as well if I can find them.'

A couple of hours later he returned to the station to inform the police that the funeral was to take place the following week. This time he also saw Treglown, who shook his hand, expressing his regret at the sad ending to such a young life. Bentley could only concur. He then gave the police both his business and home address in Brussels, along with his London contact number, 'as I'll obviously be in London until after the funeral.' He also gave his brother's last known address as 11 Mountjoy Road, SW4, after which he thanked them again, took his leave, and set off back to London.

It was a dark, wet day when the handful of people gathered in the crematorium outside Truro for the brief, very brief, committal ceremony. Out of respect, both Treglown and Willis were present. David Bentley arrived with a woman in an extremely expensive black suit, whom he introduced as his wife, Elaine, and two younger men, one apparently his personal assistant and the other an old friend of his brother. The bleak ceremony over, Bentley arranged to collect the ashes the following morning before returning home. 'He was fond of the country,' he told the police officers, 'so I think we'll just find a nice spot and scatter them here.'

He returned again briefly to Penzance for the inquest. It was a mere formality. Sergeant Willis confirmed that Mr David Bentley had identified the body as that of his brother, Graham James Bentley. The pathologist, Dr Mervyn Jones, told the coroner that Bentley's blood alcohol levels were consistent with his having been drinking fairly heavily. But he still could not say for certain what had caused his death and whether or not he had drowned.

'Why is that?' enquired the coroner. 'I thought that was relatively easy.'

'It isn't always as clear cut as people think,' the pathologist explained. 'There was water in the lungs, but not a great deal.'

Inspector Treglown then gave the police evidence, pointing out that if the young man had been drinking heavily, it might well have been sufficient to cause him to miss his footing in the dark and, in unfamiliar surroundings, to fall into the water.

'And you are certain there is no question of foul play, Inspector?'

'Quite. The only marks on the body were caused by it having being washed against the quay after death. Dr Jones will confirm that there were no other signs of injury.' The coroner nodded and recorded a verdict of accidental death, expressing his sympathy with the young man's family.

That, therefore, appeared to be the end of the matter, as Treglown commented to Jones when they met up in the bar of the local golf club at the end of the day. Jones agreed. 'But there was just one odd thing, Paul, in view of what you tell me about the family.'

'What's that?'

'You say the brother's some kind of businessman? And wealthy?'

'Very, I'd say from the look of him. Lives in Brussels. His wife's outfit must have cost him a pretty penny too. Why do you ask?'

'So the brother – our corpse – would have had a fairly cushy life?'

'I imagine so. Though Bentley says he was a bit of a layabout and bone idle. What are you getting at?'

'It's probably nothing. But from the state of his hands I'd have said he'd been used to quite hard manual work.'

Three

www.fisherking.com. Below is further information that I've managed to get hold of, though I know it's not nearly enough. But it does check out with medical books, etc. on the subject. Have taken advice from friend who knows about IT (he doesn't know why I need it) and am going to buy laptop as it takes so much time this way. Have added some material from a similar paper to 'shrimps'.

John Latymer was trying to sort out invoices when his wife called up to tell him that Becketts Tours was on the phone for him. He was surprised as his contract for the summer was over and he wasn't expecting to hear from them again until next year's itinerary had been settled. He sighed and picked up the extension.

Becketts operated on a constantly changing staff of young women, under the direction of managers who were never there. This one sounded like a twelve-year-old on work experience. 'Hello, John,' she breathed, 'this is Dawn from Becketts. Vince has asked me to ask you if you could possibly fit in another tour for us this season? We know it's short notice.' There was a pause. 'Hello? Are you there?'

Latymer was debating what Tess would say. She'd seen precious little of him during the summer and to help make up for it he'd booked a weekend in Paris.

'Sorry. It depends when and where.'

'Scotland the week after next,' Dawn explained. 'Only for a week and with a small party. There's about twelve of them, all with Scottish ancestors. It's not too bad. Straight up to Edinburgh for two days, then Glasgow for a night. After that down through Ayrshire to see the Burns Birthplace, then stopping off for a day in Dumfries. If there's time on the way back, they get to see Hermitage Castle and the Armstrong museum in Langholm. There's no extra trips or anything, they're expected to look after themselves once they get to their destinations.'

'I'll have to ask my wife,' he told her. 'I'll call you back.'

'The week after next?' Tess commented, when he explained the position. 'Why you?' He could tell she wasn't happy about it.

'The person who should have gone has been taken ill. If you really don't want me to go, I won't,' he assured her.

She sighed. 'I suppose if a week's all it is,

it won't be too bad. But no more until next Easter. Definitely no more!'

He went back to his attic and rang Becketts to confirm he would go, asking them to send him the detailed itinerary straight away. His brief exchange with Tess made him mull over once again his reasons for leaving the police force. It was true that recent changes, particularly the increasing layers of bureaucracy, had contributed to it. He'd always been a hands-on person, wanting to get out and about, and sitting in a stuffy office dealing with mountains of paperwork had left him frustrated and depressed. Then there had been his growing relationship with Tess, herself recently divorced and with a daughter just starting college. They had met at a colleague's wedding. His own marriage had foundered on his police work and once he realized it was getting serious he didn't want a repetition. So had given in his notice, taken his handshake and his pension, married Tess and bought a house in a Gloucestershire village near Chepstow.

He knew it would have been relatively easy to set up as a consultant on security or crime prevention or as a private detective, but chasing erring husbands and wives, and checking out insurance claims didn't appeal to him. Time had passed pleasantly enough at first until, as he had truthfully explained to the literary tourists, he'd become bored. In fact it was worse than that, he'd felt stifled, trapped even, in an ever more narrowing world. Becketts Tours, in spite of their demands, had provided a lifeline. But he feared he would have to deal with those demands with greater care if he didn't again want to jeopardize his domestic peace.

Sometimes the thought crept into his mind that it would make matters easier if Tess only had some outside interests of her own. She'd gladly resigned from teaching, certainly didn't miss it and seemed more than happy to spend her time on the house and garden and entertaining. Entertaining ... that was something else which had little appeal for him. Visits from old friends were one thing, supper parties with other retired couples (mostly much older) or second-home owners, something else. He had never been much good at small talk and found himself with little to say. He brought himself up short. Most men would feel themselves in clover to be in his position. He turned back to his paperwork. His briefcase was stuffed with papers, recent tour schedules, notes of people he meant to get in touch with, bits and pieces of information that might be useful in future. Much of it could now go in the bin, along with half the heaps on his desk. He began to sift through it all, coming across as he did so Liz's cuttings on the corpse in the harbour and Elliot's from his local rag. He saw little point in keeping either and was about to throw them into his overflowing waste-paper basket when a letter on the back of Elliot's cutting caught his attention.

It was headed 'Why Can't We Know What is Done in Our Name?' and was signed by a member of an organization calling itself Citizens Against Nuclear Dumping (CAND). It alleged that the Solway Firth was silting up with depleted uranium from shells fired into the sea from a secret range at Dundrennan in Kirkcudbrightshire. Unfortunately the rest of the story was missing. Nuclear waste was always good for a story, mused Latymer, as he tossed it into the basket. Then, on a sudden impulse, he took it out again and added it to a small heap of stuff he couldn't decide what to do with and banged a paperweight down on top of the lot.

He looked at the calendar. He had only just over a week to sort himself out and prepare for the trip. It was as well that he had managed a couple of tours to Scotland shortly after he had joined Becketts. He went to his shelves and dragged out his guides to Edinburgh and the west coast to remind himself where he would be going. His last tour hadn't included Dumfries, which, according to the map, wasn't too far from Kirkcudbright. If he had nothing better to do that day, then he would take up Elliot's invitation and give him a call.

The next morning he had another letter from Liz Symons. 'I'm letting you know first,' she wrote, 'before telling Becketts that they'll have to find another lecturer for mid-Cornwall next year. Pete's been offered a really good job in IT in Swindon. I can't say either of us are enthusiastic about moving from a place like this to a house on a mega-estate in Wiltshire (which is all we'll be able to afford), but at least we'll have a regular income from now on. Anyway, it's been great working with you and I trust we'll meet again some time. Love, Liz. P.S. Mystery Solved – I enclose cutting.' It was from Page 6 of the weekly paper.

FUNERAL OF MAN FOUND IN HARBOUR

The cremation took place on Tuesday of Graham Bentley (26) of 11 Mountjoy Road, London SW4. Mr Bentley's body was found floating off Newlyn Harbour on 31 August last. Foul play was not suspected. He was identified by his brother, Brussels businessman David Bentley. The funeral was attended by members of the family, friends and Chief Inspector Paul Treglown and

60

Sergeant Jim Willis of Devon and Cornwall Constabulary. Afterwards Mr Bentley thanked the police for their courtesy and assistance at this sad time. 'We are all obviously very upset by Graham's death in what can only have been a tragic accident. We would also like to express our appreciation for the work of the Devon and Cornwall police.' It is understood that Graham Bentley's ashes are to be scattered on high ground overlooking St Ives.

For reasons he was never afterwards able to explain, Latymer filed this away too.

So again he packed his bags, assumed his persona of jovial tour manager and joined the coach in London to go north. The tour went as smoothly as Dawn had promised: very few problems with plenty for everyone to do in Edinburgh and Glasgow, certainly enough for them to welcome a free day in Dumfries. When they reached their hotel on the Saturday evening, therefore, Latymer rang Elliot, who immediately offered to come and pick him up the next morning. 'No trouble,' he assured him. 'I wouldn't be going to sea today anyway.'

He was as good as his word and by midmorning they were on the Stranraer road, by-passing most of the small towns, until

61

they turned off on to the narrow road which led down to the small port on the river. It was a fine, autumnal day, and the town looked at its best. Before them was an almost idyllic scene: colour-washed cottages clustering at the foot of a picturesque, ruined castle or overhanging the tidal water in which they were reflected. It was easy to see why, years ago, painters from Glasgow had flocked to it in droves. Elliot parked his car and they walked the few yards to the small quay where a single boat, his own, was tied up.

'Where's *Lady of Annan?*' enquired Latymer.

Elliot shrugged. 'No idea. She was here last night.'

'I take it all's well there now?'

'Sort of. What happened in Newlyn seems to have put McKinley off, though. He's given up the boats, at least for now. Douglas had to find himself a new hand. Now then, how about a drink before lunch?'

There were several bars within a few yards of the quay and Elliot took him into the nearest. 'A pint?' he called over his shoulder. 'Don't worry, I'll get them.' He pushed his way through the drinkers already crowding the bar. Latymer looked around for a seat but they were all taken. 'We'll have these here,' Elliot told him as he returned with two pint glasses, 'then try and find somewhere quieter. The wife says dinner will be ready about half one.' They talked for a little while until Latymer, checking he had sufficient cash on him for the next round, remembered something. He pulled out the cuttings about the body in the harbour and handed them to Elliot. 'I thought these might interest you. After you left, they picked up a body just outside Newlyn harbour, though it appears to have been an accidental death, not the result of a fight.' Elliot balanced his drink on a nearby ledge and ran his eyes over the print.

'It's no longer a mystery, though,' continued Latymer, 'seems the man's family turned up and identified him.' Elliot finished the first cutting, then turned to the second with its photograph of Graham Bentley.

'Shite!' The exclamation came from a man who had obviously been straining over Elliot's shoulder to see what he was reading. Latymer and Elliot turned in surprise.

'That's Jeannie Armstrong's man, Euan,' he declared. 'He went off weeks ago leaving the poor girl landed with two weans.'

'I'm afraid you're wrong there,' said Latymer. 'This man's name wasn't Armstrong and he didn't come from Scotland.'

'Then it's Euan Armstrong's double,' the other retorted. He whipped the cutting out of Elliot's hand, went to the bar, shouted to the landlord and pushed the cutting at him folded in such a way that only the picture showed. 'Here, who'd d'ye say that is?'

The landlord squinted at it. 'Can't recall his name offhand, but I've seen him in the town from time to time. Doesn't he work on the boats?'

Their informant swore under his breath. 'D'ye hear that, now? I'll prove I'm right. If you'll drink up, Sean, we'll go over to the Dornoch Arms. That's where Euan mostly drank when he came over this way. They'll back me up.'

Elliot looked at the photograph again. 'I'm sure you've convinced yourself you're right, Davy, and now you've pointed it out, yes, I agree it is a lot like Euan Armstrong. Though I've never known him all that well and couldn't swear to it. I know Jeannie, of course, since she used to live here. But it hardly matters, does it, since John here says this man was properly identified.'

'I dinna care wha' the paper says, it's Euan. Now, will ye come to the Dornoch Arms and we'll ask Archie, the barman. He never forgets a face.'

Elliot looked at the clock. It was ten to one. 'Do you mind?' he asked Latymer. 'It's only five minutes walk up the road. It's easier than standing here arguing about it and I must admit it's a bit odd.'

The bar of the Dornoch Arms was slightly less crowded and the barman was wiping

64

tables and picking up glasses when they arrived. Davy wasted no time. He tapped him on the shoulder then slapped the cutting down in front of him. 'Who'd ye say that is?' he demanded.

The barman picked it up and took it over to the window. 'It looks like Euan Armstrong.' He unfolded the piece of paper and read the story above it. 'Surely to God it's not *his* body they've found down in Cornwall?'

'It wasn't,' Latymer assured him. 'A few weeks after this picture went in the paper, the man's family identified him. It seems he was a holidaymaker down from London.'

The barman shook his head. 'Well, if you say so. But it's a dead ringer for Euan Armstrong.' He turned to Davy. 'Jeannie's heard nothing then since he went off?'

'Not a word. And it's no like him. When was he last in here?'

The barman considered this. 'Oh, way back in August some time, I think. From what I've been told since, he and Jeannie'd had something of an argument and she'd stormed off with the weans to her sister in Glasgow. When she got back some days later, he wasn't there and she's not seen him since.'

'Presumably she reported him to the police as a missing person?' enquired Latymer.

'Aye, so I believe, but—' He was prevented from continuing by customers clamouring for service. 'Give us a hand, will ye, Annie?' he shouted through the door behind him.

'There you are,' declared Davy, triumphantly. 'Doesn't that satisfy you?'

'I don't see how it can,' objected Latymer. 'But if you like, when I get home I'll call the sergeant at Penzance police station and tell him about this Euan Armstrong who's gone missing. But I doubt he'll show much interest. So far as the police down there are concerned the case is closed.'

'John used to be in the police force,' Elliot informed Davy.

'In the polis? Nae wonder ye dinna believe wa' ye're telled,' bellowed Davy, resorting to the vernacular.'

'But if this other man *was* identified, then it's hard to see what John can do about it, Davy,' declared Elliot.

'Och, ye're away in a dream!' And with that, he left.

Elliot rolled his eyes at Latymer as Davy left the bar. 'There'll be no convincing him now he's made his mind up.' He paused. 'I suppose there isn't a remote possibility that this man's family could have been mistaken? I've seen enough bodies washed in after days in the sea to know how difficult it can be once the conger and crabs have got at them.'

'I realize that,' Latymer agreed, 'but as you see, according to this report the pathologist reckoned he'd only been in the water twenty-four hours at most and the only marks on him were where his body had bumped against the quayside. And the police stated categorically that they didn't suspect foul play.' The crowd in the bar was thinning out as the drinkers prepared to go home to eat. From the other side of the corridor came a buzz of conversation from those taking Sunday lunch.

'I think we'd best go,' said Elliot. 'Mary will have dinner ready by now.'

Latymer finished his pint then, on an impulse, went over to the barman. 'Just one thing, I don't suppose you remember the exact date when you last saw this man Armstrong. It might help to clear things up.'

The barman gave this some thought, then turned to the calendar hanging on the wall behind and turned the pages back to August. 'I do believe I can, as it happens. It was August 26th, the day our other barmaid had her first baby. I remember it because her man insisted on pushing his way in just as I was finally getting everyone out. We'd had a wedding that afternoon and it'd been a long day. But being as the girl worked here, I gave her man a nod and a wink and treated him to a double malt after everyone else'd gone.

'Aye, that's right,' he continued. 'Euan was in here drinking with two guys I've never seen before. He'd had a fair skinful, but that was nothing unusual when he was away from home. It was afterwards someone told me his wife had gone off to Glasgow after they'd had a row.'

'What did he do for a living?'

'Worked part-time on the boats.'

'From here?'

'No. He lives in Annan. He didn't come here all that often but when he did you always knew he was around, if you see what I mean! A bit of a braggart too, used to crack on he worked for the newspapers on the side. But if he did I don't reckon he was very successful at the reporting for I never saw anything he wrote.'

Latymer thanked him and the two men finally went back to Elliot's house for an excellent Sunday dinner. 'You'll be missing your own back home, no doubt,' commented Mary Elliot as she offered him a second helping of beef. 'You and your wife must both get tired of you being away on these coach tours.'

Latymer agreed that they did. 'It's all right at the beginning of the season, but by now I've had enough. I'm only here because the person who should've managed this one couldn't make it.'

Beef was followed by apple pie and cream,

then coffee. 'Come and sit down, Mary,' said Elliot. 'You've been jumping up and down all through dinner.'

'Yes, do, please,' Latymer agreed. 'It was very good and I'm most grateful to you.'

'John caused a bit of a surprise in the pub,' Elliot told her. 'He brought me some newspaper stories from Cornwall about a body found floating off the harbour I was in last August. The place where Harry and Andy had that fight.'

'I only brought them to show your husband that the story of a fight between two of your local fishermen was soon overtaken by something else,' explained Latymer.

'Anyway,' continued Elliot, 'it just so happens that the photograph of the dead man in the paper looks a lot like Euan Armstrong. You know, Jeannie's man. Jeannie who lived on the farm on the back road to Castle Douglas.'

'I ken well Jeannie Douglas as she then was,' replied his wife. 'Last I heard Euan'd walked out on her without any warning. Surely you're not saying it was his body they found down in Cornwall?'

'No, that's just the point. It does look like him, but it was someone else.'

'Let's see.'

Yet again John produced the picture. 'Well, it's very like. Very like indeed. But if you say you know it isn't Euan Armstrong, then it can't be, can it? And what'd he be doing so far from home, unless he'd gone on one of the boats and surely to God they'd have told Jeannie if he'd fallen overboard or disappeared.'

'That's right,' agreed Elliot, then added, 'Have you any idea where Jeannie lives now, Mary?'

She shrugged. 'Still in that council flat in Annan, I imagine.'

The rest of the afternoon passed pleasantly enough until Elliot said he thought they should be getting back to Dumfries. But as they went to the car, he turned to Latymer. 'I don't know how you are for time but do you think we could go to Annan and see Jeannie ourselves? I know it's away the other side, but I reckon I could get you back to the hotel by, say, seven o'clock.'

It was after five by the time they drove into Annan. The fine afternoon had turned to rain and Latymer was beginning to feel guilty about leaving his charges for so long. Under the grey sky Annan looked a singularly unattractive town. It took Elliot a little while to find the council flats but there were no clues outside as to who lived in which. He rang the bell of the nearest flat to be told by the occupant that he had no idea as he and his girl had moved in only a month previously. The elderly woman in the second flat they tried came out of her door and pointed upwards to the top floor. 'Number 26,' she informed them. 'D'ye ken her husband's walked out on her? Disgusting!'

They rang the bell and the door was finally opened by a thin, dark-haired young woman holding a baby of about six months, a smaller child, wearing only a T-shirt, clutching her skirts. She looked at Elliot then, past him, at Latymer. She frowned. 'What brings you here, Sean?'

'Can we come in, Jeannie? We need to talk to you.'

She held the door open. 'Go through then. I'll just put the wean down, it's taken all afternoon to get him to sleep.' She disappeared into a bedroom, the other child trailing behind and Elliot led the way into a sparsely furnished living room cluttered with children's toys. Somewhat surprisingly, a large bookcase, crammed with books, stood against the far wall. The two men sat down gingerly on the two shabby armchairs. A minute or two later, Jeannie Armstrong reappeared, the smaller child now wearing trousers and clutching half a packet of biscuits. She settled the child with some toys, flopped down on the sofa and lit a cigarette. 'So, what is it you want?'

'There's no easy way of doing this,' began Elliot. 'It's about Euan.'

She sat bolt upright. 'You've found him? Seen him?' Then, as Elliot said nothing,

'Has the bastard told you not to tell me where he is? Is that it?'

'It's nothing like that, Jeannie. Give me the picture, will you, John?' Latymer did so and Sean folded the cutting so that again only the picture was visible. He held it out to her, being careful to keep it in his hand. 'Take a look at this.'

She stared in growing wonder. 'It's Euan. Where did you get it? Why's he in the paper?' A thought struck her. 'Has he finally got that sodding story in he said he was working on?'

'This paper was published in Cornwall,' said Latymer, 'and—'

'What the hell's he doing in Cornwall?' she interrupted.

'Wait a minute, Jeannie,' said Elliot. 'Just listen to John.'

As gently as he could, Latymer explained the circumstances in which the picture had been circulated and gave her the cutting so that she could see for herself. She read the account with increasing amazement. 'I don't understand. Are you trying to say Euan *was* in Cornwall? And that he's dead?'

Latymer shook his head. 'The name of the man in the picture is Graham Bentley.'

'Oh no.' Jean Armstrong was adamant. 'I'll show you.' She rose, crossed the room and picked up several framed photographs, then a wedding album, all of which she thrust on

Latymer. 'Just see now.'

The photographs were of family groups: Euan at the christening of the first child, all four of them at the seaside, Jean and Euan in a garden. Latymer opened the wedding album. Euan standing with his best man, both of them in kilts, then posing outside a church beside a much plumper Jean who was dressed in a conventional long white wedding dress and clutching a large sheaf of flowers. 'I was five months gone with Katie when we wed,' she commented, looking over his shoulder.

Latymer closed the album and handed the photographs back. 'I don't know what to say. The likeness is remarkable but the man's family was just as definite and they must have provided sufficient evidence of identification to convince the police. There are rules about these things.'

'We'll see about that.' She began to pace up and down. Katie, aware that something was wrong, stopped what she was doing, stood up and hung on to her mother again. Jean picked her up. 'I'm going to call my sister this very night and ask her if she'll have the kids and I'll tell her why. Then I'm going down to Cornwall to tell them they've made a mistake.' Her eyes filled with tears. 'Though if I'm right, and they're wrong, it means he's dead, doesn't it?'

'Can you tell me any more about your

husband,' suggested Latymer, 'it might help.'

'He's local, born and bred here. When we met, he'd been on the boats since leaving school, though even then he was getting fed up with it. Times are very hard for fisher-men everywhere, what with the European quotas and such. Then the local weekly paper ran a competition for a first-hand account of "a day in the life of ..." and Euan won, writing about his last trip to sea and it was published. After that, he got this mad notion to be a journalist, without any train-ing or experience or anything. He took more and more time off from sea, but all he ever got in the papers were little bits and pieces, while the bills kept on piling up.

'I told him to go back on the boats full-time until we'd got ourselves out of debt. All right, so it's chancy, but even now the money can be good. But he wouldn't listen. Oh no. We began having rows about it. It was after the last that I went off to Glasgow to my sister. I thought it might make him see sense.' She stopped. 'If I go down to Cornwall, can't I ask for a ... what's it call-ed? For the body to be dug up.'

'An exhumation?' said Latymer. 'There's no question of that. Even if you could per-suade the authorities, it wouldn't be pos-sible. The man wasn't buried, you see, he was cremated.' And he showed her the second cutting.

She stared. 'So what can I do? What in God's name can I do?'

Elliot went over and put his arm round her. 'I don't understand this any more than you do,' he said, 'but let me talk it over with John and if you're determined to go to Cornwall, then we'll see what we can do.'

Latymer agreed. 'You said something about a story he claimed to be working on. Had it anything to do with the West Country? I still can't see how the dead man could possibly be your husband, but at least it would've provided a reason for his being there.'

'No,' she stated, very definitely. 'He said it was to do with something up here, but he wouldn't tell me what it was. He treated me as if I was too thick to understand. All I know is that it's some kind of scandal. When I accused him of taking me for an idiot he said it was for my own good, it was "too dangerous". But then Euan always does ... did like to make a drama of everything.'

'Do you know if he'd approached any newspaper? If so it might be possible to ask around and find out what it was he was pursuing.'

'He said he was fed up with not getting published in the papers, that no one was prepared to take him seriously because he was a fisherman and that this time he'd had a better idea. He was going to put his story out on the Internet.'

Latymer looked round but there was no sign of a computer. 'We've an old one in our bedroom,' she informed him, 'but it's not good enough for that – not that I know much about it. Euan said that he was going to put his story on some website or other, a bit at a time. He'd use those cyber cafés where you can pay to use a computer for a wee while. That way they would have no idea who was doing it. That's what caused the last big row when I finally walked out. We'd no bloody money, we're two months behind with the rent and instead of going back to sea, he was going to spend his time poncing round Glasgow playing about on the Internet!'

'Who did he mean by "they"?' enquired Elliot.

'He never said.'

Latymer looked at his watch and saw to his horror that it was after six o'clock. 'I must go, Sean. They'll be wondering what the hell's happened to me.'

Elliot stood up. 'I'll run you straight back. Look, Jeannie, leave it with us. I'll call you again within the next few days.'

She gave him a grim smile. 'You'd better make it quick. The phone's about to be cut off. I've no money and I can't get any extra from the Social yet since they say Euan might well turn up again any time. That's what the police said too. After a week they checked the hospitals and all the usual places, then said I'd best be patient and that hundreds of men left home after rows, but most of them turned up again eventually.' She showed them to the door and opened it. 'But I don't care what you say. It was Euan they found in Cornwall. I'm certain sure of that.'

Four

fisherking@appleonline.net. Just don't know how safe it is to send stuff to you, apart from that I put out on the website. I don't know if I'm paranoid, but in spite of all precautions I'm beginning to feel I'm being watched. Also a friend who I asked about e-mails says they're all intercepted by somewhere or other – Malvern? Menwith? I'll meet the contact again since you want me to, but after that think it best I lay off for a while. (Trust you've noted recent stuff on Kosovo and the Italian connection – might it apply here?) Kinmont Willie.

Chaos had reigned at the Dumfries hotel in Latymer's absence. One of the more elderly women in the party (and by far the most difficult) had slipped on the hotel steps after having her lunch and injured her ankle. As the hotel had been unable to contact the tour manager since, as the hotel manager icily informed him, his mobile phone appeared to be switched off, it had to fallen to the hotel to make arrangements to get the

78

sufferer to the nearest hospital for an X-ray and treatment. 'This meant I had to leave my post here and spend all afternoon sitting about in Casualty. I do not consider this to be part of *my* duties.'

The sufferer was now seated in the lounge, her strapped foot up on a footstool, complaining loudly to anyone who would listen. 'Oh, so you've come back at last,' she snapped, as Latymer in came through the door. 'And about time too. I thought you were supposed to be looking after us?'

'I am and I trust I do,' he responded in what he hoped was a conciliatory tone. 'But as it was a free day, there was no reason for me to stay here all the time though I never intended to be so late back. I was held up. I'm very sorry.'

The woman refused to be placated. 'You'll be hearing more of this,' she threatened.

He hadn't long to wait. Half-way through his soup he was informed that Mr Dalton from Becketts Tours was on the phone for him. 'Where the fuck were you?' he bellowed. 'You know quite well you're paid to stick with these people while they're in our care, not go gallivanting off God knows where with your mobile switched off. Mrs Breksted-Heins is very, very annoyed.'

He was right of course. All Latymer could do was apologize. 'I'm obviously very sorry about what happened, Vince, but today was supposed to be free with people going off all over the place. It's not usual in these circumstances for the tour manager to have to stay in the hotel all the time. I understand the injury isn't serious and obviously I'll do what I can to make amends to Mrs Breksted-Heins.'

There was a moment's silence on the end of the phone. 'I'm still far from satisfied, Latymer. You'd best ensure they reach London without any further mishaps. I'm most dissatisfied. We'll talk about this again.' A number of ripostes suggested themselves but Latymer contented himself with reminding Vince that he'd only undertaken the tour as a favour and that if he hadn't been prepared to do so, it would most likely have been cancelled.

The journey back to London seemed interminable. The party argued among itself about whether or not to go cross-country to Hermitage castle before leaving Scotland, but to his relief the decision not to do so was carried by a majority of one; thus ensuring the minority grumbled all the way down to the Midlands. By the time he finally delivered them to their Heathrow hotel at lunchtime the following day he was tired, bad-tempered and wanted only to get home, shower, put his feet up and watch something undemanding on television.

★ ★ ★

But it was not to be. 'Surely you haven't forgotten,' said Tess. 'I reminded you again only the other night. We're having supper with the Seftons.'

'Oh God! It'd gone right out of my head. Can't we put them off? George Sefton can bore for England. And his wife never stops talking either.'

'Of course we can't put them off. They've been so kind and helpful, knowing you've been away so much.' She paused slightly to let this sink in. 'George has mowed the lawn several times and Sheila's such a good-hearted soul, helps out with everything.' She relented slightly. 'I know it's trying when you've only just got back, but then it was fixed up before you even knew you were going to Scotland and you never said at the time that you didn't want to go.'

'It seems I don't have much choice.' Latymer sighed. 'As Shakespeare said "time and the hour pass through the roughest day" ... I suppose it won't be all that bad.'

It was worse. The Seftons had invited another couple, an estate agent and his wife who had recently moved into the village. Latymer had thought that listening to George Sefton's usual regurgitation of the day's *Telegraph* leader would be bad enough, but during supper Sefton started on one of his favourite topics: crime, its causes, the amount of it, the penalties that should be paid. Heavens above, thought Latymer as Sefton droned on, you'd think he'd spent his life in court rather than a provincial bank! Several of Sefton's remarks were obviously aimed at him, but he did not rise to them. Finally the meal dragged to its end and they went through to the lounge for coffee and drinks.

George waved a bottle at his new friend. 'Brandy, Les?'

'D'you think you should?' said his wife. 'You've had quite a lot of wine and you're supposed to be driving.'

Les winked at George. 'I'm OK, Dawn. I'm sure our ex-copper here will turn a blind eye.'

'It's not me you have to worry about,' said Latymer. 'There's nothing I can do if you get picked up on the way home.'

George erupted. 'There you are! That's what I mean about the law. The police spend all their time cruising round looking for motorists who've had one drink over the odds or drive at five miles per hour over the speed limit, while the real crooks get away with murder. All these young thugs – I'd lock 'em up and throw away the key. What do you think, John?'

That it's cliché time, thought Latymer, pushed into a response. 'And you reckon that would cure it? We've never had so many people in prison but it doesn't seem to be doing much good. What's needed is better detection, more visible policemen and less paperwork. One of the reasons I left the Force was because I was drowning in paper.'

George shook his head. 'I'd cut through all that. Flog the yobs and bring back capital punishment. That'd sort things out.'

'You're right,' agreed Les. 'People say stuff like: "Would you be prepared to pull the handle on the trap? And if not, don't ask anyone else to do it." But I tell them *I* would. Oh yes, indeed, I would.'

'And presumably you'd be equally happy to stand on the trap, knowing that you were innocent, and be hanged by the neck until you were dead,' suggested Latymer. 'We've been known to get it wrong.'

There was an uneasy silence, finally noticeable to the three women. 'John's very tired,' Tess broke in quickly, 'he's been shepherding difficult Americans around Scotland all week and only got back this afternoon. Thank goodness, it's his last trip until the spring.'

'Funny thing to take up,' remarked Les. He put on a pompous voice. 'Literary tours. Weird. Must be dead boring. Why on earth do you do it?'

'Because doing nothing was even more boring,' said Latymer, his voice rising. The atmosphere froze. 'Now, if you don't mind, I really am very tired.' He rose to his feet.

'Tess?' She shook her head at him, shrugged at the others and rose to her feet. There was a chilly silence. Sheila Sefton fetched their coats, Tess thanked her for inviting them and for the lovely meal and they left.

'I hope you're happy with what you've done,' she said as they set out to walk the hundred or so yards back to their house. 'You ruined the evening. I know you're tired, but that's no excuse. It was kind of them to ask us and she went to so much trouble.' Latymer said nothing. 'What *is* the matter with you?' she persisted. 'Did something go wrong on the tour?' He shook his head. When they got in, he went straight up to bed. However fed up he might get with the literary tours, all that stretched before him now were weeks, months of domestic routine punctuated by drinks with people like Les and George. There had to be something better than this.

The following morning he suddenly had an idea. A few weeks earlier he'd had a call from an old colleague, Keith Berry, with whom he'd always got on well. Berry told him he too had left the Force following an injury he'd received during a violent arrest and was now running a specialist crime bookshop in Bristol and they'd agreed to meet up once Latymer's tours had ended. So he rang Berry, asked if it was convenient if he came over to see him. Also where exactly he was, as Bristol's nightmare road system could defeat the best minds.

'We're close to the old Tobacco Factory. Anyone will tell you, it's now some sort of arts centre. We're in the row of shops almost opposite. You can't miss us. It says "A Taste for Crime" over the door in red.'

He felt relieved. Not only would it get him out of the house, he would be able to talk over the recent happenings with someone who knew the system. Encouraged by this, he sought out Tess, apologized for his behaviour the previous evening, putting it down to fatigue, and suggested he took her to Paris the following weekend.

The bookshop seemed rather out of the way but there were a good few people browsing around the shelves when Latymer arrived. Keith led him into a tiny back office, leaving the shop in charge of a competent young woman who was unpacking boxes of books. 'Are you able to make a living?' asked Latymer after they had briefly caught up with the recent past.

'Not bad. There's a real market for crime, fiction and non-fiction. But I don't imagine you've come here to enquire after the business or buy books. So what is it?'

Latymer gave a brief account of the body found in the harbour, the events preceding it and how half south-west Scotland, including the man's wife, were convinced the police in Cornwall had identified the wrong man.

'And what about you? I imagine you wouldn't be here if you didn't think there might be something in it.'

Latymer shook his head. 'I simply don't know. Logic, common sense, tell me that such a mistake couldn't have been made but...'

'Was the body knocked about much?'

Latymer took out the cuttings again. 'No. This, I presume, is an enhanced photograph of the corpse. You can see identification should have been easy enough.'

Berry examined the picture closely. 'But enhanced pix are rarely spot on, are they? Which is why the people up in Scotland think it looks like someone else. And you say whoever identified him actually saw the body?'

'It was the chap's brother. But now the wife of the missing man is determined to go down to Penzance and confront the local police. I've told her no one will want to know. She also talked about exhumation but that's out. He was cremated.'

Berry looked across at his ex-boss. 'I can see you still aren't happy though. I'll take some photocopies of these.' He went over to the copier. 'Is there anything I can do?'

'Would you have the time if there was?'

'Jenny out there's very competent. We

86

aren't that busy. I could make a few enquiries if you want.'

'I'm not sure yet, but I might. I must be diplomatic though. My wife wouldn't be at all keen if she thought I was contemplating taking this further. How about yours?'

'Don't think Liz would mind too much. She's put up with my leaving the police, moving here from Birmingham and starting the shop. She's been a brick.'

Two days later, Latymer received a call from Elliot. 'Jeannie's still set on going down to Penzance. Her sister's prepared to have the children and I've said I'll give her the fare. Is there any chance you could go with her or meet her there? You know what happened and you've had contact with the local police.'

Latymer's heart sank. Why in God's name had he allowed himself to become so involved. 'Look, Sean, I quite understand how she feels, but it really isn't any of my business. As I told you and Mrs Armstrong, the case is closed, the body cremated, there's nothing to be gained.'

'But you know it's not just Jeannie that thinks it was Euan they found in the water. At least if she talks to the police and they can set her mind at rest, that will be the end of it. Personally I'm still in two minds. Part of me still wouldn't be surprised if he

87

walked back in one day cool as you like. I know it's a lot to ask but couldn't you spare her a couple of days?'

Only 'a couple of days', but what on earth would Tess say? And yet ... 'Look, whatever happens, Noah's flood, Judgement Day, I'm taking Tess to Paris next weekend. If Mrs Armstrong's determined to go down to Cornwall at once, then I can't help you. If she'll wait until I get back, then I'll think about it. I suppose you could send her down overnight on the train from Carlisle and I could meet her in Penzance. In the meantime I'll keep hoping that after I've been to Paris you'll call and tell me Euan Armstrong's turned up full of apologies and begging his wife to take him back!'

The weekend in Paris came and went (mollifying Tess somewhat) but he returned to find no such good news awaiting him. After speaking again to Elliot, he finally rang Jean Armstrong. The situation, she told him, was exactly as before. People were being very good and a friend had paid her phone bill 'just in case Euan phones'. But she must go to Cornwall and put her case, with or without his assistance.

Latymer had broached the subject with Tess while they were away and in a relaxed mood, pointing out that it would take him only two days at most. 'But I can't see for the life of me why you need to go to all this trouble,' she'd objected. 'You say yourself it's all over. Obviously the woman's upset and is clutching at straws, but it sounds like a complete waste of time.'

He agreed. 'But it would help her come to terms with her husband's disappearance if she hears at first hand that the dead man couldn't possibly have been him. She's convinced she's right and they're wrong, and from the photographs one was a dead ringer for the other.'

'Maybe.' She gave him an appraising look. 'Won't you ever forget you were once a policeman? When you retired you told me you wanted to get a life, yet here you are, three years on, playing the sleuth. I didn't marry a private detective. Nor,' she added, 'did I imagine, when I agreed to move to the country, that I'd be spending so much time on my own, much as I love my house and garden. The summer tours I can just about put up with – at present. But I can't take much more of this.'

So he was feeling far from happy as he drove across the new Severn Bridge and on to the M5 two days later. The weather was dull and overcast as he reached Exeter and began skirting Dartmoor, and soon it was raining heavily. He drove into Penzance around nine o'clock and on to a bleak, windswept promenade. He booked into a pub on the front, discovered that it was too late to get anything to eat and trudged dismally off to the local Indian restaurant.

He spent a restless night, going through the story over and over again. None of it made any sense. Euan Armstrong had allegedly been working freelance and without back-up on a scandalous, possibly even dangerous, story. Jean Armstrong had been quite definite that it had a local connection though she had no idea what it was. If it was true that doing drugs was commonplace in the fishing industry, then that was the most likely subject. So it might be that inexperienced in journalism as he was, he'd found himself in too deep. If something untoward had happened to him, then logic demanded it would have done so in Scotland: there was no earthly reason for his body to turn up hundreds of miles further south.

As Latymer drove to the station to meet Jean Armstrong the following morning he felt as if he hadn't slept at all. It was still raining, the sky dark with scudding clouds, a heaving grey sea throwing waves up over the promenade. The train pulled in as he walked on to the platform and Jean was one of the first passengers off it.

'We must find you some breakfast, then we'll go straight up to the police station,' he told her. 'But you must be prepared for disappointment, possibly worse. They might simply refuse to discuss the matter at all.'

90

She nodded. 'I realize that. And it's an awful long journey. But I owe it to Euan. I still can't believe he'd have gone off like that without telling me, even if we did have a blazing row. He thinks the world of the kids.'

The only place offering food nearby was little better than a transport cafe but she assured him that a bacon sandwich and a mug of tea would do fine. He watched her as she ate her sandwich and thought that away from the flat and the children she looked less like the kind of young woman whose horizons had never broadened beyond the needs of a husband and children. He wondered if she'd ever had any other aspirations.

'What are you thinking?' she asked.

He felt somewhat confused. 'It's impertinent really. You're obviously quite a determined woman and it crossed my mind that you might have had other ambitions than early marriage and young motherhood. But it's none of my business.'

She gave him a rueful smile. 'Aye, I did for a while, when I was still at school. But you know how it is. I let things slide, took a holiday job in the summer in Kirkcudbright and one night Euan came in with some friends and we started going out. One thing led to another, I fell pregnant, we married and that was that. There was no problem about it. Marriage, I mean. He was quite happy. But it's not been easy. Like a lot of fishermen he is … was … very conventional where women are concerned. A man should be able to provide for his woman to stay home and bring up his kids. But then he tried to square that with getting into reporting. When I said why didn't he go on some sort of course and learn how to do it properly, he got mad and said he wasn't going to go back to school. So I offered to try and get a job to help out, but he didn't want that either.'

She finished her meal and they made their way through the rain to the police station, where Latymer asked if he could see Sergeant Willis.

'What's it about?' asked the desk clerk.

'Will you tell him John Latymer would like a word. He might remember me, I'm the ex-police officer who was a witness to a fight in Newlyn last August. It concerns the body you found in the harbour shortly afterwards.'

The clerk looked surprised. 'I'll tell him, certainly, but that's all been sorted out. Didn't you know? The body was formally identified not long afterwards.'

'I do know, but both myself and this lady would like to talk to him all the same.'

Willis appeared some five minutes later and looked enquiringly from Latymer to Jean Armstrong. 'So what can I do for you, Mr Latymer?'

'I don't want to waste your time,' Latymer began, 'but I feel Mrs Armstrong here has a legitimate query. Indeed she's come down all way from Annan in Scotland in the hope you can set her mind at rest. It's about the man who was found dead in the harbour last summer. I know the body was formally identified by a member of his family but both Mrs Armstrong, and many of those who knew him, are convinced that the photograph in the paper was that of her husband, who's been missing since the end of August.'

Willis looked taken aback. 'Well, I suppose you'd best come through.' He led them into an empty office and asked them to wait. 'I'll see if Inspector Treglown can spare a few minutes but I can't see how we can help you.'

Jean stared out of the window at the rain. 'They're not going to believe me, are they? You could see it in his face. "Why are they wasting our time? What's he doing bringing this neurotic woman in here?"'

She was interrupted by the arrival of Inspector Treglown. He greeted Latymer and held out his hand to Jean. 'I'm not sure I understand what this is all about, apart from the fact that this lady's husband is missing.'

Latymer explained again the reason for their visit. Treglown listened, then turned to

Jean. 'If your husband has disappeared, Mrs Armstrong, I realize you must be anxious and upset but I fail to see how you can imagine that the body of the man found drowned here last August could possibly be his. Not least because you already know the man was identified weeks ago. However distressing it might be for you to come to terms with, yours is still a missing persons inquiry. You must also know that people go missing for a whole host of reasons but only a handful are found to have come to harm. I assume you reported his absence to the Dumfries and Galloway police?'

'Straightaway. And much good it's done me,' she retorted. 'All they do is ring up from time to time to check he hasn't come home.'

'Had you any particular reason for believing your husband was visiting Cornwall?' enquired Treglown. She shook her head without speaking. 'There you are then. I'm afraid you've had a very long journey for nothing. But I can assure you without a shadow of doubt that the body found in the harbour was definitely not that of your husband. The dead man's name was Graham Bentley, he came from London, and his own brother identified him.' He sat back in his chair and smiled at Latymer in a way that signalled that was the end of the matter.

Jean caught the look. 'See you here, then,'

she snapped and produced from her handbag a photocopy of the picture from the paper and two photographs of Euan. 'Just tell me what *you* think!'

Reluctantly Treglown examined them. 'I agree the likeness is quite remarkable,' he conceded, 'and I saw the body myself. But it can only be a coincidence. May I ask your husband's occupation?'

'He works part-time on the boats out of the Solway.'

'Then both you and the police must have made enquiries among those he works with? Boat owners?'

'I don't know about the police, but of course I have. It was the first thing I did. But he hadn't worked on any boat since the middle of July. In fact the captain he often goes out with had been looking for him as he was a man short for his crew. But I'd have known if he'd been intending to go to sea, I'd have had to get all his gear ready. His oilskins, seaboots and everything are still at home where he left them.'

'If I remember correctly there was absolutely no identification of any kind on the body, was there, Inspector Treglown?' ventured Latymer.

'None at all. Nothing in his pockets. Not even loose change.'

'Didn't you think that peculiar?' Latymer persisted.

95

'As we told his brother, we assumed he must have been wearing a jacket in which he carried his driving licence, credit cards, cash and so on and that he'd left it somewhere.'

'And it wasn't *definite* that he was drowned?'

'The pathologist couldn't be absolutely certain. He did explain that sometimes there could be some difficulty.'

'And definitely no sign of foul play?'

'None whatsoever.'

This was obviously getting them nowhere. Latymer made one last attempt. 'The brother who identified the body, what was he like?'

'Businessman based in Brussels. Very smart. Forty-ish. Drove a new BMW. I can probably tell you a little more, if it will help satisfy you.' He picked up an extension phone and asked for the Bentley file to be brought in to him. 'It's in the drawer with the other closed files,' he said, emphasizing the word 'closed'. A few minutes later a constable appeared with a thin folder, which he handed to Treglown. 'Yes, here we are ... David Bentley, executive with Transeuro City Analysts ... He said something about working in the futures market, but I must admit I don't know much about that kind of thing. The brother, Graham Bentley, was a university drop-out, never held down a proper job. Down here on holiday following a broken romance, possibly stayed in Porth-leven.'

Latymer made a mental note of the name of the firm. 'I don't suppose you could let me have a telephone number for him?'

Treglown shook his head. 'You don't give up, do you? So far as I'm concerned, the matter really is closed. You of all people must know we've more than enough to occupy us without chasing after shadows.' He paused, then scribbled on a piece of paper. 'I shouldn't be doing this but here's the number he said was usually on an answerphone. I suppose you can ring it and if he doesn't want to talk to you, he doesn't have to.'

Latymer stood up. 'We won't keep you any longer, Inspector. But thank you for hearing us out.'

'I knew they wouldn't believe me,' said Jean as they went out into the street.

'Well I hate to say I told you so,' Latymer agreed, 'but you have to admit he put up a pretty convincing case for the dead man being Graham Bentley. To be honest, I think even if he did have any doubts he'd stifle them. The police here must be just as stretched as everywhere else.'

Jean sighed. 'I suppose you're right. But it doesn't make me feel any better.'

All logic should have told Latymer to leave it there, yet the force of her absolute certainty was unsettling. He thought for a moment. 'At least I know where this man David Bentley works. I might risk making a few enquiries, though I doubt I'll get any further. When are you going back?'

'There's a train this afternoon. There isn't seem much point in hanging about, is there?'

The rain had stopped and a watery sun was coming out. 'Do you feel like walking down to Newlyn harbour?' he suggested. 'At least it'll stretch your legs before the long journey home.'

'Funny business that,' Willis remarked to Treglown. 'Fancy coming all this way just because she thought the picture in the paper looked like her missing husband.'

Treglown agreed, but added, 'Though I must admit it was very like.'

'But all the way down here from *Scotland*!' He made it sound like another planet. 'If you ask me it's the old story. Hubby gets fed up with the wife and kids and goes off with a bit of totty. He'll either get tired of her and come home asking for forgiveness or set up somewhere else. It happens all the time.'

Willis was right, of course. But later Treglown suddenly recalled what the pathologist had said about the corpse's hands: that if he hadn't been told the man was an idle drop-out from a middle-class background he would have thought he'd been used to hard manual labour. And the missing Scotsman was a fisherman ... No, the case was closed.

Before seeing Jean to the train that afternoon Latymer asked her again if she'd any idea of the story her husband working on and if it might be to do with drugs.

'I asked him that. It was the first thing I thought of when he said what he was doing might be dangerous, but he swore it wasn't. He could've been lying, I suppose.'

'He might have thought it better you didn't know. If anything has happened to him, it would be an explanation. You say he was talking about using the Internet – suppose he was planning to reveal the names of dealers? Whatever he was doing, it sounds like no job for an amateur.'

'So I told him. Often.' She thanked him and he promised to keep in touch. There was nothing more to be said.

A few days later he rang the number of the answerphone the Inspector had given him and left a message. Bentley returned the call in person the following morning. The voice was well-bred and slightly bored. 'Mr Latymer? Your message was somewhat garbled. Am I to understand some woman has come forward claiming to be my brother's wife?

Graham never married and if this woman is alleging he did, I can only imagine she thinks there's money in it. An inheritance perhaps? If so, she's out of luck. All my brother left behind was debts which I've had to settle.'

There was something about the man's tone that profoundly irritated Latymer. 'No, it's nothing like that. The young woman in question saw your brother's picture in the paper and thought it was that of her husband who went missing in Scotland at about the same time.'

'Scotland! Did no one think to tell her it was Graham's body? Or that he was found in the sea off Cornwall?'

'She was told both those facts,' responded Latymer, 'but the likeness is so striking that a lot of other people also believed it was her husband, so she can be forgiven for personally checking it out.'

Bentley made a dismissive sound. 'If her friends are that concerned, they'd be better off persuading her to look for him closer to home. She surely can't believe I wouldn't be able to recognize my own brother, dead or alive.' There was a noise in the background. 'Look, I really must go. Sorry I can't be of more assistance,' and he put down the receiver. On an impulse, Latymer dialled 1471. A recorded voice informed him that he had received a call that morning at 9.07

a.m. 'The caller withheld their number,' it intoned.

He put down the receiver and rang Keith Berry. 'I see,' said Berry when Latymer had finished his explanation. 'So you want me to see what I can find out about David Bentley and Transeuro City Analysts. That shouldn't be too difficult if they're legit. And while I'm at it, I'll check out the address of the brother, I've got the cutting here some-where – 11 Mountjoy Road, SW4. Presum-ably he'll still be in the phone book. Speak to you soon.'

A little over twenty-four hours later, Laty-mer took a call from Sean Elliot to tell him that Andy McKinley, the fisherman who had started the fight at the Fish Fair, had been found dead at the foot of the castle ruins in Kirkcudbright that morning. 'They have got to do the post-mortem,' he said, 'but the police say they're almost certain it was an overdose of heroin.'

Five

fisherking@appleonline.net. No idea who
you are or what this is about but am keeping a promise made to a friend. To warn
you. Something bad's happened. He said
if it did, you'd guess why. DON'T try to
trace me.

www.fisherking.com. Those of you who
regularly visit this website will know of
the information logged here under the
heading 'WK's notes'. But there has been
no contact for several weeks. If Kinmont
Willie is still visiting the site, please make
contact. Fisherking.

'So that fight in Newlyn last August was to
do with drugs after all,' commented Latymer.

There was a pause at the end of the phone.
'That's what some people are saying but I
don't know ... It's come as a dreadful shock
here. Nobody who knows him believes
Andy did drugs, whatever the police say.
But then he'd rather dropped out of the
fishing scene since he gave up going on the

boats. He's not had any kind of regular work since, just odds and ends here and there and it's easy to get in with the wrong folk if you're hanging around with too little to do. As to the availability of heroin, it can't be as easy to get here as Glasgow but drugs can be got hold of anywhere if you really want them, can't they? But how did he pay for it? He was hardly earning anything.'

'Addicts can always find a way,' returned Latymer. 'Anyway, keep me posted.'

Why did I say that? he asked himself as he put down the receiver. This is nothing to do with me. Nothing at all. The man's dead and the manner of it explains the quayside fight in Cornwall. You don't have to look like the popular image of the addict, not all those taking heroin shamble around looking like ghosts.

Keith Berry called him a short while later. 'Thought you might be interested to know there's definitely something iffy about the Bentleys.'

'Go on.'

Berry had encountered no problems obtaining Transeuro City Analysts' telephone number. 'They do exist. So I rang up and asked to speak to David Bentley.'

'And?'

'The woman on the switchboard said, "Who?" She'd a pretty thick accent, so I said it again, very slowly and carefully. She said she didn't understand. So I spelled it out letter by letter, whereupon she bit my head off and snapped, "I heard you the first time. There is no one of that name employed here." '

'But he must be. He told the police he held an executive position.'

'That's what I said. Not about the police, but that I had been given his name as one of the firm's executives. "Then you are under a misapprehension," madam informed me. "I can assure you no one called David Bentley works here for Transeuro, nor ever has, so far as I am aware." There didn't seem to be much point in carrying on with the conversation, so I thanked her and hung up. He could've lied about working there, on the other hand he might have told his switchboard people that if they were contacted by unknown callers they were not to reveal that he did. Perhaps Transeuro are involved in shady financial dealings. I'll see if I can get anywhere asking some old contacts in the City.'

Latymer was about to tell him of McKinley's death, when Berry forestalled him. 'Oh, and another thing. Graham Bentley, 11 Mountjoy Road.'

'Don't tell me. He never lived there.'

'Better than that. There's no Mountjoy Road in SW4. Or anywhere else in London according to the *A to Z*. Only Mountjoy

Close, in EC2 and SE2.'

Finally Latymer had the chance to exchange his own news. 'How about this then?' and he told him of the death of Andy McKinley.

'Good grief, after all these years!' exclaimed Tess, as she opened a letter the following morning. 'It's from Rachel. You know, my flatmate in London years ago. She says Sue, an old friend of both of us, is stopping over in London for a few days on her way back from New York to Australia. She's been living out there for ages. It's *years* since we all met up. Rachel wants me to come up to London so that we can get together.'

Latymer smiled. 'Why don't you? It will do you good.'

'I think I will. There's so much for us to catch up on. Perhaps we can go to a couple of shows too and I can do some Christmas shopping. Sue arrives here on Friday. I could go up Saturday morning if that's OK by you. It'll only be for a few days.'

He came over and gave her a hug. 'Take as long as you like.'

'Are you saying you're glad to get rid of me?' she responded, with a laugh.

He tried not to feel uncomfortable. 'Not at all. What I might well do is take the opportunity to suss out some of the places we'll be visiting during next season's tours. Becketts are adding Shropshire as an option: Housman, Mary Webb, Ellis Peters. It would be useful to have a look round, see how long it takes to get from one place to the next, how good the local pubs and cafés are. You know I like to do my research in good time. You'll be able to reach me anytime on my mobile.'

'Good idea,' she said and went off to find out about trains.

He watched her drive away. If Tess took an early train to London on Saturday, he thought, to salve his conscience he could drive through Shropshire, stopping at one or two places on the way, then make straight for the Borders. At least he'd have a couple of days to make some enquiries. After which, all this had to stop. Having made the decision, he rang Sean Elliot's number and told his wife that he was coming up to Scotland that weekend. He also rang Keith Berry and told him what he was proposing to do.

'Would you like me to come with you?'

'It's a tempting idea. But not this time, I think.'

'This time? You intend making a habit of it?'

'No. That is, I don't see how I can. I can only go now because Tess is going up to London to see some old friends. I've told her I'm researching literary figures in Shropshire. But when I come back we'll talk again. The trouble is, once you start on something like this you want to go on until you get to the bottom of it.'

'Don't I know it. See you.'

He dropped Tess off at the station early on Saturday morning and drove straight to Shropshire. The weather was fine and he made good time to the Clun villages, took a brief detour along Wenlock Edge, before heading for the motorway north of Birmingham. The sky steadily became more overcast as he skirted Manchester and by the time he passed Preston it was already getting dark. As he drove through mile after mile of bleak, empty countryside he wondered what it must have been like to make the journey centuries earlier when there were footpads and highwaymen to contend with, not to mention the reivers, the bloodthirsty brigands of the Borders.

By the time he turned off on to the Stranraer road, he was tired, stiff and cursing his decision to go back to Scotland. It was late by the time he arrived in Kirkcudbright and found a bed at the Dornoch Arms, but at least they had been willing to give him a hot meal. Afterwards, still feeling cramped from the car, he went outside to stretch his legs. The sky had cleared and it was a crisp, cold night with an almost full moon. He crossed the main road and went down through the nearly empty car park to the castle. The gate leading to its inner court was securely closed for the night. Dead on cue, an owl hooted from somewhere above. He walked around the outside wall, wondering where McKinley's body had been found, until he came to a small row of traffic cones. A dangling piece of yellow and black tape was stretched around them. There was nothing else, presumably the police had finished searching the immediate area.

Lady of Annan and *Tam o' Shanter* were both tied up against the little quay. Well, he would see Elliot in the morning. He shivered in a sudden wind. Quite suddenly the town and its river felt alien to him. Like a foreign land, which in a way, he supposed, it was.

Elliot came looking for him as he was finishing his breakfast. 'Good to see you again, John,' he said, shaking him warmly by the hand. 'Jeannie Armstrong was very grateful for what you did for her.'

'But I didn't do anything. The police stuck to their story and that was that.'

'I feel even worse about you coming up here then,' said Elliot. 'It's probably just another waste of your time.'

'As it happens the trip to Cornwall wasn't entirely wasted,' Latymer rejoined. 'Don't tell Jean Armstrong yet as I don't want to raise any false hopes, but there's definitely

108

something wrong. Whoever the man was who was identified, the address given for him doesn't exist. Not only that, I've real doubts about the supposed brother.'

Elliot took this in. 'Well! You can tell me all about it later, and I think you're right – it's better kept from Jeannie for the time being. Now there's Andy's death.'

'It definitely was a heroin overdose?'

'No doubt at all, according to the post-mortem. But they admit there were no obvious signs of addiction. No needle marks, apart from the one for the dose that killed him. What they're saying is that he must have been smoking it and then decided to start injecting and misjudged the dose. He'll go down as just another drug death statistic. His girlfriend is absolutely convinced he never did drugs. You might like to have a word with her.'

'And how is Jean Armstrong coping now?' enquired Latymer as they left the hotel. 'She wrote thanking me for my help, telling me she was putting the children in a nursery and starting on some kind of computer course. And she'd no intention of giving up until she's found out what's happened to Euan.'

'I can believe that,' agreed Elliot. 'I'm surprised at how determined she is. What's happened has changed her. She never used to be like this. She says she's certain, whatever the police say, that Euan is dead and that she won't rest until she gets some answers.'

'I've known it happen before,' Latymer acknowledged. 'People who have never been able to string more than a few words together become articulate, and folk who've never questioned authority before in their lives turn into obstinate fighters when something bad happens that directly affects them.'

'You'll be able to see for yourself,' Elliot told him. 'She's coming over to have dinner with us today. But first I'll take you down to where they found the body, then we'll call in on Sally – that's his girlfriend.'

Latymer had rightly surmised McKinley's body had been found in the taped-off area. 'He couldn't have fallen from anywhere,' Elliot told him as they both looked up at the ruin. 'The gate to the inside was locked and he'd hardly have climbed over it, it's spiked at the top. But the odd thing is that a few odds and ends, including his flat key, were found inside, yet the official who looks after the site and knows everyone in town, swears that he never saw Andy in the castle that day, or any other, that he can remember.'

'If he'd fallen from anywhere inside there would have been ample evidence,' Latymer commented, 'but that's not to say he died in the immediate area. Did the police say anything about that? If he did die some-where else and was moved afterwards they should be able to tell.'

'Not that I know of. So far as they're concerned it's just another drug death.'

'Do you know when he was found?'

'About four o'clock in the morning, I think.'

'Have you talked to anyone who saw or spoke to him the previous day?'

'He spent the night before that with his girlfriend. He told her he'd got a permanent job lined up at last and they went out to celebrate. But she can tell you herself, she lives just round the corner on the High Street.'

I wonder how many other people know I'm in town, thought Latymer, and why. They'll think I'm some kind of private detective muscling in making enquiries best left to the Dumfries and Galloway police. Elliot led the way to a terrace of colour-washed houses. The door was opened to them by a red-haired young woman whose swollen eyes demonstrated that she'd been crying.

'Is this a particularly bad time, Sally?' began Elliot. 'We know how upset you must be. But I'd be grateful if John could ask you a few things. Like you, I find it almost impossible to believe Andy took drugs.'

'Is he polis?' she demanded suspiciously,

111

eyeing Latymer.

'Ex-police,' he told her. 'Very much *ex-police*. I got involved in all this because I just happened to be there when Andy had his fight with his skipper. In fact I called the ambulance when I saw he was hurt.'

'It was John who went down to Cornwall with Jeannie to see if she could find out any more about Euan,' added Sean.

Sally nodded. 'You'd best come in.' She led them through into a neat sitting room. 'I'll just let mother know what I'm doing.' She reappeared a few minutes later, having washed her face. 'Aye, Euan Armstrong going off like, that's strange too. Andy could never understand it. They were friends, you know. And I hear Jeannie's still convinced that man found dead in Cornwall was Euan. So what is it you want to know, Mr...?'

'Latymer, John Latymer. I'd be most grateful, if it's not too painful for you, if you could tell us anything you can about Andy, particularly his behaviour during the last few days before he died. I take it you don't believe he was a heroin addict?'

'He wasn't. Most definitely not. Surely I would have known, if anyone did? We've known ... knew ... each other since we were seven years old and both in the same class. We spent all our time together, we were going to get married as soon as he'd found a decent job. Everything started to go wrong

112

after that bloody trip to Cornwall.'

'Because of the fight?'

'Aye, because of the fight. We all know how some men on the boats get a skinful when they come ashore, then start smacking each other. But not Andy. And to have pulled a *knife*. What got into them? They'd worked together for years.'

'There was a suggestion then that it had to do with drugs,' said Latymer. 'I was told they've a big problem down there. I know it was what some local people thought at the time.'

Sally shook her head. 'No. No, I'm sure it wasn't drugs. He smoked fags, but then who doesn't? But nothing else. When he got back from Cornwall after being in hospital, he was different. Really worried about something. It preyed on his mind. I was pretty amazed when he decided to give up the boats, fishing was his life. Harry Douglas came round and tried to patch it up, but it was no good. After that Andy just drifted, doing what work he could, a bit of labouring, some driving.

'Then, suddenly, he brightened up. Said he'd met a man who'd offered him some interesting work. He wouldn't say what it was, only that it was legal and well paid and he'd tell me all about it once it was definite. So we went out to celebrate, to the posh hotel in Gatehouse of Fleet, then back to his place to bed...' Her voice broke. 'He got up in the morning right as rain. He said he'd things to sort out and he'd see me the next day and we could start making real plans for the wedding. I never saw him again until someone came running to tell me they were putting him into the ambulance and by that time he was already dead.'

'Presumably the police searched his flat?' queried Latymer.

'Oh aye. But there wasn't much to see. It's really only a big bedsit, with a shower room off. He'd not got much in it but even so it was always a tip. I'd told him that once we were married and set up home, he'd have to change his ways.' Her voice faltered. 'The police told me they found nothing. Not a trace of drugs.' Her eyes filled again with tears.

'Are you sure there's nothing else you feel you should tell us?' asked Latymer, gently.

She hesitated. He could have sworn she was weighing up what to say. Then she set her shoulders and lifted her head. 'No. No, nothing else.'

'It certainly doesn't sound as if he was experimenting with heroin,' commented Latymer, as the two men left the house. 'But if what she says is true his change in behaviour started after the fight in Cornwall. Yet all that does is bring us back again to the possibility of an involvement with drugs –

it's a vicious circle.'

'Well, I can't see the police here changing their minds,' declared Elliot, 'they don't believe anyone else was involved.'

Latymer gave a wry smile. 'Just like the police in Cornwall and the body in the harbour. You know that young woman and I don't, but I felt she was holding something back. But if she was, God knows what it is.'

The bar of the Dornoch Arms was busy as they went in for a drink before dinner. There was no need to introduce the subject of McKinley's death: it was already the main topic of conversation. There seemed little or no consensus of opinion as to the truth of the matter. 'I reckon that while he wasn't an addict himself,' opined one woman, 'perhaps he'd started dealing in the stuff, since he'd no proper job any more. Then thought he'd try it just the once and gave himself too much.'

'Or got into trouble with some big bastard he owed money to for his habit who did it for him,' added another.

'You're away in a dream,' bellowed a young man with a pint in one hand and a whisky chaser in the other. 'You've been watching too much TV. D'ye reckon someone we all know like Andy would start dealing drugs in a place this size without us all knowing about it? As to trying it himself the once ... well, that I don't know. We've all done daft things in our time.'

'I don't believe he ever took drugs,' his companion chimed in. 'My sister knows Sally Black really well and she says she'd never have stuck with him if he'd been doing them or even just messing about with them.'

Elliot shrugged. 'There you are, you see. It's a mystery.'

His wife put her finger to her mouth when they arrived at the front door. 'Jeannie's wee boy's asleep upstairs and we want to keep it that way while she has her dinner. The little lass is in the old high chair. I dug it out from the back of the garage.'

'Did they have much to say about Andy McKinley in the pub?' Mary Elliot enquired, after the pudding had been cleared away.

'Plenty. But none of it to any good purpose,' replied her husband. 'He *might* have been on drugs, he'd *never* been on drugs, he was *dealing* drugs, he was experimenting with them. No one has a clue what happened.'

'His girlfriend swears he wasn't a user,' added Latymer, 'and that she would definitely have known if he was. She was very convincing.'

'Aye,' agreed Elliot, 'and she said again that he'd just been offered a good job somewhere. They were going to get down to planning the wedding day. If that's right, then surely the last thing he'd have done was start fooling about with heroin.'

Jean shivered. 'First Euan, now Andy McKinley, who next? Look, you may think I'm paranoid, but I've been thinking. D'you reckon there was something they *both* knew, which they shouldn't?'

'It's a thought,' Latymer conceded. 'Are you any nearer to finding out what your husband was working on before he disappeared?'

She shook her head. 'No, but even I'm coming round now to think it must have been to do with drugs. I can't think of anything else so risky. At first I thought it might be to do with fraud and council contracts – there's been a lot of rumours and it's the kind of thing he might well have decided to look into. He's never trusted politicians from any party. But he definitely spoke of danger and whatever's gone on in our local planning department, we're hardly talking about the Mafia.'

They left the table and Jean put the little girl down to play with her toys. 'As soon as I got back from Cornwall, I turned the place upside down to see if he'd left any notes or papers I still hadn't come across. Then, when I started my course, I thought about the computer, but I wasn't sure what to look for or how to do it. So I asked one of the other students if he'd come round and have

117

a look but there was nothing much on it at all. He reckoned Euan must have saved what he was doing on to floppy discs. And the computer isn't up to getting on to the Internet.'

She picked up a carrier bag, took out a file and handed them some A4 sheets. 'I did find these though, stuck under the printer. But as you can see, it's nothing much. Just bits and pieces.'

There were a couple of stories on the effect of EEC rulings on local fishermen, reasonably well put together but hardly newsworthy; also the draft of a feature on the bird life of the Solway.

Latymer skimmed through it. 'He was interested in birds then?'

'Only quite recently. He'd a really expensive pair of binoculars. A friend told me the last time she'd seen him he'd been over Dundrennan way watching birds with them. Getting them caused a row too, but he claimed someone had given them to him. Not that I believed him.'

The name rang a faint bell. 'Where's Dundrennan?' enquired Latymer.

'A little way down the coast,' Elliot told him. 'It's only claim to fame is its ruined abbey.' He frowned. 'I suppose it's possible that while he was out birdwatching he might have seen something he thought a bit odd. A boat where it shouldn't be, or which was strange to this area. People rowing ashore in a funny place. And perhaps they saw him.'

'Then there's this,' added Jean. 'It's a bit weird. My friend said it looked as if it was the last page of a document of some kind. We couldn't make head nor tail of it but thought it might be something to do with EEC quotas.'

There was very little on the sheet of paper, which seemed to be a continuation of some kind of table:

BQS

Inner Solway Shrimps	2.5	to 3.8
North Solway Coast Crabs	14	16
Lobsters	850	1800 (1997)
Wick	Not analysed	

Intervention level for food is 1.250

'First lobsters, then pigeons, now spinach.'

Six

www.fisherking.com. Click on Lobsters. 'First Lobsters, then Pigeons, now spinach (not shrimps here). The new Ministry of Agriculture, Scottish Environment Protection Agency Data is out. A selection of figures for contamination with Technetium-9 follow which give an idea of how it spreads. I've removed the data for 1992–94 so that the table fits on an e-mail plus attachment.'

They stared at the sheet of paper in front of them.

'What the hell is that about?' exclaimed Sean.

Jean shook her head. 'As I said, the only thing we could think of was that it was something to do with quotas and fishing. Or EEC regulations.'

'But that would hardly explain the pigeons and spinach,' commented Latymer. 'So you've no idea what this might mean, Sean?'

'Not a clue. 2.5 and 3.8 of a shrimp! And what wasn't analysed at Wick? Or happened to 1800 lobsters in 1997? Perhaps it's some kind of joke.'

'Anyway I'll leave it with you,' said Jean. 'We must go or I'll miss the last bus. When do you go back, John?'

'The day after tomorrow at the latest or I'll be in dire trouble at home. I'll call you before I do. Even if this is part of some table of data, I don't see how it could possibly result in some shocking revelation in a newspaper.' They all laughed. Later he would recall just how wrong that was.

The next morning was very overcast but time was short and he must make the most of it. He got out his map of central Scotland. Where was it Armstrong had been seen shortly before he died? Dundrennan. That was it. The remains of the abbey were clearly marked. Well it might be interesting to go out there and see where Armstrong did his birdwatching; if that's what it was. But before he left the hotel, he rang Keith Berry.

'How's it going?' Berry sounded cheerful.

'I don't think it's going anywhere,' Latymer admitted. 'Except that few people here, including McKinley's girl, believe he took drugs. Armstrong's wife doesn't seem to have got any further either. She made me think though. Was there something both these men knew which they shouldn't, as a result of which someone, somewhere decided they had to be got rid of? I know it sounds far-fetched.'

'Who? Local villains? Drug dealers? I suppose if the would-be hack had crashed into a major organization of some kind and told his friend, it might be possible. But not very likely. What are you going to do now?'

'Go up the coast a few miles. It seems Armstrong had developed an interest in birdwatching. Or claimed he had. If he really was, then I suppose it's possible he saw something dodgy going on while he was doing it and threatened to publicize it.'

'When do you get back?'

'Tomorrow or my life won't be worth living.'

'If you do go up there again, let me come with you. Two heads are better—'

'I've no intention of coming up here again.' Latymer meant it. He put down the phone.

He drove up and out of Kirkcudbright through trees on whose branches only a few, battered leaves still clung. The view of the coastline on the other side of the river was a fine one until the road abruptly flattened out and bore sharply left across open scrubland with the sea some distance away on his right. A sign pointed to Dundrennan and onwards from there to Dalbeattie, while on the seaward side there was now a high fence, partly topped with razor wire. Every few feet or so along its length were notices saying: 'Warning. Danger Area! Keep Out. Ministry of Defence.' A mile or two further on, he passed a gate and a road leading down to a cluster of drab buildings. From then on he noticed that all the lanes and paths to his right, which must once have led down to coves or beaches, were closed to the public except for one sign-posted to 'Port Mary'. He stopped the car, got out and walked across the road. There was little to see. Behind the fence, the ground rose slightly, blocking off any view. A greyish blur on the horizon may or may not have been the sea.

He continued on to Dundrennan. Out of season the small town was almost deserted. The abbey ruins were extensive, even impressive, but a chill wind had got up and a light rain was beginning to fall. There was nothing to tempt him to linger. He went into a newsagent's shop to buy a paper, then, noticing they also sold maps, bought a detailed Ordnance Survey map of the area and went in search of some coffee.

He was the only person in the chilly lounge of the small hotel. The attitude of the young woman who plonked his coffee down in front of him deterred him from asking if she would put the gas fire on. He opened the map and spread it out on the table in front of him. To his surprise a large area to the east of Kirkcudbright right down to the edge of the Solway Firth was peppered in red with the words 'Danger Area'. Nor did the warnings stop at the coastline, but went right out into the Firth itself and even into the Irish Sea. He looked at the road he had taken between Kirkcudbright and Dundrennan but could find no Port Mary marked anywhere along the coast. He must have misread the signpost. He finished his coffee, glanced at the day's headlines, and went in search of the young woman who had brought him his coffee.

'You on holiday?' she enquired as he counted out the change.

'Taking a break,' he replied, 'in Kirkcudbright.' He gave her the money. 'I see the Ministry of Defence has fenced off a big area back along the road. What do they do up there?'

'It's a firing range,' she answered, shortly.

That made sense and explained why the maps were marked 'Danger' miles out from the coast. 'I take it they fire out to sea then? It must be pretty hazardous for shipping.'

'The skippers get told when they're going to do it.' It was obvious she had no wish to prolong the conversation.

He returned to his car. A firing range. Hardly conducive to attracting tourists, but then that wasn't a priority for the MoD – look at Dartmoor. He set off back towards

Kircudbright and was deep in thought when he noticed again the sign to Port Mary. It definitely pointed down towards the sea. He pulled in and referred to his new map. No, it definitely wasn't marked. So what was down there? On an impulse he turned left and followed the sign. He drove cautiously for the lane was very narrow with endless blind corners, but eventually it widened out and he found himself at a dead end. On his right was what had once been a farmhouse, immediately ahead a reinforced metal gate and fence marked: 'No Entry. MoD Property'.

A track bore off on his left. Another notice, with an arrow pointing down it, informed him that this was a day when the beach was open. Open for what? Presumably, as on Dartmoor, it meant there was no firing on the range that day; therefore the public had access. Presumably the elusive Port Mary was at the end of the lane and he envisaged a small quay where boats could tie up when the ranges weren't in use, though this didn't explain why it wasn't marked on his map. The track wound on for another mile or so, crossed a burn, then ended without warning in a clump of straggling trees at the edge of a small bay. Shallow cliffs curved round both sides of it but there was no sign of a quay or anywhere a boat could easily be beached.

The scene around him was bleak. The rain, which had looked as if it might hold off, was getting heavier by the minute. The 'beach', such as it was, was made up almost entirely of shingle and large pebbles, leading down (since the tide was out) to flattened and broken rocks. The burn he'd crossed earlier trickled sluggishly across the shingle into the open water; while beside it tufts of the fleshy-leaved plants common to exposed beaches wilted in the wind. It was distinctly unappealing. The rain blew into his face from across the Solway. Who on earth would bother to find their way to such a place, even when the road was open? Of 'Port Mary' there was no a sign.

Then he heard the sound of a vehicle from behind him and turned to see a dark grey car bumping down the track. It emerged at the top of the beach and the driver pulled in and parked beside his own. Some other tourist in search of Port Mary? Or a local? Perhaps people fished off the beach, though it didn't look likely at present as the tide was out. If it was a local perhaps they could explain what had happened to the supposed port and why the signpost pointed to a place that no longer existed. He retraced his steps.

The driver of the grey car, his window wound down, was puffing on a cigarette and staring out to sea. He looked at Latymer without a change of expression and answered his 'good morning' with a grunt.

'Not much of a day for the beach,' Latymer persisted. 'Or do you come here to fish?'

The driver stubbed out his cigarette. 'Why do you want to know?'

'I just wondered that's all. Do you know why the sign up on the main road says Port Mary when there's no port here?'

The man merely shrugged and took out another cigarette. There was nothing to be gained by hanging around in such a dismal place, so Latymer turned his car and made his way first along the track, then up the lane and on to the main road. He must ask Sean about Port Mary. Also what kind of firing ranges required danger notices covering half the Irish Sea.

He was within a mile or so of his destination when he realized that the grey car he had left on the beach was now behind him. For a brief moment the thought crossed his mind that he was being followed, but when he turned into the hotel car park it continued past without even slowing down. However, all questions about the mysterious port and the use of the firing ranges went right out of his mind when he walked into the hotel bar to find Sean waiting for him. He motioned at the newspaper under Latymer's arm.

'You've seen it then?'

'Seen what?'

'The piece in the *Herald*. It seems Jeannie's gone public about Euan.'

'No. I've only looked at the headlines.'

The two men sat down together and Latymer opened his paper. The story was not hard to find. It was headed 'WOMAN DEMANDS TO KNOW FATE OF HUSBAND. "I will never give up until I know the truth," declares Jean Armstrong.' Underneath, was a large picture of her with her two children and a smaller one of Euan.

'Did you know about this?' queried Latymer.

'I'd no idea. Jeannie never let on yesterday. You were there yourself most of the time.'

Readers were informed that Mrs Jean Armstrong's husband, Euan, had gone missing at the end of August and that in spite of the efforts of herself and the Dumfries and Galloway police nothing had been heard of him since. 'We'd had a row,' she was quoted as saying, 'and I'd gone to my sister in Glasgow for a few days to let things cool down. Even so, Euan would never have walked out on us like that. He's devoted to the children. But the police seem to think it's just another broken marriage story.'

Euan Armstrong, it continued, had worked as crew on the boats fishing out of the Solway Firth for most of his working life but had recently tried to break into freelance journalism. His wife claimed that at the time of his disappearance he had been working on a story he had described to her as 'dangerous'.

But there is a macabre twist to the tale. Several weeks after her husband went missing, Jean Armstrong was shown a picture in a Cornish newspaper of a man found dead in the sea off the Cornish port of Newlyn. 'It looked exactly like Euan,' she says, 'and it's not only me that thinks that, so do people here that know him.'

Although she was told that the dead man had already been identified and the body cremated, Mrs Armstrong's quest has taken her down to Penzance in Cornwall. 'The police there agreed the photograph of my husband was very like the dead man but said that it definitely wasn't Euan. But if it wasn't, then where is he? Why hasn't he contacted us?'

A spokesman for Dumfries and Galloway police stated that everything possible had been done to discover the whereabouts of Euan Armstrong. 'In the light of what Mrs Armstrong told us, we ourselves contacted the Devon and Cornwall police and are entirely satisfied that the man found dead in

129

Cornwall was properly identified by members of his family. We must also emphasize that we still regard this as a Missing Persons Inquiry. There is no reason to believe any harm has come to Mr Armstrong.'

The piece ended with a plea to Euan to contact either his wife or the paper to let them know that he was safe and well. A police telephone number was also given for anyone who either knew where he was or thought they might have seen him.

'Well, that'll set the cat among the pigeons,' commented Latymer.

'D'you think anyone will ring in? That is, if Euan himself doesn't?'

'Hundreds of people, I should imagine. They always do. You wait, he'll have been seen in every town and city between Glasgow and Penzance. On Eurostar. Driving through Greece! Hours of police time will be spent following up the supposed sightings and, if my cynical experience is anything to go on, none of them will come to anything.'

'So she shouldn't have gone to the press?'

Latymer looked thoughtful. 'I don't know. My instinct was to keep it low key.' He felt in his pocket for some change and, in doing so, realized he'd left his mobile phone switched off since the previous afternoon.

Quite possibly Tess had tried calling him once she'd discovered he was still not home. Guiltily he switched it on and learned that she had. Excusing himself briefly, he went outside and dialled her friend's London number.

'Where on earth are you?' she demanded when she'd been brought to the phone. 'I thought you were bound to be home by now. It can't have taken all this time for you to drive round Shropshire.'

He economized with the truth. 'I decided to go a bit further, on into Wales,' he told her. 'There's been talk of a Dylan Thomas tour. I didn't think you'd mind as you were away yourself.'

'I suppose not,' she replied, somewhat mollified.

He changed the subject. 'Are you having a good time?'

She was, she told him. They'd been to the Tate Modern, up on the London Eye and were going to the theatre that evening. 'I'll be home the day after tomorrow. Presumably you're on your way back now?'

'More or less,' he lied. 'What time shall I meet you at the station?'

'Don't bother. The trains are so unreliable. I'll get a taxi.'

The conversation ended amicably and he rang off. But one thing was for sure. He had to be home by the following night as he told

Sean when he rejoined him in the bar. 'And I'm off to sea first thing in the morning,' said Sean. 'But I'd be glad if we can keep in touch. I suppose you must think it a wasted journey.'

'Logic tells me I should. But instinct? Well, that's rather different. I just don't know. Oh, and by the way, I went out to Dundrennan this morning, past that Ministry of Defence place. I understand it's a firing range. I bought a map while I was there and was amazed to see how big the area marked "danger" is. Why do they need so much space simply for target practice?'

'But it's not a range for rifles or assault weapons,' Sean explained. 'It's for firing shells.'

'*Shells!* Aren't they frightened of hitting something out to sea?'

'They haven't done so yet. So far as we know, that is. They always relay warnings when they are firing.'

'And the shells? Are they live?'

'It seems so.'

'Hell's teeth! Well, rather you than me.'

Sean shrugged. 'Oh you get used to it. After all, they've been doing it for years.'

The two arranged to meet later. Sean went off to his boat to make ready for sea the next day while Latymer, after a short walk round the town, went back to the hotel for some lunch. He was just about finishing it when

Sally Black came into the room. She was carrying a cardboard box.

'Is there anywhere we can talk?' she said uneasily, looking round.

'Let's see.' Towards the back of the hotel was a somewhat gloomy lounge which he had never yet seen used. As usual it was empty. They went inside and sat down.

'That story in the paper about Jeannie Armstrong,' she began without any preamble, 'it looks as if she still really believes the man found dead in Cornwall was Euan. Could it still be? In spite of what they say?'

'The police would have to have made a very big mistake. More to the point, so would the man's brother who identified his body. It hadn't been in the water long. It wasn't disfigured in any way – or so I'm given to understand – so it's hard to see how he could have done. Why?'

'When you came to the house, you asked me if there was anything else I'd like to tell you. Look,' she continued, awkwardly, 'I didn't know whether to trust you or not. To be honest, I'm still not sure but I can't keep it to myself any longer. You see, something funny happened just before Andy died. I told you he hadn't been the same since that business down in Cornwall and when he came back and found Euan missing, he was really worried. I kept asking him what was wrong, but all he'd say was that he'd a lot on his mind. Decisions he had to make and it was best he didn't involve me. It wasn't like him.

'As time passed and there was still no sign of Euan, it seemed to affect him more and more.' She lifted up the box and put it on the small table in front of her. 'The last time I saw Andy he asked me to take this home with me. He said Euan had left it in his flat and asked him to keep it safe for a week or two. But then Andy went off to Cornwall with the other lads and when he got back, Euan had disappeared. Andy hung on to it for a bit, not knowing what to do with it, then the day he went off for his interview he said he thought I'd better get in touch with Jean Armstrong and give it to her. I meant to, but after what happened it went clean out of my mind until you came to see me, then I remembered. It might have nothing to do with anything and I wouldn't know, I've no idea how these things work.' She opened the box and he looked inside. It was a laptop computer.

'You didn't think of giving it to the police?'

'I told you. I forgot about it. Anyway, why should I? It was Euan's computer, not Andy's.'

'What do you want me to do with it?' asked Latymer.

'Take it off my hands. Give it to Jeannie. I don't care. All I know is that I want rid of it.'

'Don't you think it might still be better to give it to the police?'

'I want nothing more to do with the police. They won't listen to anything I say.'

He nodded. 'Very well. I'll take it over to Mrs Armstrong and see if there's anything on it that might be of use. But if I think it contains information the police should know about, then I'll have no alternative but to tell them. You do understand that?'

She looked far from pleased. 'OK, then. But I don't want to know. Tell them all Andy was doing was keeping it for Euan.'

After she left, he considered what to do next. He was no computer expert. He looked in the box again and saw that there were also a couple of floppy discs. Presumably Euan had backed up his work. And there was, of course, the possibility that the hard drive contained the information for the story Euan had been working on. He came to a decision. He would drive over to Annan so that he and Jean Armstrong could look at what was on it together and see if it made any sense. Then, however late it might be, he would drive on home that night.

He walked down to the quay and told Sean what had happened.

'Pity I'm going to sea tomorrow,' he said. 'I'll be interested to know what you find there.'

'I'm leaving too,' Latymer informed him.

'I've decided to push on home after I've seen Jean. I'll either leave the laptop with her or, if she prefers, take it with me. There's a couple of discs too, which I can look at on my own computer. Whatever we might find, I've already warned Sally that if I believe the police should know about it, I'll have to tell them. Especially if drugs are involved.'

Jean greeted the discovery of the laptop with amazement. 'I'd no idea he had one. However did he pay for it? His credit card statements have kept coming but I haven't dared open them. I didn't want to know.' She went over to a small pile of envelopes on a shelf. 'I've kept them though.' She brought them over and opened them.

They were dated respectively August, September, October, November. The first statement showed a debt of £1,000 carried over from July, of which £100 had been paid off. The September statement showed the debt had been cleared. 'How on earth could he have found £900?' she commented in amazement. 'He never had that kind of money. And it must have been about the time he disappeared.' They checked through the rest to discover that no further pur-chases or withdrawals had been made.

'Well,' said Latymer, 'let's plug this in and see what happens.'

The result was something of an anti-climax. Whatever might have been stored on

136

the computer itself had obviously been wiped, except for some odds and ends filed under 'DUS', which meant nothing to either of them. 'Presumably he backed stuff up on the discs,' Latymer commented. He clicked on 'chooser' to discover Armstrong's server. 'Let's see if his e-mail files tell us anything.'

There was the usual selection of files labelled 'in', 'out', 'sent', etc. but they were all empty. Either Armstrong didn't make use of the facility or was sufficiently concerned someone might see what he had stored on his laptop to regularly check them and delete the contents. He tried 'sent/received' and was connected to the server. There was one message dated mid-October. He and Jean gazed at the screen, transfixed.

It was from 'fisherking@ appleonline.net' and was addressed to 'kinmontwillie'.

I am now seriously alarmed not to have heard anything from you for so long, even though you did say that you would not be in touch for a while but I'd at least expected a report on the last meeting. If you're still visiting the website, you must know I've been appealing for you to contact me. So far I have not, as I promised, contacted your wife. Two days ago I received the following disturbing communication: 'No idea who you are or what it's all about but am keeping a promise made to someone. To warn you. Something terrible's happened. He said if it did, you'd guess. A Friend'. Fisherking.

Seven

Jean turned to Latymer. 'See? I knew it! I knew it! Something bad *has* happened to Euan.' Latymer had to admit he was shaken. It was beginning to look as if she might be right.

'Who is this "fisher king"? What does it mean?' she persisted.

'I've no idea.' Latymer paused. 'I've a vague memory that the Fisher King had some kind of a connection with King Arthur, though it's years since I last read any of the Arthurian stuff. Yes, that's right. It's to do with the quest for the Holy Grail. One of the knights, I think it was Sir Percival, comes to a poisoned and blasted land ruled over by the mysterious Fisher King, who is suffering from an unexplained disease or a wound that won't heal. It was some kind of punishment because he was supposed to have kept the Grail safe, and it had gone missing.'

'But what's that got to do with anything?'

'I can't imagine.' He stared at the screen again. 'I wonder ... it could be this "fisher king", whoever he is, has a website. Let's see.' He logged on to the net, typed in 'fisherking' then hit 'search'. Within a short while a list appeared. There was a novel with that title, an opera by Michael Tippett in which the Fisher King appeared as one of the characters, a number of academic papers on the meaning of Grail legend, a host of sites to do with King Arthur and Camelot and, finally, 'fisherking, ecological consultant: www.fisherking.com'. That must be it. He typed it in.

He was totally unprepared for the torrent of information. 'Good God! Look at all this. I wonder if Euan downloaded any of it? Possibly he saved it on to a disc. Otherwise, if he'd printed it all off, you could hardly have missed it lying about in the flat. There's pages and pages of the stuff.'

'But what's it about?'

'A major health hazard in the Solway Firth. This early stuff doesn't say exactly what. It mentions cancers and a leukaemia cluster. This must be what Euan was working on, Jean, not drugs. He was on to something quite different, presumably to do with pollution.' He scrolled down – 'Kinmont Willie'. 'I assume this is Euan, since the e-mail was addressed to him under that name, presumably because he didn't want people to know who was doing it. But why Kinmont Willie?'

140

Jean smiled. 'It's the name of one of the famous bad lads of the Borders. Back hundreds of years ago. Always against authority. He made a famous escape from Carlisle castle. Aye, that would amuse Euan.' Then her face changed. 'Do you think this is so serious it could have put his life in danger?'

'I can't tell you at this stage. I'll have to wade through it all. Look, as an ex-policeman it's hard for me to say this, but there are people prepared to do almost anything to prevent information coming out that a government would rather we didn't know. But I may be going over the top. It could simply be to do with some public health issue the relevant local authorities aren't taking seriously.'

'So what do we do now?'

'I'd already decided to drive back home tonight. I think I should take the laptop with me. Download some of this material and also take a look at the discs to see what might be on them too. After that, I'll e-mail Mr Fisher King myself and ask him when he last heard from Kinmont Willie and if he has any idea of his whereabouts. Then, if he replies, I can take it further and see if he'll tell me exactly what it was your husband was up to. The other reason for taking the computer away is because it might be safer with me. Though possibly I'm getting paranoid!'

141

She smiled. 'Well at least have a cup of tea before you set off.' She went out towards the kitchen, flicking on a tape recorder as she did so. The music that came out was unfamiliar to Latymer. The tape had started halfway through a band of something vaguely folk, but with an odd persistent drum beat. Then came the pure, clear voice of a girl singing in a language totally unfamiliar to him. Jean reappeared with a teapot and two mugs on a tray.

'Whatever's this?' enquired Latymer, motioning towards the sound.

'She's singing in the Gaelic,' Jean informed him. 'Some of the songs are in English though. Haven't you heard them before?' He shook his head. 'It's a group called Capercaille. Very popular up here. This is from their last CD. It's called *Delirium*. Euan was very fond of it. We both were.'

She began pouring out the tea, at which point the telephone rang and she went over and answered it. 'Yes, this is Jean Armstrong.' There was a silence. 'I see. Is that right? No, I don't know what it means either, but thank you for telling me.' She put down the receiver. 'That was the *Herald*. They've had two telephone calls today from hotel managers, one in Carlisle and the other in Glasgow. Both said the same thing. That they had seen a man answering Euan's description back in the summer. That he'd

142

stayed overnight and asked if it was OK to plug in his laptop as he'd a business letter he needed to send. Why on earth would he do that? Surely he didn't think I'd be so furious with him for buying it that he daren't use it at home?'

Latymer began to feel cold. It was a symptom he recognized from the past when he first began to suspect he'd uncovered something nasty. 'One reason could be that he felt it safer to put information on to the fisherking website from various neutral locations. Probably a different one every time. That way he would be more difficult to trace.' It was beginning to look as if Armstrong had stumbled across a major story. If so, then inexperienced as he was and determined to keep it to himself, he would have been quite out of his depth.

Jean caught his mood and shivered. 'That man in Cornwall. Was it really someone else? Or do you now believe it *was* Euan?'

'I don't know,' he told her. 'I really don't know.'

He finished his tea, put on his jacket and replaced the computer and discs in the cardboard box. Jean Armstrong turned off the tape recorder and took out the tape. 'Here,' she said, 'take this. It might help pass the time on the journey. I've got it on a CD, this was the one we used in the car. It's off the road at the moment, I can't

143

afford to tax it.'

Latymer got wearily into his car, after stowing the box away in the boot. It was going to be a long and tiring drive. He made straight for Carlisle and from there on to the motorway. The temperature had dropped sharply and as he crossed the Border it began to snow. Halfway through Cumbria, he realized he was both hungry and thirsty and pulled into a motorway café. As he ate he watched the snow swirling past the windows and considered what to do in view of the rapidly worsening weather conditions. Perhaps the sensible thing would be to stop off somewhere near Manchester and find a room for the night, then continue on in daylight. Yes, that might be best. He finished his meal, drank a second cup of coffee and returned to his car. There was already an inch or so of snow on the windscreen and he brushed if off. Parked opposite was a grey saloon. The events of the morning came back to him suddenly. The car on the beach at the non-existent Port Mary had been grey and its driver had followed him back on to the road ... He shook himself. He was definitely getting paranoid.

He pushed on. The rain changed to sleet. He put on the radio but there was nothing he really wanted to listen to. He pulled Jean Armstrong's tape out of his pocket and fiddled it into the slot. The rhythmic beat of the music flooded the car. He still wasn't sure if he liked it, but it was better than driving in silence. From time to time he looked into his mirror but it was impossible to make out exactly what was behind him on the road, apart from the heavy lorries. He must stop this, he told himself. There were thousands of grey cars on the road and if he'd been that worried back there in Scotland, then he should have made a note of the number, he'd had ample time.

He reached the signs to central Manchester, decided against the city centre for the night, carried on south for a short while then finally left the motorway at Knutsford.

There was a hotel immediately on his right and he parked the car, went in, and asked for a room for the night. It had been cold outside and the lounge bar was very warm. He no longer wanted to eat, but he certainly felt like a drink. He had a double malt, then another. He wondered if it was sensible to leave the laptop in the boot and decided it was best to bring it in. The snow had stopped and it was freezing hard. The change of air and the whisky made his head swim slightly. The box containing the computer, labelled 'Kellogg's Corn Flakes', was exactly as he'd left it. He carried it into the bar, had another whisky, said goodnight to the barman and went up to bed, promising himself he'd leave at the crack of dawn.

The combination of cold, tiredness, alcohol and all that had gone before, put him out like a light and when he finally surfaced and looked blearily at the clock in his room he saw it was after nine o'clock. He leapt out of bed, shaved and dressed, and raced down for his breakfast. 'I overslept,' he told the young woman who came to serve him.

'Didn't you ask for a call then?' she enquired.

'I didn't think I'd need it.' It wasn't all that drastic, he told himself, as he decided after all to have a decent breakfast; there wasn't too much of a hurry since Tess wouldn't be home until the following day.

It was nearly ten o'clock by the time he went to his car. It was as he had left it. Everything was there: his anorak, the breakdown triangle in its yellow plastic case, the box in which he kept such items as screen defroster, a chamois leather, and other bits and pieces. He put his bag and the computer box in and slammed down the lid. There were two notices in the hotel car park warning visitors that the adjacent motorway encouraged thieves and that the management was not responsible for theft from vehicles. He opened the door. No problem, his radio and tape recorder were still in place.

The frost had been very heavy. It was thick on the windscreen and the car park looked like a skating ring. He would have to be very careful driving out. He sprayed the windscreen to clear the ice and set off gingerly towards the entrance to the car park. Almost at once, in spite of turning on the heater, the windscreen iced up again and he pulled over and braked to try and clear it. Nothing happened. He braked again, but the car kept on going until it hit the wall at the side of the car park with a dull crunch. He got out and surveyed the damage: a nasty dent to the wing but that was all. He started the car and tried the brakes again. Nothing. The pedal went right down to the floor.

Wearily, he took out his mobile phone and called the AA. They would, they said, be some time as the bad weather was causing many problems, so he should wait in the hotel until their man arrived. He pushed the car to the side to clear the entrance, cursing his luck, and sat down to wait. It was over an hour before the AA man turned up, whistling cheerily and chatting about the host of accidents caused by the ice on the roads. 'They don't clear or grit them like they used to,' he commented, 'then you get all these idiots who think they're immortal.'

He tried the brakes. 'Something's gone badly wrong here all right. There's no brake power at all. You had it serviced recently?'

147

'Three weeks ago.'

'Well there's nothing I can do, the car needs putting up on a ramp to find out what's happened. The best thing is for me to get you and the vehicle to a garage so that they can fix you up. There's one we use just down the road.'

This was getting worse and worse. Was he never going to get home? But there was nothing to be done except follow the expert's advice. Twenty minutes later he was towed ignominiously into a garage forecourt where the AA man explained the position to its proprietor, had Latymer sign to the effect that he had properly attended the call, then left for the next breakdown. The proprietor came out, looked at the car, shook his head gloomily and informed Latymer they were up to their eyes in work and it would be late afternoon at least before they could even begin to sort his problem out.

There was no help for it but to lie. 'But I can't wait that long.' He felt in his breast pocket as if about to take out a warrant. 'I'm a plain-clothes policeman. Detective Inspector Latymer, West Midlands police. I've been in Scotland and it's absolutely vital I get back to Birmingham.'

The proprietor shrugged. 'That's not my fault.'

Latymer took out his phone, walked a few yards away and pretended to call a number.

'I'm stuck in Knutsford, sir,' he said, loudly. 'The brakes are playing up on the car and they're telling me at the garage here they can't fix it until this afternoon.' He paused. 'I know that, sir. Yes, and it does look as if McGarry was involved in that drugs haul ... very well, I'll ask him again.' He turned to the garage owner. 'My chief says surely you can do something for me? We're talking possible murder here.' Then he took a risk. 'Do you want a word with him?'

'Oh, very well,' snapped the garage owner, 'tell your boss we'll do our best.'

'He says he'll do his best,' Latymer informed his non-existent recipient. 'Right, sir, be with you as soon as I can.'

Ten minutes later the car was up on the ramp and a mechanic examining the brakes. 'Fuckin' 'ell,' he said, after a minute or two. 'You got someone who doesn't like you? Someone you put away, p'raps? You being in the police.'

'All policeman do,' replied Latymer. 'Why?'

'Some sod's cut almost through your brake pipes. That's why.'

Latymer walked a few yards down the road and rang Berry. 'How'd you get on?' he enquired. 'Was it worth it?'

'You tell me,' said Latymer. 'Someone sabotaged my brakes last night outside a hotel in Knutsford. I'm lucky I wasn't killed

149

on the M6.'

'Christ! Come and tell me all about it as soon as you get a chance.'

He drove back on to the motorway, his mind in a turmoil. The hotel was literally yards from one of the most dangerous and congested stretches of motorway in the country. All things being equal, he would have driven out of the hotel car park almost straight on to the slip road and braked while waiting to join the pounding, nose-to-tail traffic travelling between Manchester and Birmingham. At which point his brakes would have failed. The hard frost had probably saved his life or at least kept him from serious injury. The mechanic was right of course. Most policemen made themselves enemies, though mostly it amounted to nothing more than muttered threats from the dock or threatening letters. But he was no longer a policeman and this was altogether different.

It had taken several hours for the garage to complete the repair and it was late afternoon by the time he turned into the road in which he lived and realized, with a sinking heart, that his misfortunes hadn't ended in Knutsford. The house was ablaze with light. He opened the door and saw Tess's bags in the hall. He called her name and she came down the stairs, her face frozen.

'I came back early,' she told him. 'Liz had

to go back to Australia suddenly. Her husband's had a heart attack.'

'I see.'

'And don't try and tell me you've been in Wales all this time.'

'The car broke down, Tess. You can check with the AA if you like. The brakes failed. I've been hanging about in a garage most of the day. I saw no need to call you as you weren't due home until tomorrow.'

She ignored him. 'You've been back up to Scotland again, haven't you?' He tried to speak. '*Haven't you?* Don't try to lie to me. I've just played a message on the answerphone from your girlfriend, this Jean Armstrong. She said she hoped you'd got back safely and that when she came back from doing her college course this afternoon, her flat had been broken into and everything turned over.'

Eight

'Go on,' continued Tess. 'You'd better return her call.'

Latymer dropped his bag down on the floor. 'Jean Armstrong is not my "girl-friend". You know very well that's not true.'

'Do I?' Tess gave him a bleak look. 'Do I? All I know is that you went off to Cornwall with her; then, as soon as my back's turned, you rush up to Scotland having lied to me as to where you actually were.'

He felt unutterably weary. The events of the past few days had taken their toll. Now this. He went back to the car and retrieved the computer. Tess stood and watched as he shut the door and placed it on a small table, then went into the kitchen.

He followed her. 'For God's sake, will you be sensible and listen to me, Tess! Come and sit down, let's have a drink and I'll try and explain. You know all about Jean Armstrong's husband's disappearance and the body found in Cornwall who was a dead ringer for him. Well there's been an un-expected development and Sean Elliot pleaded with me to go up there. I told you the brakes failed on the car, but since you're accusing me of God knows what, then you'd better have the truth. While I was stopping over in Knutsford last night – Knutsford, mark, not Jean Armstrong's flat – someone cut through my brake pipes. Had I not had to brake sharply before I got out of the hotel car park to clear the windscreen, I'd almost certainly have been killed on the M6 which is only a couple of hundred yards away.' He felt in his pocket. 'And here's the receipt for the hotel and that from the garage for the work they had to do.'

She said nothing but went into the sitting room and poured out two drinks. He took off his coat, then joined her. 'I did go to Shropshire. You can check that too if you like. Then I went on to Scotland via the Welsh border. You see there's been another death. One of the fishermen involved in that fight in Cornwall back in the summer and a close friend of Armstrong. He died of a heroin overdose but almost all those who knew him swear he'd never been a user. Before he disappeared, Armstrong had left with him a laptop computer and some discs. That's what's in the box in the hall. I've had no real chance yet to see what might be on it, but it seems Armstrong was on to some pollution story. I'll know more when I have a look in the morning.'

'But what then?' demanded Tess. 'What if you do find something sensational? You're not a journalist. You have no contacts. And if it's true what you say, that someone deliberately meddled with the car, then you must tell the police. The *police*, John, since you're no longer a policeman! As to the rest, how many times do I have to say it? Whatever you think might be going on up in Scotland, it has nothing to do with you.'

He was at a loss to know how to make her understand. 'I only wish I could see it that way, but I can't. Yes, I know, I'm no longer a detective, that it should all be behind me and anyway the local police are satisfied Armstrong's friend died of a drug overdose. Even though his own fiancée swears that couldn't have happened. But the facts are that Armstrong's vanished, his close friend is dead and someone tried to prevent my reaching home. Now Jean Armstrong's been burgled. At the very least I need to know what Armstrong was working on. And now, if you'll excuse me, I'll ring his wife.'

Jean sounded very subdued when she answered the phone. She'd realized something was wrong as soon as she opened the door and found books and papers strewn all over the place. 'At first I thought it was simply burglars but then I saw the TV and video were still there, and Euan's camcorder, which seemed very strange. But they'd

154

turned out all the cupboards, there were jars and crockery all over the floor, even the stuff from under the sink. The box I kept bills in had been emptied. Then I went into the bedroom thinking perhaps they'd taken the old computer, but it was still there. I can't tell if anyone else has been on it or not, but my notes for my course were all spread out on the bed. What do you think it means?'

'That someone was looking for something specific.' He hesitated, hoping that she would realize he was referring to the laptop.

There was a pause. 'That's what I thought. But who?'

'I don't know. But whoever they are, they must be pretty desperate.' Then he told her about the car. 'I think,' he added, 'that we should be careful in future what we say on the phone. By the way, have you told the police?'

'What's the point? They don't believe anything I say.'

'Tell them, just so that it's logged. And I'll be in touch one way or another.' He left it at that.

The atmosphere over breakfast the next day was chilly, Latymer's efforts to draw Tess out on her trip to London answered mainly in monosyllables. It was clear she felt her trust had been betrayed. They'd seemed so well suited at the beginning, both feeling they'd learned from their previous

155

marriages, eager to start a new life together away from old ties. He'd realized that Tess was naturally conservative, that her own world was one of order and familiarity. Outside her domestic preoccupations, her views on most matters were conventional. She held a touching faith in the forces of law and order, had in part been attracted to him because he had spent his working life as a policeman. Now, for the first time, he saw a gap widening between them.

Awaiting him was a thick packet from Becketts Literary Tours listing the names and addresses of those booked on the first tour of the season, along with a detailed itinerary of hotels, places of interest and dates for lectures, all of which he would have to check out. It took most of the day to do so but this time, instead of finding it interesting, even fairly enjoyable as he had in the past, the task now seemed unbelievably tedious. The prospect of a whole summer conducting tour parties around the country's literary sites made his heart sink.

Finally, when all had been done, he took out the laptop computer and the discs, but before investigating either further, logged on to fisherking.com from his own machine. At least the site was still there. He was beginning to wonder if he'd either got it wrong or it had somehow disappeared during the last forty-eight hours. There were a number of headings and he chose 'Background Information'. There was an awful lot of it. He clicked on to 'A Beginner's Guide' and read:

IT'S CHEAP, PLENTIFUL AND TOXIC

Depleted Uranium (or DU) is a radio-active heavy metal left over when the radioactive isotope uranium-235 is taken from naturally recurring uranium to fuel nuclear power stations and build nuclear bombs. This cheap and plentiful by-product is almost twice as dense as lead. It is valued by armies for its ability to punch through armoured vehicles.

A report by the US Army Environmental Policy Institute said that DU had both chemical and radiological toxicity ... The risk is greatest from ingesting DU or inhaling particles. DU poses a great threat to the kidneys, where high concentrations can lead to organ failure. There is also a radiological hazard, mostly due to short range alpha and beta radiation that can cause DNA damage and thus, in theory, lead to cancer. Source: *Daily Telegraph*.

There was plenty more. Suggestions that depleted uranium shells might be responsible for what had become known as Gulf War Syndrome, discussions as to the possibility of similar contamination following the conflict in Bosnia. But why should 'fisherking', whoever he or they were, be interested, let alone Euan Armstrong? What would interest a fisherman-turned-journalist in depleted uranium shells in Iraq? He downloaded some of the basic information on depleted uranium even though he could not see its relevance. After an hour or so Tess called up to tell him their meal was ready. He stopped with some reluctance as the last document he downloaded was some kind of table, at least half of which appeared to be missing. It detailed pollution data from the Irish Sea and Solway Firth, much of it attributed to the outlet waste pipe from the nuclear reprocessing plant at Sellafield on the Cumbrian coast.

But it also expressed concern about levels of radioactivity in seafood in the Solway Firth. That certainly brought things nearer to home. He was certain now that this was what Armstrong had been working on when he disappeared. He found the figures and the information hard to understand, not least a statement couched in semi-joking terms. 'For the first time results from vegetable plots near Sellafield, where seaweed is used as a fertilizer, have been published. These show that spinach has been found with a staggering 8,400 Becquerels per kilogram, almost seven times higher than the EU intervention level following a nuclear accident! *First Lobsters, then Pigeons, now Spinach!*' He had made the link but was at a loss to know what it meant.

The next morning he tried again. This time he chose 'Queries'. There were a number, mainly from women using only their Christian names, asking about possible threats to their children. One in particular interested him. 'Like many others in this area,' she wrote, 'I am becoming seriously alarmed. A public health official on the Dumfries and Galloway Health Board told me that the statistics from 1980 to 1997 showed no evidence of a high risk of leukaemia in children living near the range. But how do we know if that's really true?'

A range ... did she mean a firing range? Of course! The firing range near Dundrennan close to the beach and the non-existent Port Mary. Where he had been joined by the stranger in the grey car. And now, he thought seriously for the first time, possibly beyond. Perhaps, after all, the grey car in the motorway services in Cumbria had been the same one. If so the implications were deeply unpleasant. Had he been followed first to Jean Armstrong's flat, then on to the hotel in Knutsford? So what was so special about that particular firing range?

The first piece of information was from the the *Glasgow Herald*:

About 7000 shells, containing depleted uranium, have been fired over at least eight years at a range in Kirkcudbright, alongside the Solway Firth. Now the Government's Defence and Evaluation Research Agency, which monitors the range, has announced new experiments are to be carried out 'to determine the rate and nature of the corrosion process of DU both in the soil and the seabed'. The range is causing concern because the MoD says it can trace hardly any of the rounds fired into the sea. Dr Richard Dixon, of Friends of the Earth Scotland, said the MoD was doing little to solve the problem. 'We want this area cleaned of shells because there is a risk to the food chain.'

In another document, an Emeritus Professor of Chemistry then explained what happened to the shells fired into the sea...

'Since the depleted uranium penetratror is fully exposed after firing, the DU will leach into sea water and be eroded by wave action, etc. This way the sea environment will be contaminated. The best markers for such contamination are seaweeds, fish and crustaceans ... Today

160

the genie is out of the bottle and we have an uncontrolled and unknown situation. The precautionary principle would indicate that the situation should be carefully monitored and that people must be informed of the risks.'

There then followed a spate of comforting reassurances on public safety by spokespersons for the Ministry of Defence and government scientists.

This was all very worthy, thought Latymer, good material for Friends of the Earth and Greenpeace but hardly the stuff of a headline story for an amateur hack. There was obviously no secret about the existence of depleted uranium in shells used in the Gulf and Bosnia. As to more local implications, while it may not have been widely known elsewhere, presumably the population of Dumfries and Galloway had lived for years with the knowledge that such shells were regularly lobbed into the Solway Firth, without losing sleep over it.

And yet ... just suppose Armstrong had got on to some kind of a cover-up? Could go public on the fact that there was a real hazard from the shells quietly rotting just off the coast. The ramifications, if there really was such a hazard, were enormous. It would cost a vast amount of money to remove the shells from the silt, even if it was certain

161

they could be found. And if people then began to come forward with tales of ill health and demanding compensation, the bills would go through the roof. Far easier and cheaper to keep repeating the mantra that there was no problem and ensure, by one means or another, that the truth did not get out. No one wanted any unnecessary fuss: 'Not In My Term of Office' was a useful motto. The next move was obviously to contact 'fisherking' direct. But before doing so he must talk to Keith Berry.

'There's no doubt then that the brake pipes were sabotaged?' The two men were sitting over coffee in a café close to the bookshop. Latymer produced the bill from the Knutsford garage. 'I see. Have you reported it?'

'Tess has been on at me to do so, but no. Just at this moment I don't want to draw more attention to myself.'

'How is Tess?'

'Don't ask! We're barely on speaking terms. I think she now accepts I'm not having a raging affair with Jean Armstrong but won't forgive me in a hurry for deceiving her about going to Scotland. I suppose I can't blame her. But it's brought up again all the arguments about my having supposedly given up policing. She says she married an ex-copper not a private detective.'

'So what next?'

'When I get back I'll e-mail this "fisher-king" and see what, if anything, that produces.' He reached in his briefcase for a small file of papers then handed them over to Berry. 'These are copies of what I've downloaded so far. I'm no expert in this field but it does look as if the information's pretty sound. Have a read and see what you think.'

Berry took them. 'And then?'

'I think that will have to be it if I'm to restore domestic harmony.'

Berry lent across the table. 'Promise me one thing, John. If you do decide to take it any further, go back to Scotland say, take me with you.' He paused. 'You must think as I do that spooks could have been involved in this. At least I can watch your back.'

Latymer drove back through the middle of Bristol. It was raining and the Christmas decorations festooning the streets and shop fronts dripped dismally but, he thought, Tess and I might be able to sort ourselves out over the coming holiday. He returned home and sent an e-mail to 'fisherking', saying that he was acting on behalf of Mrs Jean Armstrong who was very anxious to know if he had any information on the whereabouts of her husband, Euan, known to him as 'kinmont willy'. He received no reply. For the time being he would do nothing more.

* * *

Christmas and New Year passed pleasantly enough, but much remained unspoken. On the surface all was well: they entertained and were entertained. Gave each other gifts. Tess's daughter and her husband came to stay for a few days, she excitedly informing her mother that by the summer she would be a grandparent. Jean Armstrong and the Elliots sent Christmas cards. But underneath, it felt to Latymer as if they were merely going through the motions. So far as Tess was concerned, Latymer had destroyed her trust.

A note from Jean added to the season's greetings in her card (addressed to both of them) informed them that her course was going very well and that she expected to be able to get a job in the New Year. But of Euan, there was still no sign. 'I simply can't believe,' she wrote, 'that if he was still alive, he wouldn't have sent presents to the children.' Tess read it without comment.

Then, interestingly, a few weeks into the New Year, the papers were full of claims by servicemen that they had been made ill by contact with depleted uranium shells. He read the stories with interest, but there were no further revelations, nothing more than the information he had downloaded from the fisherking website. The media frenzy lasted a few days, then it died away and interest turned to other matters.

***

The letter from Sally was forwarded on to Latymer by Sean Elliot.

Dear Mr Latymer

I don't know what you're going to think of me, but I still wasn't straight with you. I was very frightened after Andy's death but I've been thinking a lot over the New Year, my first without him, so this is it. I told you he was never the same after he came back from Cornwall and that he was worried about something. One night, it got really bad. He'd been depressed all day, then he went out and got really pissed. He came back out of his head and started rambling. 'I saw it,' he kept saying, 'I saw it. A guy's hand poking out. You see the ice had started to melt.' I asked him what he was talking about but he just went on and on about the ice, then he clammed up and said it was best I didn't know. In the end I got real mad and told him there was no way I'd marry him if he didn't trust me. This is as near as I can remember what he told me: 'I know I'd had a skinful but when I saw that I thought, Fucking hell, what's Harry got me into? So I went looking for him to ask him and he went for me. We nearly did

165

for each other. And now I can't get it out of my head. Keep dreaming about it. The hand in the ice. Afterwards Harry kept saying I was so pissed I was seeing things, but I wasn't. There was a *dead man* down there in the hold of our boat, packed in the ice. And I should have gone to the police.'

I told him to go now then, it wasn't too late, but in the morning he said it was nothing, to forget about it. He'd been drunk and having another night-mare. I wanted it to be true, so I left it at that. But now I believe he was telling the truth. He did see a dead man in the ice and look what happened to him.

A dead man in the ice. The implications stared Latymer in the face. He went up to his study and switched on his computer to see if there were any e-mails from Becketts Tours and found one entitled 'change of personnel'. Becketts personnel were always changing. But there was a second message too. He clicked on to it. It was very short.

'We must meet. Fisherking.'

Nine

Latymer had a disturbed night, laced with uneasy dreams. One was a familiar nightmare which had recurred since childhood. He was walking along a deserted beach. It was very bleak and empty and overhead was a lowering sky. Suddenly his feet began sinking into the sand. At the same time, he realized he was being pursued by some unknown terror but the faster he tried to run, the deeper his feet sank beneath him and the slower he moved. Then his pursuer or pursuers were right behind him, but he daren't turn round and look at them for fear of what he might see. Now he was unable to move at all ... He awoke in a cold sweat, his heart pounding.

'What's the matter?' queried Tess, sleepily. 'You've been tossing and turning all night, then you started jabbering. I was about to wake you up.' It was still dark outside the bedroom window. 'What time is it?'

He leaned over and looked at the clock. 'Half past seven. It must be raining again. I thought it was much earlier than that.' He

167

got out of bed. 'I'll make some tea.' The kitchen was warm from the Aga. He plugged in the kettle, unhooked two mugs, then gazed out of the window in the growing light. Everything outside was as neat and orderly as it was in the kitchen. Under the old apple trees there was a small drift of snowdrops. Tess, assisted by a local man, had worked wonders in the garden. It was a good place to live, they were not under any financial pressure and he had his summer job for interest. What on earth was the point of jeopardizing all this? He made the tea, waited a little while as it brewed, then took the mugs upstairs and handed one to his wife.

She sat up and took it from him. 'It's this wretched business again, isn't it? What's happened now?'

'I've tried to leave it alone, Tess, I really have. But whether I wanted it or not, I've become involved and I feel responsible. Yesterday I'd a letter from the fiancée of McKinley, the fisherman found dead of a drug overdose.'

'And?' Tess's face took on the frozen expression he was learning to expect. 'I don't think I want to hear this.'

'You asked me what was the matter! When I saw Sally – that's the young woman – I felt she was holding something back. Now she tells me that before he died, McKinley told

168

her that when they were in port in Cornwall, he'd discovered a dead man concealed
in the ice in the bottom of the boat.'

'So why in God's name didn't he immediately tell the police?' demanded Tess.

'It seems it's just about the last thing any
sea fisherman would do. The less they have
to do with the police the better. When
there's a problem, the tradition is they sort
it out themselves even if it results in rough
justice.'

'Even murder?' Latymer said nothing.
'Did he know who it was?'

'I don't think so. Sally says all he saw was
a hand sticking out of the ice.'

She stared at him. 'And you *believe* it?

'In this context it makes an awful kind
of sense. If I killed someone and wanted
thoroughly to confuse forensics, packing the
body in ice would be a good way to do it.
Then, to make things even more difficult for
the investigators, how about conveying it
hundreds of miles from the place where the
killing took place and throwing it overboard
for good measure? Mind you, the obvious
place to do that would have been well out at
sea, not just off the coast. I wonder what
went wrong?'

Tess finished her tea and slammed down
the cup. 'The literary tours have gone to
your head. Perhaps you should think of
writing a crime novel.' She got up. 'I'm

going to have a bath. I suppose you're going to tell me next you know who it was.'

'I think it was Euan Armstrong.'

Later that morning he sent another e-mail to Fisherking. 'Re your e-mail. I live near Chepstow and for this and other reasons such a meeting would be very difficult for me at present. Why do we have to meet? Won't e-mails or the telephone do?'

The answer came within the hour. 'Because I'm dying. That's why. Fisherking.' Latymer sat down and made a call to Keith Berry.

This time he asked Berry to come over to see him as Tess was out for the rest of the day. 'Some place you've got here,' he commented admiringly, looking around. 'Makes my flat over the shop look like a slum. How'd you manage it?'

'I still had money from the sale of my other house after I split up with Linda. And Tess got a good price for hers.' He paused. 'Who knows? The way things are going a flat over a slum might well be an option – not that yours is.'

'Can't be that bad, surely?'

'Can't it? If I could get her to understand. I've no intention of making a habit of this kind of thing, but now it's got this far .... Anyway, now you're here, take a look at these.' He handed him Sally's letter and copies of the Fisherking e-mails. *'Is* it

170

drugs?'

Berry glanced through the papers. 'So. Let's suppose this chap Armstrong had been poking around and fell over a major local drugs operation. It doesn't need rocket science to work out that the kind of people involved aren't particularly picky about how they deal with those who interfere in their business. Obviously the skipper of the boat must be involved.'

'Indeed.' Latymer referred to a notebook. 'Harry Douglas – that's the skipper's name. But was he acting on his own or were there others, higher up the chain, who told him to get rid of the guy who was asking all the questions? If Douglas's usual part in the operation is limited just to bringing the stuff in under cover of his legitimate fishing, it would be logical for whoever disposed of Armstrong to make use of him to dispose of the body. Except that he didn't do it in time and found himself tied up with it still aboard in a harbour crowded with people attending a carnival. Next thing, McKinley sees the body and the plan goes even more wrong.'

Berry frowned. 'But surely the rest of the crew, including McKinley, had to be in on it? And if that's the case, then any one of them could shop Douglas, not just Mc-Kinley.'

'I don't think all of them need have been.

One would be enough. It would take two to get the body out of the ice and over the side. Presumably for one reason or another there was never an opportunity until they'd actually got to Cornwall. I know from Elliot that they hadn't done any fishing on the way south as the weather was poor. But I can't understand why Douglas took such a risk. Oh, possibly you're right. They were all in on it and Douglas and McKinley really fell out over the cut each was to get. It'd make more sense. Presumably the local police questioned the other crew members after McKinley's death if only for confirmation he did drugs.'

'It puts "Bentley" in the frame too,' responded Berry. 'Presumably he's all part of the set-up and when he realized something had gone wrong, he went down to Cornwall and put on that charade for the benefit of the police. God knows how you'll prove any of this, though. But what about "Fisherking"? Are you going to see him?'

'I want to but how on earth am I going to tell Tess?'

'Ask her to come with you. And if she won't, and you're still set on going, then take me. It'll be quite like old times.'

'Give me a day or so to summon up the courage, then I'll let you know.'

He began in as placatory way as possible

172

and at first Tess said nothing. He explained that as well as the letter from Sally Black, he'd had an e-mail from a dying man who wanted to speak to him urgently. Therefore he felt he should go to Scotland again, but very definitely for the last time. 'So why don't you come with me? I know it's hardly the best time of year, but I'm sure we could find somewhere nice to stay. And if you're still worried about Jean Armstrong you could meet her and see for yourself that you've nothing to fear. I'll go and see this man, he sounds quite genuine, then we could go on to Edinburgh for a few days.'

'You've not taken in a word I've been saying to you,' she blazed at him, her face white. 'You've become obsessed with this ... this farrago to the point where you're unbalanced. Out of your head. You should see a doctor.'

This was even worse than he'd expected. 'Tess, I'm obsessed, as you call it, because I can't get to the bottom of this. Because the more I find out, the nastier it gets. I agree that from the start it should have been a matter for the police. But we're talking about two separate police forces hundreds of miles apart. Dumfries and Galloway haven't over-exerted themselves because, so far as they're concerned, Euan Armstrong has simply run out on his wife and family. And McKinley? He's just another statistic on the drugs deaths register. As for the Cornish police, I can't see the remotest chance of finally convincing them that the body they found in the harbour was wrongly identified without new evidence. Don't you see? By sheer coincidence, I'm the link between the two cases. That's what's driving me on.'

'So you know better than two police forces!'

'I'm not saying that. They've made perfectly reasonable assumptions, based on what they know, and have closed their minds to any other possibilities. I see this as my last chance to persuade them otherwise.'

'Then you're on your own,' she told him. 'And I mean it. Really on your own. I've no intention of coming with you on a wild goose chase. If you go to Scotland again, then you must take the consequences.'

'What are you saying?' he demanded.

'That it's this crusade of yours or me. You can't have both. This isn't what I married you for. For our home to be turned into some kind of private detective agency, for all and sundry to ring up, write letters, send e-mails. I thought we both knew what we wanted. It seems I was wrong.'

'Are you really telling me that our relationship means so little to you? That you're prepared to break up our marriage over this?'

'It's not me that's wrecking our marriage,'

Tess retorted. 'Go to Scotland by all means. But don't rely on my being here when you get back.'

He nodded. 'Then that's a risk I must take.'

He rang Berry and made arrangements to pick him up from Bristol the following day. Then he mailed 'fisherking' asking where he lived. In return he received a telephone number and a note asking him to call it when he reached the area. For the first time he began to feel faintly ridiculous. It reminded him of the spy stories in which the hero was told to sit on a bench in St James's Park with a copy of *The Times* and await further instructions. What if the whole thing was a giant hoax?

It was a relief this time not to have to drive all the way. Berry was happy to do most of it which was as well, since for the first part of the journey all he could think about was Tess. She'd stayed humped under the bedclothes when he got up and had refused to say anything at all when he attempted to say good-bye.

By early afternoon they were in Cumbria. Over to their left a watery sun glinted off the dramatic peaks of the Lake District, clear on the skyline. On either side of the road, moorland rolled away as far as the eye could see, with little sign of human habitation anywhere. 'You must be a glutton for punishment if you keep coming up here,' commented Berry. 'What a wilderness!' He looked over to a bleak hillside, on which sheep grazed. 'I hate to think what it must have been like doing this trip years back.'

'Pretty appalling,' responded Latymer. 'If the natural hazards and the highway robbers didn't get you on the way up north, the bandits of the Borders – the reivers – would have taken you apart when you got up past Carlisle.'

'Well, let's hope your "fisherking" comes across. We're going to need a whole lot more than we've got to stand any chance of interesting Dumfries and Galloway police.'

'I suppose we could try and persuade Sally to give them a statement as a start. But then I suppose Douglas would be questioned and all he'd need do is stick to saying there was no truth in McKinley's story and that there were plenty of witnesses to the fact that he'd been roaring drunk when he started the fight. Even if we asked them if they've suspicions Douglas is involved in drugs, it's unlikely they'd tell us.'

They crossed into Scotland and Berry asked where next. 'I don't want to alert everyone in Kirkcudbright straightaway to the fact that I'm back,' Latymer told him. 'There's a place called Castle Douglas just off the Stranraer road. I suggest we find a

176

bed for the night. The forecast is for snow. We'll have something to eat then I'll call Mr Fisherking.'

He was going round in circles. Berry was right, it was all surmise. He was no longer so sanguine now about meeting Fisherking. The man's interests were obviously ecological and he'd more or less ruled out the possibility that the information on the website about depleted uranium shells had any bearing on Armstrong's disappearance, however many thousands of them were lying rotting at the bottom of the Solway Firth. The only hope was that he knew more about Armstrong's activities and movements immediately before his disappearance than Jean.

Before he called the number he rang Tess but there was no reply. He tried her mobile but it was switched off. She must have gone away. She obviously hadn't wasted any time. He wondered where she could be. Possibly with her daughter in Somerset? He'd no idea of the number, so rang Directory Inquiries, only to be told the number was ex-directory. Thoroughly depressed, he rang Fisherking's number. He was answered by a woman with a pleasant voice and a slight local accent. She was obviously expecting him.

'Are you in Kirkcudbright? Castle Douglas? Ah well, in the morning drive to

Kirkcudbright, cross the bridge and turn sharp left. It's a minor road signposted to Borgue. It runs along the shore. After a couple of miles, you'll come to a bay, opposite St Mary's Island. There's a place you can park your car, near some trees. I'll meet you there. We're a wee bit hard to find.'

'What time?'

'About eleven, if that's fine with you. James gets little sleep now but sometimes dozes off late on. He's very tired these days.'

Latymer considered whether or not to tell her that he had a companion with him, then decided not. He'd meet that one when it came. In the event, Berry made his mind up for him. 'Why don't I go and scout around in Kirkcudbright while you go and meet Mystery Man? I can look up this chap Elliot, if he's around, and the young woman. You never know, I might come across something. It could be a fresh eye will see something you've missed as you've been so close to it all. Presumably you can drop me off there?'

'No problem.' He opened up a map of the area. 'See, I'm meeting Mrs Fisherking, or whoever she is, just the other side of the water from Kirdkcudbright. It might be as well if we stayed there tomorrow night anyway. We'll book in somewhere before I go off to meet her.'

Berry peered at the map. 'I see what you

mean about the ranges. The whole area's plastered with danger signs. It must be pretty odd living up here knowing what's going on. Perhaps we shouldn't rule out any theory yet.'

It was already snowing by the time they set off the next morning and Latymer had visions of the weather really setting in, marooning them on the Borders for days. He turned off the main Stranraer road, drove down to Kirkcudbright, booked both of them in to the Dornoch Arms and after they'd both had coffee, left Berry sitting in the bar reading his paper. He drove back out of the town, crossed the bridge and turned on to the minor road described to him. About ten minutes later he found the bay, parking unknowingly in almost the same spot where a man had been killed six months earlier. There was no one about. He got out of the car. As he did so, the snow began to fall more heavily. The sky was dark and overcast, the water a curious light green. He looked at his watch. It was just eleven o'clock, the time they'd arranged. Shivering, he got back inside and as he did so a battered Land Rover pulled up and a woman jumped out. She was wearing a thick jacket, her face muffled by a scarf.

'You're Mr Latymer? You can leave your car here and come with me. It won't come to any harm.'

'I'd rather not. When I left it in a hotel car park shortly before Christmas, someone cut through the brake pipes.'

'Then you'd better follow me. But I must warn you the lane up to the farm is bad enough at the best of times and appalling in the winter.'

He followed behind the Land Rover at a sedate place through the driving snow. He wondered who she was. Secretary? Wife? Partner? She led him back on to the main road, then turned in the opposite direction to that which he had come until they reached a signpost to 'Borgue', continued on for a further mile then slowed down and turned sharp right. She hadn't exaggerated the state of the unsurfaced track. Where it wasn't pitted with deep potholes, sharp stones projected out of the covering of snow and he began to fear for his exhaust and sump. They bumped slowly on for another ten or fifteen minutes until he saw lights ahead and they drove into a gateway opening into a farmyard to be greeted by barking dogs. He parked beside the Land Rover outside a substantial, double-fronted farmhouse.

The woman came over. 'Don't worry about the dogs,' she shouted, calling to them by name. 'They're fine if I'm here. Come in out of the cold. I hope you haven't damaged your car.' She opened the front door into a lighted hallway. 'Heavens, I haven't even introduced myself.' She put out her hand. 'I'm James's wife, Fiona.' She unwound the scarf and took off her jacket. Unwrapped, she was an attractive woman of about forty, with dark hair and eyes. In other circumstances he could imagine her being a lively companion. 'Leave your coat here then I'll take you to James, he's at the end of the passage.'

They walked through to what he judged must be the other end of the house. Fiona knocked on the door. 'Are you fit, James?' she called out, 'I've got Mr Latymer here. It's blowing up a blizzard outside.' She opened the door, motioning to Latymer to enter. 'Go in. I'll away and make some coffee.'

The room he entered was large and shabby but comfortable. A wood-burning stove glowed in a stone fireplace. Opposite to it, a man lay propped on cushions beside a desk on which was a computer, printer and telephone.

'Do sit down, Mr Latymer,' he said. 'Find a seat near the fire, you must be perished.'

Latymer judged the speaker to be in his late forties or early fifties, but it was hard to tell as he was so obviously a sick man. He was completely bald, which suggested chemotherapy and his complexion had a yellowish look he had seen before on the terminally ill. 'You are...?' he enquired.

'Garleston. James Garleston.'

'Otherwise "fisherking"?'

'A conceit, I admit. Do you know the legend?'

'I recognized it as being to do with King Arthur. Or at least the quest for the Holy Grail.'

'Very good. Then you'll know that the Fisher King is the mortally sick ruler of a poisoned land. I'm no king or ruler, but I am a sick man and all around us is a poisoned land. Or so I believe.' The door opened and his wife appeared with a tray and three mugs, which she handed round. Garleston smiled. 'Come and join us, Fiona.' Then, to Latymer, 'We have no secrets from each other.'

Latymer took the mug of coffee offered to him. 'Why have you brought me up here?'

'Because from what I've heard, you're a man who doesn't let matters rest when you think there's been an injustice. Therefore I think it essential that we trade information while we can still do so. I have leukaemia and was in remission again for a while, but now the disease is winning. That being the case, there's little more that can be done for me. You obviously know of my concern?'

'I've seen all the stuff on the website about depleted uranium shells and their dangers. And that there are thousands of them in the

Solway Firth, which did surprise me. But that's not my prime concern. I'm trying to find out what's happened to a young man called Euan Armstrong, who's been missing since last August. The man you corresponded with under the name "Kinmont Willie". Why did you do that?'

'We both thought it best he keep up the pseudonym, though I imagine it didn't take long for those who really wanted to know to discover his true identity. Armstrong was an oddball in many ways. With no real experience and not, I believe, much talent he was desperate to make a name for himself in journalism. Of course most people around here know of the shells in the Solway, but he came to me because he thought it might make a story. I saw him because I badly needed a leg man to do research for me and I thought we might be of mutual benefit to each other, though I warned him it might prove hazardous. When you begin prying into such matters, it's not too dramatic to say that you raise dark forces. Anyway we had a deal. I'd stake him to do the research and when I thought the time was right, he could publicize it as he chose.'

The snow was now whirling against the windows. 'I don't know how much time you can spare, Mr Latymer,' Garleston continued, 'but given the weather, we could give you a bed for the night and then we could

183

talk properly. I tire easily and need regular periods of rest.'

What do I do now? thought Latymer. Tess had accused him of becoming obsessed. Was Garleston then just another obsessive with a cause, further exacerbated by his illness? During his police career he had come across people convinced that 'they' (often unspecified) were against them or that they were the victims of some kind of devilish plot. Occasionally they turned out to be rightly paranoid. Now he was being invited to spend a night with complete strangers, miles from anywhere and a blizzard outside. Common sense demanded he leave at once. There was also Berry, stuck in Kirkcudbright on his own without a car.

'It's very kind of you,' he said, 'but this time I came with a friend who's expecting me back in Kirkcudbright later.'

Garleston frowned. 'I thought you'd come up here on your own.'

'I believe someone tried to kill me the last time I came. I wasn't prepared to take unnecessary chances this time round.' Garleston appeared unsurprised.

'Do you think you could ring your friend and explain?' enquired Fiona. 'He'll see for himself how bad the weather is. And James really can only sustain conversation for limited periods. There's a phone in the hall as well as in here, if you prefer. If you can't get him, then leave our phone number. There's no mystery, we're in the book.'

In the circumstances there seemed no help for it if he was to have any benefit from his journey. He rang the Dornoch Arms and was in luck, for Berry was still in the bar. He briefly explained the position. 'I think you should stay,' Berry responded. 'If this mystery man really has something to tell you, then you'd better hear it. Give me the phone number so I can contact you if I need to, and I'll see you in the morning. Your friend Elliot's away for a few days with his wife, but I'm on the case – I've got the names of the other crew members. One lives nearby and I'm going to go and see him, the other's a bit further out. I'll see how the weather goes.' Latymer put down the receiver then, on an impulse, rang Tess but again there was no reply from the house or her mobile.

'I'm afraid my wife took a pretty dim view of my coming up here again,' he told the Garlestons as he came back into the room. 'I think she must have gone away for a few days. She thinks I've become irrational and obsessed over Euan Armstrong.'

Garleston nodded. 'I see. So tell me what *you* think has happened?'

Latymer went yet again through the whole story, the fight, the body off the Cornish coast, its identification by a man who appeared to have lied to the police as to who

185

he was and his own part in the subsequent chain of events, ending with Sally's information that McKinley had seen a body in the ice in the boat.

'And you believe it was that of Euan Armstrong?'

'Jean's not heard a word from him since last August, not even over Christmas. She says that even if they'd fallen out for good – which she swears they hadn't – or he'd gone off with some woman, he'd have sent the children presents.'

'And you say the man who identified the corpse – David Bentley? – is a fake?'

'When my colleague checked out the firm he was supposed to work for, he was told no one of that name worked there or ever had. Next he discovered that the brother's address didn't exist.'

'Have you told the police in Cornwall?'

'Not after the reception Jean Armstrong and I had when we arrived suggesting their corpse was the wrong man. The inspector in charge did say the man in the harbour was a "dead ringer" for the photograph of Armstrong Jean showed him, but put it down to coincidence. And there's no way of proving anything now since the body was cremated. He more or less patted her on the head and told her to go back home and wait for her errant man to return.'

'Poor woman,' broke in Fiona Garleston.

'It's because I feel sorry for her that I've let myself get so involved. That and actually having witnessed the fight that seems to have triggered the whole thing off.'

'Is it possible this man Bentley could have made a genuine mistake?'

'I find it difficult to believe. The body wasn't marked, had hardly deteriorated at all – as it wouldn't, of course, if it had been packed in ice. The best I can come up with is that Armstrong, while researching for you, was also working on a drugs story, the kind of thing that would be dangerous enough for an experienced reporter with full newspaper or TV back-up. Possibly he suspected Harry Douglas, the skipper of the boat in question, of running drugs or had been given a lead of some kind. Then, instead of passing it on to a professional, he decided to go for it himself and began digging around until either Douglas or those for whom he worked decided he was becoming a nuisance and was best got rid of. It could be "Bentley" is the man in charge of the whole operation. It would explain his appearance in Cornwall.'

'It's a very persuasive theory,' commented Garleston. 'But after we've had some lunch and I've taken my medicine and had a rest, I'll explain why I think you're wrong.'

Ten

At about the same time as Latymer had been making arrangements to visit the Garlestons, Jean Armstrong had just finished settling the children for the night when the doorbell rang. She'd become wary of answering it since the break-in and she put the newly purchased chain across. A woman stood outside, woolly hat pulled well down over her head. She looked down at the chain. 'You expecting trouble or something?' Jean looked at her blankly. 'It's Sally, you daft cow! Sally Black. Andy's girl.' She loosened her coat and a faint whiff of alcohol reached Jean.

'Come in,' said Jean, hastily removing the chain, 'it's just that I had a break-in before Christmas. I didn't recognize you under all that gear. I take it it's still snowing?'

'Aye. And bitter cold with it.'

Jean ushered her into the living room. 'I've just got the weans to bed. Take your things off. Do you want some tea?' Sally nodded and Jean went into the kitchen and put the kettle on. 'I can't offer you a ciggy, I'm

188

trying to give them up. Apart from anything else I can't afford it. So what brings you to Annan?'

'I've come to see you,' said Sally. 'It's taken a couple of stiff drinks to do it. We've got to talk.'

From the kitchen came the sound of the kettle boiling. Jean left the room to return a few minutes later with two mugs of tea. Sally had picked up the Armstrongs' wedding photograph from the dresser and was looking at it. 'You've still heard nothing from Euan, I take it?'

'No. Not even at Christmas.'

'And nothing more from the police?'

Jean shook her head. 'Not for ages. They've been convinced right from the start that he's gone off with another woman. I've not been able to change their minds.'

'And what do you reckon?'

'I believe he's dead. I have all along.'

There was a pause, then Sally put the photograph back. 'I know he is. At least I'm almost certain.'

Jean stared at her open-mouthed. 'What are you trying to say? Are you now telling me you've known it all along? And done nothing? Said nothing?'

'Hang on a minute, will you? What do you think has made me come over here in weather like this? I had to get a lift to Dumfries, then a bus and Christ knows how I'm going to get back. It's half eight already and I'm supposed to be at work in the morning.' She hesitated. 'It's hard to know where to start.'

'How about with the truth?'

'First then tell me what the police said when you went down to Cornwall with that man Latymer because you thought they'd found Euan.'

'They said it couldn't possibly be, though the inspector admitted, after seeing his photo, that Euan was a dead ringer for the man they'd taken out of the sea. But the reason it couldn't be was because the dead guy's own brother identified him. Of course by the time we got there, it was all done and dusted and the body cremated. But whatever they say, I *know* it was Euan and the body was found within a few days of his going missing. I'm still raging. I know I'm right but *nobody* believes me. I don't even know if John Latymer does. Right, now I've answered your question, tell me what the hell all this is about.'

'There's no easy way to say this.' Sally paused. 'Look, Andy told me that when they got into port in Newlyn, there was a dead man on board, packed in the ice in the bottom of the boat.'

Jean stared. 'I can't believe I'm hearing this. And he let it go at that?'

'You've heard all about the fight in

Cornwall. Although Andy was pretty drunk, he went straight up to Harry and asked him what the hell was going on. Then they had the fight and he landed up in hospital. Afterwards, as soon as he got back home, Harry came to see him and Andy said it again. But Harry just laughed. Reminded him that he'd been absolutely wrecked from a day on the piss and then been knocked out cold. There was no dead man in the ice in the boat. The other two crewmen would vouch for that. Then he offered him his job back. Alright, any normal person would've gone straight to the police in Cornwall in the first place but you know our men. They just don't do going to the police. Andy told Harry that no way would he go back on the boat, but I think for a wee while he thought Harry was probably right, that he'd imagined it all. But he kept getting bad dreams.'

She paused. 'He only told me all this the night before he died, after waking up yelling his head off. He went on for ages before going back to sleep. But when I tackled him about it again in the morning he said he'd been having a nightmare and to take no notice. All he was interested in was the new job he'd been offered. But I was sure he was lying.'

'And it was Euan? He actually *saw* Euan?'

'He only really saw a hand and a bit of an arm above the wrist, but there was a funny

191

three-cornered mark on the back and Andy said Euan'd done it when a chisel slipped when they were both at school. At first he was so shaken he didn't take it in. Did Euan have a mark like that?'

Jean sat down again. 'He did. And Andy's story's right. He did do it at school though it wasn't very noticeable. But there was no mention of any such mark on the hand of the man they found in Cornwall. Perhaps they didn't notice it. It's too late to find out now.'

'So,' continued Sally, 'think about it. Andy finally tells me all this and what happens? He's found dead of a drug overdose. Just coincidence? Or did he decide to tell someone else too? I've been trying to find out who'd offered him this job, if it ever existed, but I've got nowhere and I didn't see any point in going to the police, since they're convinced Andy must have been doing drugs even if it wasn't a regular habit. But he didn't, Jeannie, he really didn't. I suppose I should have told Latymer this too. He must wonder where I'm at. First I tell him nothing, then I give him the computer Andy was keeping for Euan without telling him any more, then I thought perhaps I'd better tell him Andy said he'd seen a body but I imagine he's lost interest for he hasn't replied.'

'I see.' Jean got up. 'What now, then?'

'I don't know. That's what I've come to ask you.'

Jean began pacing up and down. 'Even if we both go to the police, I don't believe we'd get anywhere.'

'We could tackle Harry head on,' suggested Sally.

'If he's covering up a murder then he's hardly going to admit it. He's got a pretty dodgy reputation, you know. From what Sean Elliot says, there's been rumours he brings the stuff in.'

'Do you think it was to do with drugs? Euan's death, I mean.'

'He was on to something. The daft loon was determined to prove he could make it with the media. About all he did tell me was that it wasn't to do with drugs. Let me think. If, like you say, John Latymer's lost interest, then why don't we try and make some enquiries ourselves?'

'Any chance of some more tea?' enquired Sally.

'Tea? If you'll stay here with the weans, I'll go round to the co-op and get a bottle of wine. We need to make some plans. And you can stay the night, if you don't mind sleeping on the sofa. I was going to Kirkcudbright in the morning anyway. The Elliots are picking me up – Mary thinks I can do with getting out more. They've been over in Canonbie, visiting her sister. It'll be a squeeze but I'm sure you can come back with us. Ring the shop in the morning and tell them you've been held up by the weather. And I'll give John Latymer a call and tell him what we intend to do.'

Throughout that strange afternoon and well into the evening, Garleston told his story, interspersed with periods for medication and rest. Fully aware that time was running out, he was determined to talk until overcome by exhaustion in spite of obviously being in pain. He had, he told Latymer, been a professional soldier but after over twenty years' service and following the Gulf War, he decided to leave the Army. Shortly before doing so, he and Fiona had bought the farmhouse on the Solway coast. He was a Londoner, and something of a rolling stone, but she was a Borderer and he'd always promised her that one day they would end up north, near to her old home. She loved gardening and planned to turn her knowledge to good use, rearing and selling plants in a small way, but shortly before Garleston left the Army for good, he began to feel ill.

'I was sent to see the medics and the first thing they discovered was that my white blood cell count was three times what it should be. Then they did some more tests and told me it was leukaemia, in the long run probably untreatable. You can guess how we felt.'

At first he'd thought it was just terrible bad luck but soon he began to think again. 'I'd been in the Gulf, you see. And I started hearing and reading about the men and women who had developed what came to be known as Gulf War Syndrome. It wasn't all leukaemia of course. Some had cancers of different kinds and others simply a whole list of symptoms that didn't add up. Since when, as you might know, they've been fighting even to get recognition that there's a problem, let alone its cause. All I do know,' Garleston added, bitterly, 'is that nearly five hundred of us have died. Five hundred of us!

'I began looking into possible causes, in between relapses: radiation, chemical weapons, inhaling smoke from burning fuel dumps. They've all been suggested, along with the cocktail of drugs given us before we left the country. Another suggestion is depleted uranium shells. Now that really is ironic. I'd no idea when we bought the house here that there was a range out there across the water designed to test the bloody things! For all I know I've brought myself to a place possibly contaminated by the very stuff which could have made me ill in the first place.'

Then, when he had started going to the

local hospital, he heard rumours of others who had become ill. So he had set about trying to discover if there was a noticeable incidence of unexplained illnesses along the Solway coast, but drew a blank when it came to obtaining official statistics: either there were hardly any or they were not made public. Meanwhile his treatments were becoming more frequent and tiring.

'Hence the "fisherking" website. I wasn't fit to traipse around the countryside. Setting up the website was my way of encouraging information to come to me.' And it did. Stories of cancers, leukaemias and strange maladies, the source of which seemed to be impossible to trace. 'It's all anecdotal, of course. What's needed is a proper epidemiological study. As to causes, well ... I hate to think of the amount of radiation sloshing around in the sea outside from the nuclear reprocessing plant down the coast at Sellafield alone. Then there's pesticides – after all it's a rural area. And last but not least, the depleted uranium shells from Dundrennan. Anonymous correspondents have left e-mails claiming there's been numerous misfirings and that sometimes the road near the base is covered with a strange red dust.'

Among those who contacted him in this way was Euan Armstrong. 'You didn't know him, of course, and I told you he was an oddball, but he was an engaging character and very keen. So we did the deal I mentioned and I offered him a small retainer to keep his ear to the ground and see if he could track down any cases of illness in the area that might be relevant. Or anything else he thought might be useful, and he was most enthusiastic. But I soon realized he wasn't equipped to deal with the dark forces he eventually found himself up against.'

The second mention of 'dark forces' had Latymer worried. Was Garleston, perhaps due to the drugs he was taking because of his condition, now starting to believe in the occult? His own unwanted involvement had already thrown up not only one, but two possible murders, as well as drug dealing and Gulf War syndrome. If he was now also to be invited to enter the realm of Denis Wheatley and *The Devil Rides Out*, he would make for home without further delay.

But it soon transpired that what Garleston had in mind was something more material than demons. After a while Armstrong began to believe he was being watched and followed, although he had been unable to pin any single incident down. He was also convinced that on one occasion his car had been broken into, although nothing had been stolen. He told Garleston he was going to leave his laptop (which Garleston had paid for) with a friend for safe keeping. For a while he carried on with the research and, given his inexperience, had at least managed to compile a respectable list of people within a radius of ten miles who had suffered ill health of one kind and another, collating it with the distance they lived or worked from the firing ranges.

Then one day, towards the middle of August, Armstrong told Garleston frankly that for the first time he was really alarmed. He was becoming worried for his wife and family and had decided to drop the whole thing and return to fishing, though he wouldn't explain why. 'It was quite sudden. He'd agreed to do one last thing, then that would be it, he said. After that I never heard from him again. I didn't worry at first, I thought he'd decided to put it all behind him and gone back on the boats, like he said. Then I was told he'd run off after a row with his wife. But as time went on, I became very uneasy. It didn't sound right.'

'If he was feeling watched, who was doing the watching?' queried Latymer.

Garleston shrugged. 'MI5? Special Branch? Even the Modplod – the Ministry of Defence Police. Some private agency hired by one or other of them. It has been known. Anything nuclear and a lot of people have a vested interest as you must know.'

'I kept as far away as possible from the security services,' Latymer told him, 'including Special Branch.'

'Too many cut corners, perhaps?' suggested Garleston.

'That in part. But do you really think it was true that he was under surveillance?'

'Yes, I do. Not least because shortly after he disappeared I had to spend a night in the hospital and Fiona stayed there with me. In the morning we came back to find the place ransacked. It wasn't very clever. There were files pulled out of the cabinet and spread around the floor, and someone had been on the computer. But there was nothing left on the hard disc of any real use and the handful of important files on disc were elsewhere. It might be that they just wanted to scare us, rather than hope to find anything incriminating. I trust you believe me. From what Fiona says, last time you were here someone interfered with your car.'

Latymer agreed this was so and explained the circumstances. 'And all right, I had been down to the coast near the ranges and it could be that I was followed back into town, but what happened later would fit my drugs theory just as well.' He recalled suddenly the story of Armstrong's newly acquired interest in birdwatching. 'It could be when he was looking out for you at what was going on in the Solway, he saw something else entirely and aroused interest of a quite different and criminal kind. I take it you yourself have received no direct threats?'

Garleston gave him a bleak smile. 'Why should anyone bother? All they have to do is wait.' He went back over aspects of his story again in more detail, but towards the end he was drifting in and out of sleep and his wife urged him to stop. Latymer too could hardly keep awake and eventually they all went to bed. It had been a strange day followed by a weird night and the image of the shadowed room, with its glowing stove and the sick man, caught in the lamplight, was to remain with him for a long time.

Eleven

The day had started promisingly enough for Berry. Immediately after breakfast he'd gone to see the first of the crew members on his list. Rob Campbell was an open-faced, straightforward looking young man of about twenty. He was, Berry told him, doing some research into young people and drugs and had been told of the tragic death of Andy McKinley. 'I went to see his fiancée and she's convinced he didn't do drugs – though I suppose that's what she'd want to think. She said you might know,' he lied.

'Don't know that I do. I could hardly believe it myself,' Campbell told him. 'I'd have sworn Andy didn't do them, unlike...' he stopped, then continued, 'someone else I know. That's all. I told the police when they came here to see me. They said it could've been a one-off. You'd perhaps be better off having a talk with them.'

'And the other member of your crew? He lives near here too, doesn't he? Would you have his phone number?'

Campbell gave it to him with obvious

201

reluctance, presumably not wanting to get further involved. 'He lives with his mother, though I doubt you'll find him in.'

Outside in the street, Berry rang it. A woman's voice answered. No, she was sorry, but Kevin wasn't home. Had gone off first thing that morning she didn't know where. Could she tell him who called? Berry said not to bother, he'd call back. Latymer had given him the Elliots' number, saying that if he explained who he was then he was sure Sean would be very co-operative. But there was no reply, except for the mechanical voice informing him that the person he'd called was unavailable. A final call to Sally Black was greeted with evident suspicion. He eventually prised from her mother the fact that Sally spent the night with a friend in Annan, having been unable to get home, but had phoned to say she was getting a lift back later on and would go straight into work. Cold and frustrated, he took himself back to the warmth of the hotel.

After an hour spent impatiently struggling with *The Times* crossword, he decided to try Elliot again, first taking the precaution of telephoning to see if he was back at home. This time he was in luck. He explained who he was, why he was there and that Latymer was spending the day with the person who set up the fisherking website. Would it be convenient therefore for them to meet?

'Stay where you are,' replied Elliot, 'and I'll be with you shortly. We've been away for a few days and have only just got back. We're later than planned as we made a detour to bring Jean Armstrong and the kids back with us. I take it you know all about her?'

He arrived twenty minutes later. 'I didn't know John was planning another visit,' he told Berry. 'I suppose it's because of Sally's letter. Actually we gave her a lift back too. She'd spent the night with Jeannie in Annan. But why didn't John tell me he was coming up here?'

'Wife trouble, I think. It seems she's pretty fed up with all this. It was all done rather at the last minute.'

Elliot nodded. 'I had the impression things weren't going too well. Makes me feel somewhat guilty but I did tell him to drop it rather than upset his family. So, I take it he's managed to track down the mystery man?'

'Seems he's local to you. A man called Garleston. James Garleston. John says he's lives out at the back of beyond on the other side of the river and that Armstrong had been doing some legwork for him. That's all I know. John will be able to fill you in better when he comes back tomorrow morning.'

'Garleston is "Fisher King"? That explains a lot. He's a nut.'

'You know of him then?'

'Ex-army officer. Reckons he's a victim of

some kind of poisoning. He hadn't moved in here more than five minutes when he started asking questions about the Dundrennan firing ranges and pollution and so on. Got on people's wick, especially those who rely on B and B for a living. Then it all went quiet and I heard a rumour he was ill. So he's been carrying on his campaign on the Internet? *Is* he sick?'

'Apparently he's got leukaemia and it's terminal.'

'Poor sod. I suppose that might turn anyone a bit daft. But I don't see where Euan comes in.'

'Neither do I. Look, John's suggested that I find some way of meeting Harry Douglas, the skipper of the *Lady of Annan*. I understand he's something of a dodgy character and I don't want to stir things up, but is there any way we can bring up the matter of McKinley without his becoming suspicious?'

'We can try,' said Elliot, doubtfully. 'But we'll need to have some reason for your being here. We can hardly tell Harry that you and John Latymer have come all this way to see him because Andy's girlfriend claims he had a dead man in his boat last August!'

'Well, I suppose since I run a bookshop, second-hand as well as new, I can say I've been up here seeing some dealers before the

204

various book fairs in the spring.'

'And why Kirkcudbright?'

Berry thought for a moment. 'Dorothy Sayers! The crime novelist. She set a book here about the artists' colony in the 1930s. I can't remember all that much about it except that the killer's alibi hung on local train times and the crucial clue was a tube of white paint. I'll say I'd been told there was someone here with Sayers first editions, but had drawn a blank. If he asks, that is.'

Elliot looked at his watch. 'Well, obviously none of us are at sea because of the weather. Harry lives over the river at Gatehouse of Fleet. We could try his local pub. He might well be there since he's nothing else to do. There's a second-hand bookshop further on in Newton Stewart; we could say we were on our way there and stopped off for a pint.'

The snow was beginning to let up as they drove into Gatehouse and parked outside the pub. They were in luck for Douglas was sitting in a corner with another man. He waved a hand at his fellow skipper then looked inquisitively at Berry. 'Keith Berry,' said Elliot, by way of introduction. 'He's been spending a few days in Kirkcudbright.'

Douglas laughed. 'Surely not on holiday in this weather? Can I get you both a drink?' He went off to the bar and Elliot and Berry joined his companion, who introduced himself as 'Mick'.

'I'm not a masochist,' Berry informed Douglas as he came back with the drinks. 'It's just that there are a number of book fairs coming up and I wanted to see a couple of dealers in Edinburgh and Glasgow. Then I was told of someone in Kirkcudbright who had a collection to sell, but it seems I was wrong. No one there knew anything about it.'

'I came across Keith trying to track down his supposed collector and suggested he might like to go on to the second-hand bookshop in Newton Stewart, since the guy doesn't appear to exist.'

'And what do you do?' Berry asked Douglas.

'Same as Sean. Or almost. Different kind of boat that's all. This weather buggers us both up.'

'The wife talked me into visiting her family since I was at home and couldn't get out of it,' Elliot informed them. 'We only got home this morning. So I escaped to the Dornoch and found Keith there, also at a loose end. I feel I've done my duty and Mary's got plenty to do back home. We brought Jeannie Armstrong and her weans back with us for a couple of days. We also gave a lift to Sally Black, poor girl, she'd been staying over with Jeannie.'

'Why "poor girl"?' enquired Berry, innocently.

'Her boyfriend, Andy McKinley was found dead recently of a drugs overdose,' Elliot informed him. 'He was one of Harry's crew.'

'That must have been tough for her. Is there much of a problem around here?'

'I suppose there's a problem everywhere these days,' observed Douglas.

'McKinley was a surprise though,' continued Elliot. 'I'd never heard he'd a habit and his girlfriend swears he didn't do drugs. What do you think, Harry?'

Douglas shrugged. 'So far as I'm concerned, he did his job OK. That is until we went down to Cornwall last summer and he went bananas.' He turned to Berry. 'Went for me with a knife! We both ended up in hospital. There was no reason or explanation for it, so it could be he was high on something or other. And afterwards he refused to go to sea again. It's sad, but it happens to a lot of youngsters these days.'

Elliot got up to buy another round of drinks, after which the conversation became more general until Douglas made a comment about Jean Armstrong. 'I presume she's still no news of Euan?'

'Not a word. She's sure he's dead. You probably heard she went to Cornwall back in the autumn after she saw a picture of a dead man found in the sea down there. She showed it to me and I have to agree it did look very much like him; but it wasn't, of course. The guy's own brother had identified him.'

Douglas shook his head. 'It's pretty obvious he went off with another woman. I don't reckon anyone else believes he really is dead, though Jean Armstrong might prefer to think so, rather than that he got fed up and dumped her and the kids. I'm told they used to row like cat and dog.' He turned to his friend. 'Isn't that so, Mick?'

'Aye. And after all, Jeannie had pissed off to Glasgow and left him. She could hardly blame him for walking out.'

They all finished their drinks and got up to go. 'Well, we'll be off to Newton,' said Elliot. 'Grab a bite over there.'

'Glad to have run into you, Harry,' declared Berry, truthfully. 'I must admit I was feeling pretty pissed off sitting in Kirkcudbright in the snow.'

'What kind of books are you looking for?' enquired Douglas, as they went out into the cold. 'Anything in particular?'

'I specialize,' Berry informed him. 'In crime. Especially true crime.'

The response drove Mick away at a run. They got into Elliot's car and drove off leaving Douglas still standing on the pavement, staring after them.

Twenty-year-old Kevin Tyler was having not

only a frustrating day but a bad day; a very bad day. It was over two weeks since Harry had paid the crew off from the last trip, the weather was far from promising and he was almost out of cash. The last two trips had been quite profitable and should have seen him all right until the next time and would have done; had it not been for his habit. He'd started on the boats as soon as he left school. Actually *before* he left, until he got caught. Then, following a row with his mam he'd gone up to Peterhead and signed on as crew on a beamer, one of the bigger boats, and had never had so much money in his pocket in his life.

He'd first tried smack as a dare about eighteen months ago when he was still based in Peterhead and for a while bragged that he could take it or leave it. By the time he'd discovered that wasn't true, he'd got himself into a good deal of trouble up north, had returned home and signed on as crew with Harry Douglas. Which was how he'd become so dependent on Harry. It hadn't taken Harry long to realize what was going on but, somewhat to Kevin's surprise, they'd done a deal. Harry wouldn't grass on him to the local police so long as he did his best to keep out of trouble and agreed to assist Harry when, from time to time, he needed an extra pair of hands. On occasion he had even provided Kevin with the necessary when he'd been unable to get it elsewhere, though he made it clear he didn't like doing it. One thing was certain, though. If he ever so much as breathed a word about Harry's possible involvement in the trade, retribution would be fast and final.

He had to admit Harry was a slick operator. His import trade was carefully concealed within his legitimate business and he made a point of ensuring that he only picked up the extra cargo from time to time and never in the same place. Likewise, he rarely delivered to the same dropping off point twice. There had been one or two close shaves, but on the whole the system appeared to work well. Kevin had no idea whether or not his fellow crew members were aware of the situation. If they were, then they never spoke of it.

Almost out of money and with the stuff far harder to get hold of in Kirkcudbright than it had been in Peterhead, he'd asked Harry if he could let him have some on tick. 'I'll work it off, I promise,' he told him. 'You can easily take it out of my share when we get back. And if I don't get it, I'll not be fit to work.' This time Harry had been singularly unsympathetic. 'Then you'll have to stay ashore,' he told Kevin. 'You sort yourself out. I wouldn't let you have it even if I could, it's too bloody risky since Andy died, but as it happens I haven't got any anyway.'

So Kevin had gone into Dumfries with the small amount of money he had left, having learned that there was a small dealer there who operated down on the car parks by the river. It had taken some time to find him and even longer to cut a deal and that at an extortionate rate. By this rat's standards, thought Kevin, Harry appeared generous to a degree. It had taken him all the money he had with him to purchase a meagre, overpriced amount of smack, resulting in his having to hitch a lift back to his mother's house. (He'd been forced to move back in with her having been thrown out of his flat for not paying the rent.)

He'd been somewhat disconcerted when the dealer asked him about Andy. 'Heard you'd an overdose up your way a wee while back,' he'd commented. 'If it's true, I would not have thought you needed to come here.' Kevin had mumbled something in reply. Andy's death had made him shiver. He was as sure as anyone could be that Andy simply didn't do drugs, never had. After all he should know. He wondered if Andy had realized that he was a user, but then Andy had been pretty laid-back. He might not approve but he'd leave it at that.

Until the trip to that bloody awful hole in Cornwall. That was something he tried not to think about, even though it haunted his worst dreams. Scoring in Newlyn had been easy-peasy. No problem at all. But the whole trip had been a strange one. Harry had been on edge since the very moment they'd cast off and had twice told him that beween Scotland and Cornwall he would have a very special job for him, one that no one else must know about. Naturally he'd assumed it was to do with picking up drugs and was interested to learn exactly how Harry proposed to do it this time round but three days passed without his being told anything else, during which time the weather worsened. They had often fished in poor weather before but for some reason Harry had pressed on south without even making the attempt.

He'd no idea what caused the fight between Harry and Andy in Newlyn. Had Andy just cottoned on to Harry's other activities? Whatever it was, both men had ended up in hospital and, when Harry came out, they sailed without Andy. Before they'd sailed in the small hours of the morning, Harry had sent Rob down to his bunk telling him to get some sleep as it would be a hard voyage home with a man short. Within half an hour Rob'd been out like a light and, having checked this out, Harry had set off. But almost as soon as they'd left the harbour safely behind, he'd put the helm on automatic and pushed Kevin down below, threatening him with God knows what if he made a noise. Then he'd started moving the ice around until he caught hold of a large bundle of something wrapped in a thick cloth. It was heavy, an awkward shape, hard and stiff and cold.

Harry thumped him then whispered, 'Don't just stand there staring, help me get it up on deck.' They did so with extreme difficulty, Harry obviously concerned that the activity might rouse Rob. 'It's something I was asked to dump out at sea on the way down, but it never seemed the right time. We can't take it back with us, it's got to go. I've been tipped off we might be stopped and searched. We'll go a bit further out into the bay first.'

He went back to the helm. It was quite dark, there was no moon, no other boats about. The water was slapping noisily against the boat. He left the helm again and joined Kevin. 'Now, take the edge of the cloth with me and roll what's there out over the side.' The object hit the water with a dull splash, floated on the tide, then disappeared. 'It looked like...' Kevin swallowed, 'it looked like a body.'

Harry was about to say something when a sleepy Rob appeared from below. 'I thought I heard a bump and a splash. Why've we stopped?'

'We bumped into some old fishing gear, that's all. I stopped to make sure we'd not got tangled up in it. Go back to bed and I'll wake you up again in a couple of hours.'

'What was it?' persisted Kevin when Rob had gone back below. 'Surely you wouldn't throw that much stuff overboard like that. It'd be worth millions.'

Harry turned and grabbed him by the throat so hard he'd nearly choked. 'If I ever learn you've said one word of what you've seen tonight, I'll break your neck,' he told him. 'Don't even think about it. Or that you can run away and I won't come after you. Or send those after you who'll do it for me.' The matter had never been referred to again but from time to time Kevin had thought about it. What had they put over the side? *Could* it have been a body? The body of a grass, perhaps? It was the stuff of nightmares.

He gave himself a fix in Dumfries, reckoning he'd be able to get through without another dose for some time yet. After that, he'd no idea what he was going to do. His mother would be waiting with a meal ready for him when he got back. He felt very guilty about her. At first she'd kept asking what was the matter with him, but of late she'd stopped doing it. Perhaps she didn't want to know the answer. Gradually he began to feel better. He made his way to the bus home and drifted into a dream.

★ ★ ★

214

Elliot had invited him back for the evening and some supper. Jean Armstrong had opened her eyes wide when he'd explained that Berry had come up to Scotland with John Latymer, who was over the river visiting someone near Borgue. It had been a pleasant enough meal, devoted to ordinary topics, after which Jean settled her children down for the night. 'Are you sure it's all right for me to meet Sally for a drink?' she asked Mary when she came back down-stairs.

'No problem,' Mary assured her. 'You go along and enjoy yourself. You can't get out much of an evening and it'll help cheer Sally up. You've had a hard time the two of you.' She looked out of the window. 'It's frosty, but it's not snowing now.'

'I'll walk into the town with you if I may,' said Berry. 'I feel like an early night.' He thanked the Elliots and he and Jean set off towards the middle of the town. At first there was a strained silence, then she said, 'I didn't expect John to come back. Sally says she wrote to him but got no reply.'

'It was her letter that decided him, that and some e-mails from a man calling him-self Fisherking. That's where John is.'

'Sally and I'd decided to make some enquiries ourselves since we thought John'd given us up. That's why I'm meeting her tonight.'

Berry stopped. 'I can't prevent you, of course. But if what's been happening is as serious as I think it might be, you'd be putting yourselves at risk. If you can find anything out casually, then fine, but it would be advisable to let either John or I know if you do.' They continued walking. 'Why don't I at least buy you and Sally a drink? Give what I've said some thought.'

'I'll go round to the house then,' said Jean, 'in case she's changed her mind. From what she's told me, she's done an awful lot of sitting home of an evening.'

Berry went into the bar and a few minutes later she reappeared with Sally. She had obviously explained the position. He greeted her and bought them their drinks. They were in the raised part of the bar, almost hidden from the rest of the room, when a thin, pale-faced young man came in and ordered a pint.

'That's Kevin,' said Sally. 'He works with Harry on *Lady of Annan*. Now he almost definitely *does* do drugs. He was one of the people we were going to tackle.'

'Then why don't you?' Berry stepped back further out of view. 'See if you can find anything out. He's obviously more likely to talk to you than to me.'

Kevin was sitting on his own in a corner when the girls went over to him. 'Why, look who's here,' commented Sally to Jean.

'Mind if we join you?' she asked.

Kevin felt uneasy. Sally Black never voluntarily sought him out, indeed rather the reverse. He'd once heard her refer to him as 'that slimeball Andy sails with'. She sat down motioning Jean to sit beside her.

'You'll remember Jean? She married Euan Armstrong.'

He nodded. 'Have you heard anything more of Euan, Jean? I was told he'd gone missing.'

'Nothing since last August.'

'Oh, I'm sorry,' he said. And meant it.

Sally gave him a less than pleasant smile at this. 'Funny isn't it? Here we are, the two of us, Jeannie and me. And both of us have lost our men. Quite a coincidence.' Kevin agreed it was. 'And neither lost at sea. One's disappeared and the other's dead.' Kevin didn't know what she was getting at but whatever it was he didn't like it.

'You were there, weren't you, in Cornwall?' she said, suddenly. 'When it happened.'

'When what happened?' He swallowed and went even paler.

'Why, that fight of course. The one that put Andy in hospital. What do you think we meant? What was it about? The fight, I mean. I never did know.'

'I've no idea. They were probably both pissed.'

'Harry Douglas pissed!' Sally sounded incredulous. 'He's never pissed. Andy said he was the most careful drinker he'd every come across.'

Jean lent towards him. 'How is Harry?'

'Harry?' Kevin's voice cracked in his throat. 'OK, I suppose. Haven't seen him since I was paid off. Why?'

'Just wondered, that's all. Busy is he?'

'In this weather? Why ask?'

'I was thinking of his other business interests,' Sally persisted. There was a pause as the statement hung in the air. 'About that fight in Cornwall back in the summer. Could it be to do with drugs? Andy said Cornwall was full of them, that there were pubs there where you could buy anything you wanted.'

'Harry doesn't do drugs, if that's what you're getting at. I'm sure of that.' Kevin began to perspire and feel slightly sick. The stuff he'd bought in Dumfries obviously wasn't as good as that he usually bought. Perhaps he'd better give himself the second fix. The girls smiled at each other and settled back. They seemed in no hurry to leave.

'So here we all are,' said Jean. 'Except, of course, for Euan and Andy. They aren't here any more.' She stopped smiling. 'What *is* this all about, Kevin?'

Kevin shivered. 'I don't know what you're

on about.' Oh God, he really must get away. He downed the rest of his drink in a single gulp.

'You're not looking too good,' commented Sally. 'Aren't you feeling well?'

'I think I must be going down with 'flu.' He stood up and rocked slightly on his feet. 'I'm off.' He stumbled out of the bar without looking back.

'Well now,' said Sally. 'I'd say we'd got a result though I'm not sure what it is. If we can get at Harry through him, then we might have something to go back to the police with.' She sighed. 'I suppose we'd better tell Berry.'

It was bitterly cold as Kevin made his way across the car park and down towards the river. *Lady of Annan* was tied up at the quay and he jumped down on to the deck, made his way to a sheltered spot out of the wind and gave himself the second shot. It was the first time since becoming hooked that he'd had so little access to the stuff and he'd no money. He couldn't keep asking his mother for a sub. Having been off work a fortnight, he'd signed on but the giro wouldn't arrive for another four days.

There was no help for it. He'd have to try Harry again. Surely with his contacts he could get him *something*. But that still left the question of money. As the drug began to take effect, he felt better, more optimistic.

He still had a couple of pounds in his pocket, thanks to the girls buying him a drink. The girls. What did they know? And all that business about Harry? A thought struck him. Suppose he went to Harry and told him that Sally and Jeannie Armstrong were asking questions about him, hinting at things. Of course, he hadn't said a word or given anything away. He rattled the coins in his pocket, went along to the local taxi firm and asked the driver to take him to Gate-house of Fleet.

Twelve

By the time the taxi deposited Kevin Tyler outside Harry Douglas's substantial double-fronted villa in Gatehouse of Fleet he was beginning to think that this might not, after all, be a good idea. However he hadn't enough money to go back again after paying off the driver. There were lights on in the house, so at least someone was at home. Finally, after walking up and down in the cold for several minutes, he went up the path to the front door and rang the bell. The door was opened by a woman he assumed must be Mrs Douglas. Although he'd worked for Harry now for some time, he'd never met her. Harry kept his work and home lives strictly separate.

She peered out into the gloom. 'Yes?'

'Mrs Douglas? I'm Kevin. Kevin Tyler. I crew on Harry's boat. Is he there? D'ye think I could have a word with him?'

'I expect so. You'd best come in.'

He followed her into the hall. The house was as neat as a pin, a nicely furnished, well-decorated, suburban home a world away from that of fishing and light years from that of drugs. She opened the door on the left. 'You've a visitor, Harry.'

Douglas looked up from watching television. His eyes widened in surprise and he looked far from pleased. I shouldn't have come, thought Kevin. Now what do I say?

'What are you doing here?' enquired Douglas, without any preamble.

Kevin looked at him, willing him to understand. 'I thought you might like to come out for a drink,' he said, tamely. Then realized that if Harry said yes, he'd no money to pay for it.

Douglas looked hard at him and a look of realization crossed his face. He nodded. 'Very well, just a quick one.' He turned to his wife. 'I won't be gone long, Eileen, there's that programme I want to watch.' He went out into the hall and took a thick jacket and scarf off a peg, then turned to Kevin. 'Come on then.' Once outside he walked on slightly ahead, crossed the road and went into the public bar of a pub, the one he didn't usually drink in. Kevin looked round. There were few people there on such a cold night, as a result of which, the barman had turned up the piped music just about as far as it would go to help pass the time. Two ancient regulars sat at the bar roaring at him over the top of the music while, in a murky corner, a courting couple were locked in an embrace.

'Right,' said Douglas. 'Mine's a half and half.'

It was rapidly turning into a nightmare. Kevin's stomach churned. 'I haven't any money, Harry. I'm desperate.'

'Haven't you signed on?'

'Aye. But I won't get anything until the giro. I've borrowed what I can off Mam. She's pretty hard up.'

Douglas lent across to the barman. 'A half and half. And you? ... A pint of dark.' He paid for the drinks, then led the way to the other side of the room. 'So how did you get here?'

'By taxi. I used all the cash I'd got left.'

'So what the hell is this really about?'

Kevin wiped his face. 'You must have guessed.'

Douglas regarded him with cold fury. 'If you mean what I think you mean, are you out of your mind that you've come chasing me over here?' He dropped his voice as far as was practicable against the background din. 'What did I tell you when we first made a deal? I wouldn't shit on you to the police and you'd keep your mouth shut, do what you were told when asked and, when we're ashore, keep out of my way. I don't have to take you as crew, you know. There are plenty of experienced men out of work now who'd be glad of a berth.'

223

'Not right here on the spot though, Harry,' Kevin replied, unwisely. 'Not since Andy died.' It was true. There had been talk.

The mention of McKinley was a definite mistake. Douglas took a mouthful of whisky. 'Don't bet on that. Now drink up and get the hell out of here.'

'But I'm desperate, Harry, absolutely desperate. Like I told you, all my money's gone. I spent the last of it buying lousy stuff in Dumfries this morning.'

'Tough,' responded Douglas.

'But you don't understand.' Kevin was nearly weeping. 'I get out of my head if I try and come off it. I'm frightened of saying things.' He paused. 'Do you know who I met in the Dornoch Arms tonight? Jeannie Armstrong and Sally Black. Together. Cooking something up. And asking questions about Andy. And Euan.'

Douglas's eyes widened. 'But I take it even you weren't stupid enough to give them any answers.'

'And about you as well.'

Douglas exploded. *'Me!* What for fuck's sake did they ask about me?' His voice rose even above the sound of the music, causing the barman to look across at them. Douglas smiled back, then turned to Kevin. 'Treat this as a normal conversation if you don't want me to take you outside and beat your head in.'

'They kept on about Andy dying and Euan not coming back. They said it was a weird kind of coincidence and now there were the two of them, left on their own. Then they asked about you. Hinted there were rumours of ... you know. Of course I said you were OK and that there was no truth in it, it was all talk.'

There was a pause. 'I see,' said Douglas, slowly. 'Now I understand. Those girls aren't the only ones you're been talking to, are they?' Kevin stared. 'You've been shouting your mouth off to Elliot, haven't you? And that bookseller fellow.'

'Bookseller?' Was Harry losing his marbles? 'What bookseller? I've never met any bookseller. I don't know who you're talking about or what you mean. And I haven't talked to Elliot.'

Douglas said nothing for a minute or two, then appeared to make his mind up. 'Very well, I'll believe you this time. But don't you ever dare pester me here again. Do you understand?'

Relief flooded through Kevin. 'So you will help me?'

'This once. As it happens I can give you enough of what you want to see you through until tomorrow night. And I'll dock the cost from your wages before you get a penny of them. In exchange for which, I want some help from you tomorrow night.' He handed

Kevin a fiver. 'Get us another two drinks and mine's a tonic water this time.' He took his mobile out of his pocket. 'I'll make this call outside. And nip home.'

Five minutes later he reappeared. He sat down beside Kevin and pushed a screw of paper into his hand. No one noticed. 'Well that's all sorted. Tomorrow. Midnight. Kirkcudbright. Over the bridge and wait in the lay-by for a white Transit. I'll meet you there. And no questions,' he added as Kevin opened his mouth.

They finished their drinks and went outside. 'When do you reckon we'll be able to go to sea again?' asked Kevin.

Douglas sniffed the wind. 'Hopefully within the week. It's partly a question of the quotas too. Might as well save up our days until the weather's OK. I'm off, my programme's already started.' Kevin felt in his pocket for the change from the fiver. 'Keep it,' said Douglas. 'There's a phone box round the corner where you can ring for a taxi.' He crossed the road and went into his house without a backward glance.

Kevin felt the comforting screw of paper in his right-hand pocket. In the other he had a ten pence piece for the phone. Good old Harry. It'd been worth all the hassle. It had all come all right in the end.

As they left the bar the barman had looked after them, then shaken his head at the two regulars. 'Bold as brass that one. God only knows what the polis are about, everyone knows what goes on.'

'Aye,' responded the older of the two. 'And look at the state of that wee fella with him.'

'You know who he is, don't you,' added his companion. 'Maggie Tyler's son, Maggie Murdoch that was. He's called Kevin. Father came from England and married her. Died five or six years back. She deserves better.'

When Latymer came down into the farmhouse kitchen the following morning, he found Fiona already up and dressed. Music played in the background. She looked worn and tired, which was hardly surprising, but offered him breakfast, which he accepted gratefully.

'I've dosed James up and he's asleep. We both know this can't go on for much longer,' she commented as she set a plate of eggs and bacon down in front of him. 'But please try and help him if you can. If you really could find out what happened to Euan Armstrong it might bring this whole thing out into the open.' Latymer didn't know what to say. He was feeling increasingly out of his depth. He'd fully intended to go straight back to Kirkcudbright when Fiona briefly disappeared returning with a carrier bag which she handed to him. Inside were several folders tied with string and an envelope in which there were more computer discs.

'It's the stuff Euan did for him towards the end,' she told him. 'James wants you to have it. Do you think you could take a quick look at it before you go? Though I'll quite understand if you feel you must get back to your friend.' He looked at the bag with little enthusiasm but when he thought of what she was going through he couldn't bring himself to refuse. Her face lit up when he said he would.

'I'll stay a little while then I'll have to take the rest away,' he told her. 'I'll ring Keith and see what he says.' But Mr Berry, the receptionist told him when he rang the hotel, was already out and about, so Latymer left a message to say he'd be back later in the day. Fiona took him through to Garleston's study, explaining that James was in bed in another downstairs room and unlikely to get up that day.

'Obviously you can use his computer and if there's anything else you want, just ask. I'll be sitting with him but I'll come out from time to time to see how you're going on. And if you need me, just tap on the door on the left.'

Latymer took out the files and flipped through them. There was a great deal of material on the subject of Gulf War

Syndrome in general and depleted uranium shells in particular, most of which he recognized from the information he'd previously downloaded from the fisherking website and which had been supplemented by Garleston. There were also lists of names and addresses of people who were suffering from cancer or leukaemia or, if they were already dead, details of their family background.

Some of these were broken down further into more detailed medical histories and there was also a list, under the heading 'unexplained symptoms', of people who were complaining of illnesses or general malaise for which there seemed to be no identifiable cause. There was another, handwritten, list of the dates and times when depleted uranium shells had been fired from the Dundrennan base, to which was attached a grainy colour photograph showing a red deposit along the roadside verges. One folder contained a thick wad of printed matter on emissions from the Sellafield nuclear reprocessing plant only a few miles further south as the crow flies. Attached to one of the documents inside was a letter to Garleston from an anonymous Sellafield employee informing him that the situation regarding the pollution of fish and shellfish in the Irish Sea was far worse than was officially admitted.

But it was a second anonymous letter in a folder of its own which stopped him in his tracks. In it the writer claimed familiarity with the Dundrennan base and offered to reveal startling information if a meeting could be set up. It was dated 15 August 2000. On this one Garleston had written 'send Euan'. Did he go? Latymer wondered. And if he did, did he take the basic precaution of telling someone else when and where the meeting was to take place? It's what any real professional would do. Somehow he doubted it.

He combed through the rest of the folders but could find no report of such a meeting. He began to examine every paper in every file in earnest. At lunchtime Fiona brought him a bowl of soup and more coffee and he thanked her. By this time he was on to the computer discs but, like the folders, there was nothing to indicate that Armstrong had ever kept his appointment with the anonymous source, so close to the date of his disappearance. Time passed and he was suddenly aware that it was getting dark. Presumably, if Berry had needed him, he would have telephoned but he really had to go. He tapped on the door and she came out to him. 'I really must go now.'

'Have you found anything useful?' she asked.

'I'm not sure. Do you know anything

about a meeting Armstrong might have had with some anonymous source?'

She shook her head. 'No. If there was such a meeting then James never said anything to me. If he's feeling better this evening, I'll ask him.' They went through to the kitchen and the back door. He was suddenly aware of the music and smiled at her. 'I know this. It's called *Delirium*. Jean Armstrong gave me a tape of it.'

'You like it? Oh, so do I. Especially this track, it's kind of hopeful – the idea of a new beginning, waiting on the shore for the wind to turn. It promises better times. If not for James, then for others.'

He went out to the car, carrying the carrier bag of files and discs and she came out with him. She looked up at the sky. 'At least it looks as if the weather's improving. How much longer will you be here?'

'Another day or two at most. I've too much to sort out at home and my friend has his business to run. I want a word with Sean Elliot, though, if I can get hold of him before we go.'

'If you can possibly come over and see James again, we'd be very grateful. But whatever you do, take care.'

'Don't worry. I'll do that all right.'

'That's the last thing Euan Armstrong said to me,' she responded. 'And look what happened.'

Behind the tiredness he could see for the first time what an attractive woman she might be in different circumstances. She was a gallant soul. On an impulse he gave her a hug then, suddenly aware of what he was doing and how pleasant it was, broke away, embarrassed. Momentarily she clung to him. He put her gently away. 'Don't you wish he'd drop all this? So you could make the most of the time you have left together? He isn't going to change the world, it's too late.'

She smiled up at him, then her eyes filled with tears. 'Don't you see? This cause of his is what's keeping him alive. I truly believe that without it, he'd already have left us.'

He bumped off down the lane and, when he reached the main road, rang Tess again. There was still no reply. He tried not to think of the difference in the way Fiona Garleston reacted to her circumstances compared to Tess. Tess with her comfortable home and income, her garden and her social life. Fiona with a dying husband, surrounded by mystery and ahead of her an uncertain and possibly lonely future.

He found Berry waiting for him in the hotel. 'What do you reckon then?' he asked as soon as Latymer had taken off his coat. 'Did you get any further?'

He produced the carrier bag. 'I don't know, nor if it's worth staying up here any longer,' he said, wearily. 'I feel I've dragged you up here for nothing. We'll give it one last go and call round on him tomorrow morning. I told his wife I'd try and come back. Then we'll decide what to do. In the meantime, I've got quite a lot to tell you that is interesting.'

'It's nothing to what I've got to tell you,' retorted Berry. 'I suggest we leave any discussion until this evening. Sean Elliot's invited us round for drinks after dinner and I think he should be in on it all.'

Kevin arrived at the specified lay-by dead on midnight. He hoped Harry would have brought some more stuff with him. What he'd taken was beginning to wear off. It was dark and cold with little moon. He stamped his feet impatiently. Finally he saw the lights of a car approaching. It pulled up beside him and Douglas got out, turning off the lights as he did so.

'Sorry about the delay. The van'll be here in a minute.' As he spoke other lights appeared and a battered white Transit pulled into the lay-by. Douglas went over and spoke to the driver, then opened the back door. 'OK,' he said. 'Get in.'

Kevin did so. 'Aren't you coming then?'

Douglas shook his head. 'Things to see to. They'll tell you what to do. I'll give you a call when I'm ready to go back to sea again.

See you soon.' He slammed the door to and banged on it twice to tell the driver he could go. He watched its lights disappear into the distance for a few minutes, than took out his mobile and began to dial a London number. But before completing it he changed his mind, returned to his car and drove off back to Gatehouse.

It was pitch dark in the back of the van and there were no seats. It was being driven fast and Kevin was finding it difficult to stand upright. He felt his way round cautiously and came across what felt like a pile of sacks. He sat down on them. The van left Kirkcudbright behind and turned out on to the Dumfries road. It was then Kevin became aware that he was not alone. There was someone else in the van, he could hear breathing.

'Who's there?' he demanded. There was no reply. 'Why don't you say something? Have you got the stuff Harry fixed for me?'

'Harry's fixed it for you all right,' responded a voice from the gloom. Kevin was turning towards it when he was felled by a stunning blow to the head.

Thirteen

Late that same evening Latymer, Berry and Elliot were sitting at the kitchen table in the Elliots' cottage. Jean Armstrong having left unexpectedly early claiming she had home-work to do on her course and Mary had left the men to it, preferring to watch television in the sitting room. Latymer heard Berry out then thumped the table, stood up and began to pace up and down the room. 'So what you're telling me, Keith, is that the silly girl has known all along that the body in the ice was that of Euan Armstrong? And she said *nothing*? In fact getting any and every piece of information out of her has been like drawing teeth.'

'I knew the two of them were up to some-thing,' commented Elliot, 'from the way they were whispering to each other in the back of the car when I drove them back from Annan.'

'For goodness sake, sit down, John,' said Berry. 'Let's look at it rationally. In fairness, Sally was well and truly frightened. Andy claimed to know something and Andy was dead, but had it really happened? He'd been drunk at the time, she might even have begun to wonder if he had tried drugs, and anyway he'd told her to forget it, he'd been having a nightmare. Eventually she'd plucked up enough courage to trust you up to a point, but when you didn't reply to her letter she assumed you'd lost interest and that she was on her own. That was why she persuaded Jean Armstrong they could go it alone. It was fortunate I was able to intervene.

'I let them talk to a rather unpleasant lad called Kevin – incidentally the fourth crew member, the one I'd not been able to track down – and from what the women told me I certainly got the impression he knew something. I suggest we tackle him ourselves tomorrow.'

Latymer nodded. 'I just hope you've made those two young women see sense.'

'I told them in the strongest terms what they might be up against and to come to us if they have anything else to say. They're right out of their depth.'

'Well, I'll do my best to keep an eye on them when you've gone back,' Elliot assured them, 'but obviously I'm not here all the time and the weather forecast's finally improving. And not before time – we've been stuck here for days. I'll be going to sea again very soon. When do you go back to

England?'

'That must be very soon too,' said Latymer. 'I promised Fiona Garleston I'd look in again before I left and we'll do that in the morning. And I'll also try and see Jean Armstrong too. The day after tomorrow I reckon. I'd be grateful if you'd keep in touch, though.'

'Of course.'

'So what do you really believe it is: drugs or nuclear waste?' asked Berry as they made their way back to the hotel.

'I'm totally confused. It could be either, or a combination of both.'

He awoke the next morning with a thick head from a dream in which Garleston, his bald head shining in the moonlight, was leading him and a chain of other people hand in hand in a mad dance across the Solway sands to the accompaniment of loud drumming. He switched on the light and looked at his watch: seven o'clock. He might as well get up. The imagery of the dream stayed with him. Surely he'd seen something like it somewhere? Finally he dragged from his memory that it was a *danse des morts* on the walls of an ancient church in a village in the Lot et Garonne, visited on some holiday years ago. A small plaque beneath it informed the interested that it dated from the time of the Black Death. Black Death, dark forces ... Here we go again! He shook

237

himself wider awake.

As soon as they finished breakfast he and Berry set off for the Garlestons. At least this time it wasn't snowing. They drove beside the bay, past the place where Fiona had met up with him, Latymer then trying to decide which track led up to the farmhouse. Having made the decision, he drove slowly along it, cautiously negotiating the potholes. As they turned the last corner they saw the ambulance. As they drew up, two paramedics were wheeling out a stretcher, one holding a drip high in the air. The face of the blanketed figure lying on it was concealed by an oxygen mask. Latymer left the car as Fiona Garleston, wrapped in a heavy coat and holding an overnight bag, came out of the house and locked the door behind her.

'I'm so sorry,' Latymer apologized, 'I promised I'd try and come back and I'd no idea things...'

'He felt terrible all night,' she explained. 'But he wouldn't let me send for the doctor. Then this morning he was taken really bad and I called for the ambulance regardless.' Her voice broke. 'We're away to the hospital. I don't imagine he'll come back again this time.' Latymer pressed her hand in sympathy. The stretcher was lifted into the ambulance, she climbed in after it, and it set off back along the track, Latymer and Berry bumping along behind. As it reached the road, the driver put on the lights and the siren began to blare.

'Well there's obviously nothing more we can do here,' commented Berry. 'What next? I suggest we track down this fellow Kevin and see what he has to say.'

It was a milkman who'd come across what looked at first sight like a bundle of old clothes lying in a back alley in Carlisle. At first he just glanced at it as he went by with the crate he delivered every day to the side entrance to a small office block, but on his way back to his float it occurred to him it might well be a rough sleeper. Perhaps he should see if the man – at least he thought it was a man – was all right, since it had been such a perishing night. As he got nearer he could see it was indeed a man, lying in a huddle face down. 'You OK, mate?' he enquired. Then, as there was no response, he repeated his query. Still no reply. He bent down and shook the man's shoulder. His hand came away sticky.

With an awful sense of foreboding he returned to his float and drove it as near as he could so that its lights illuminated the scene. There was a good deal of blood, some of it splashed on a nearby wall. Cursing the fact that his employers wouldn't give him a mobile phone and that he didn't own one himself, he spent an infuriating ten minutes searching for a public call box to call the emergency services. When he finally found one he asked for both police and an ambulance then reluctantly returned to await the arrival of one or the other or both.

The police car arrived first and parked at the end of the alleyway. A sergeant got out, followed by a constable. 'I take it that it was you who called us?' he said as he came over.

The milkman confirmed that it was. 'And now you're here, can I go?'

'Hang on a minute.' The sergeant shone his torch down on the injured man, then knelt down beside him, felt for a pulse in the neck, looked at the constable and shook his head. A squeal of brakes heralded the arrival of the ambulance, which parked beside the police car. 'You sent for an ambulance as well?'

'I didn't know whether he was alive or dead, but he looked pretty bad to me.' The milkman looked at his hand again in disgust as two parademics arrived with a trolley. 'Rough sleeper?' enquired one.

'Maybe,' returned the sergeant. 'But from what I can see, this one isn't going to wake up again. I reckon we're all too late.'

'Better just check.' The paramedic bent down and also felt for a pulse. 'You're right. He's gone.' He wiped his hand on a cloth. 'Nasty. Been in a fight, I imagine, or mugged. Anyway, I take it you don't need us right away?'

'Not really. I'll have to get our people down here now. All the usual. But thanks for being so prompt.'

'No problem. That's what we're here for.' They took the trolley back to the ambulance, which reversed out of the road and went on its way.

'*Now* can I get on with my round?' demanded the milkman. 'I'm hours behind. I'll lose my job if I'm not careful.'

The sergeant turned to the constable. 'Make a note of his name, employer and home address, then get a brief statement about how he came to find this chap. After which,' he continued, turning to the milkman, 'you can go, but we'll probably want to talk to you again later in the day.'

Half an hour later, the area was securely taped off and a second police car was on the scene, along with the police surgeon, photographer, and the Scenes of Crime officers. 'That's some whack he's got on the back of his skull,' commented the police surgeon as he bent over the corpse. 'Done with something like a tyre lever, I imagine.'

'He's also had a good kicking,' remarked the sergeant.

'That too,' returned the doctor. 'It'll have to be confirmed at the PM, but I'd say he was dead or dying though before that

241

happened. The bleeding into the brain would have been enough. And if the blow hadn't been fatal, he'd probably have died of hypothermia anyway, the night being so cold.' He pushed up the man's sleeve. 'Oh, here we go! Take a look at these.'

The sergeant looked closely at the needle marks. 'Well, little doubt what's at the bottom of this one.' He looked across to the photographer. 'OK if I turn him over?' Then to the constable. 'Give me a hand.' Some of the kicking had obviously been to the face. 'What a mess!' The young constable felt his stomach beginning to churn. 'His own mother wouldn't recognize him now.'

The doctor looked again at the man's arm. 'Using for a good while by the look of him. Let's see the other one. Yes, there you are, you see.' He yawned and rubbed his cold hands. 'Looks like he either couldn't pay his dealer and got beaten up or dealt himself and ran into some dissatisfied clients. Any identification?'

The sergeant felt the man's anorak. 'Nothing in his outside pockets except some small change.' He felt inside. 'Doesn't seem to have had much on him, no credit cards, there's a counterfoil for the pools ... Here we are ... a note on the back of an envelope, looks like a shopping list.' He turned it over. 'Addressed to Mrs Morag Tyler, Kirkcudbright. His wife perhaps? I'll get on to

Dumfries and Galloway straightaway and tell them what's happened and get them to send someone out there to see her. At the very least he'll have to be identified. Any idea of when it might have happened, doctor?'

'Well, rigor's setting in fast but you'd expect it in this weather. I'd guess – and it is a guess – sometime around one or two o'clock this morning. I'll know more when I've done the post-mortem. If you can get him to the mortuary sharpish, I'll try and fit him in at the end of the afternoon.'

The two men drove back to Kirkcudbright in silence, thoughts still going round and round in Latymer's head. He still wasn't completely convinced that Garleston was on to a major pollution scandal but whatever the truth of the matter, he felt desperately sorry for him. And even more for Fiona. He was sure she was right, that this time he wouldn't return home except in his coffin. But she'd cope somehow, she was that kind of person. If only he had seen the anony-mous letter earlier he could have asked Garleston there and then if Euan had kept the appointment and, if so, what he had learned from it, a point he made to Berry.

'Great words "if only",' returned the latter, '– think of all the times we must have said it when we were both in the Force. "If only" a young woman hadn't been in the wrong place at the wrong time, "if only" he'd followed up one clue rather than another, "if only" some dumb superintendent had been prepared to listen to us!'

When they got back he once again rang home. To his surprise, this time Tess answered. She sounded very cool. 'Where've you been?' he demanded. 'I've kept on trying, as I promised, and getting no reply. I was beginning to worry.'

'Not enough to come back,' she retorted.

There was no answer to that. 'Look, Tess, there really has been something bad going on up here. Keith agrees and if you don't believe me, I'm sure he'd be happy to talk to you. We've decided we'll give it one more day at most, tell the police what we think even if they don't want to know, then come back. Please just try and understand why I feel so strongly that I have to do this.'

He heard her sigh. 'I don't know.' She told him she had, as he suspected, been staying with her daughter. 'Diana thinks I should leave you,' she told him. 'But Peter takes your side, says it's me who's being unreasonable. That you're only doing what you were trained to do, even if you aren't in the police any more.'

'And what do you think?'

'I don't know what to think.'

'I'll ring you again tonight and regularly

until I come home. At least don't do anything until I get back and we talk this thing through. If you'll let me explain properly what's been going on up here, then perhaps you'll finally be able to see it my way.' Even as he spoke, he felt more doubtful. 'Are you sure you're prepared to break up our marriage over this one issue, however strongly you feel about it?'

'All right.' She sounded doubtful. 'But promise me you'll keep in touch.'

'I promise.' He got back into the car.

'How was it?' enquired Berry.

'Well let's say at least we're back on speaking terms.' What he wasn't prepared to admit even to himself, let alone Berry, was just how much it would really matter to him if Tess carried out her threat.

The woman on the reception desk at the hotel greeted them in a great state of excitement. 'There's been a phone message from Sean Elliot. He says will you go straight up to his house.' Then she paused to make the most effect. 'It seems the police have found a *body*!'

The two men looked at each other and Latymer's blood ran cold. Sally Black? Jean Armstrong? Had they already put themselves at such terrible risk before confiding in Berry? This time they wasted no time walking but took the car. Elliot was outside

245

his cottage talking to a young constable. He briefly introduced them.

'The receptionist told us the police had found a body,' said Berry. 'Is it true?'

'Young man of the name of Kevin Tyler,' the constable informed them. 'I've just had to break the news to his mother. I've left a WPC up there with her. We understand he was a fisherman working out of here.'

'The man we were talking about last night,' added Elliot. 'The fourth member of Douglas's original crew.'

The constable frowned. 'Talking about him? Why should you be doing that?'

'Someone had brought his name up, I can't remember who,' continued Latymer, smoothly. 'I think it was to do with some rumour that he did drugs. We were discussing what a problem it was.'

'It seems he was found dead in a back alley in Carlisle this morning,' Elliot informed them.

'How did he die?' asked Berry.

'Blow to the head and a good kicking,' said the constable. 'It seems whoever told you they thought he did drugs was right. Arms like a pin cushion, according to the Carlisle police.'

'His mother lives a couple of miles out of town,' explained Elliot. 'Mary's gone up there in the police car to see if there's anything she can do.' He turned to the constable. 'Tyler had been staying with his mother since coming back here from Peterhead. I suppose he'd gone to Carlisle to buy drugs.'

'So you might say that he did drugs was common knowledge?' The constable made a note in his book.

'As we said, it was rumoured,' returned Elliot. 'I'd have thought you lot had a good idea too. Perhaps you should ask some of your colleagues. He's not the only user on this stretch of coast and it's the second drugs-related death we've had in this community in a matter of weeks. Why you don't do more about it, beats me.'

The policeman looked uncomfortable. 'The powers-that-be believe we should concentrate on the big fish since we're so under-resourced. That they can always pick up the little people any time they want as they know where they are. I'm not saying I agree, but that's how it is. Well, I'd better get on my way, I've a good many people to see. It's kind of your wife, Mr Elliot, to go up to the lad's mother. We'll need a formal identification too but the Carlisle police are hoping someone else will be willing to do it. He's an awful mess.' As he spoke a police car drew up. 'Well, I'll be on my way. I might need to talk to you again, Mr Elliot.'

'Then you'd better be quick about it, I'm off back to sea in a day or so. I've a living to earn.'

'Going to sea with Captain Douglas will soon be as popular as signing up for the *Marie Celeste*,' commented Latymer dryly, as the car disappeared.

Elliot shrugged. 'It's a bad business but life must go on. I've got to get down to the boat. There's a small oil leak somewhere and I've an engineer coming to fix it. I'll see you both later.'

Kevin's death merited a brief item on the local television news after the main news bulletin at one o'clock. The body of a young man, thought to be that of Kevin Tyler from Kirkcudbright, had been found in Carlisle in the early hours of the morning, the local reporter informed viewers, and the police were treating it as a suspicious death as it appeared he had been violently attacked. There then followed an appeal for possible witnesses and a telephone number to ring.

They were in the middle of their lunch when a frightened Jean Armstrong telephoned. Latymer took the call.

'The man found dead in Carlisle, John,' she began without any further explanation, 'it's the same guy Mr Berry saw us talking to the other night. Kevin Tyler. It was on the local news just now. But why was he in Carlisle?'

'Where are you now?'

'Back home in Annan.'

Latymer felt uneasy about saying too much over the phone. 'Do you think it might be an idea if we went back to see Sally?'

'Yes. And I'd like to see you as well before you go back.'

He thought for a moment. 'I think Keith warned you as to what you might be getting into. Now you can see it for yourself. I promise I'll see you before I go and, in the meantime, be very careful indeed and don't talk to anyone unless it's the police.'

He put the phone down and returned to the table.

They finished their lunch and went down to the shop where Sally worked. 'She's just slipped home for a minute,' the owner informed him. 'Had some telephone call that upset her. I've told her over and over not to bring her mobile into the shop. If she hadn't got it with her whatever it was could have waited until she'd finished work!'

Sally opened the door to him herself. 'Is it about Kevin Tyler? Jeannie called me. She said it was on the news on the telly. You'd better come in, but I can't stay long. I must go back to work.' She led him through to the small sitting room. 'Are the police sure it really was Kevin they found in Carlisle?'

'Quite sure. Though he has to be formally identified.'

'Did Jeannie ask you to come and see me?'

249

'She thought it a good idea. Now listen to me, there's no point in going on now about your not telling me all you knew earlier, but if you are hanging on to any more information then for God's sake tell us now. It could be a matter of life or death.'

She looked shaken but wary. 'Are you serious?'

'Deadly serious. Now tell me one thing. Did Andy at any time see Armstrong's face?'

'No, as I told Mr Berry the other night, he recognized a scar on the back of his hand. He said it didn't sink in straightaway, but afterwards he remembered Euan had one just like it. It wasn't usually all that noticeable but as the hand was very white, it kind of stood out.'

'You really should have gone to the police,' said Berry.

'Why should the police believe me? I told you again and again, since they're so sure Andy was a drug addict, they'd just say he'd been seeing things. Kevin Tyler was different, he really does – did – do drugs. You saw him, Mr Berry, and the way he fairly ran out of the pub. He couldn't wait to get away.'

'You do realize you now have to go to the police.'

'I've already told you. It would be a waste of time. They won't believe me.'

'Then we'll come with you,' Latymer assured her. 'I take it the headquarters is in

250

Dumfries? I'll find out if they'll see us first thing tomorrow morning. And I think Jean Anderson should be there too.' She began to protest. 'No, this has gone far enough. You must tell them exactly what you've told me.'

Yet again Latymer went through the Garleston files just in case he'd somehow missed a vital note, while Elliot ran Berry up the road to show him where the firing ranges were. But there was definitely no report back from Armstrong. He wondered how Garleston was faring and rang the hospital to find out. In answer to the demand to know if he was a relative, Latymer mumbled 'close friend' and was finally informed that Mr Garleston was very poorly indeed and that his wife was with him. Did he want to leave a message? He told the nurse to tell Mrs Garleston that John Latymer had enquired after her husband and was thinking of them both.

As he finally put the folders away, Berry arrived back. 'I rang the police in Dumfries and made an appointment to see them in the morning with both women. They didn't sound particularly enthusiastic. How did you get on?'

'We weren't able to get down to the beach you spoke of, it was one of the days when the road is closed. It's hard to imagine looking out across the water that there are thousands of nuclear shells lying in the mud. I have the feeling Elliot would rather not know about it. Drugs he can get his head round, anything that might interfere with the fishing or spoil the local tourist trade is something else. I suppose you can't blame him.'

Latymer smiled. 'An Enemy of the People.'

'What?'

'A play by Ibsen. It's about an effort to cover up a possible epidemic in a holiday town in Norway in the nineteenth century. Officialdom were far less scared of the disease taking hold than that publicity about it might affect business. There must be many people living around here, as well as Sean Elliot, who feel exactly the same. I suppose poor James Garleston could be seen as just that.'

The violent death in a Carlisle backstreet of yet another young drug addict wouldn't normally have merited even a paragraph in the national press. But it just so happened that one of the broadsheets was planning yet another series of features on drugs, their use, the culture, and whether or not the law really did need to be changed, following recent signs that a re-think might finally be on the way.

The journalist charged with the task of

putting together the first piece (the usual one on the use of drugs amongst the young and the hazards to those involved) was going through the information he had got together so far when a more senior colleague dumped a torn-off piece from a Press Association report on his desk. 'This must be one of the latest,' he said, pointing to the heading 'Drugs Killing in Carlisle'. 'It'd give you an intro.'

So the reporter rang the police in Carlisle and was put through to the officer handling the press. It was, the officer sighed wearily, unhappily no big deal. Such a death hardly made the front page even locally. No, the dead man – Kevin Tyler – didn't live in Carlisle but some distance away near Kirkcudbright. Oh, and he was a fisherman and that made it the second drugs-related death in the fishing fraternity from that same small port recently. Which all went to show how prevalent drug abuse is in the fishing fleets these days.

Cause of death? The pathologist who had just carried out the post-mortem confirmed it was due to a blow to the head with a blunt instrument which had fractured the skull and caused bleeding into the brain. He'd also been the victim of a vicious kicking, but by that time he must already have been dying. The investigation was proceeding. Yes, it might well be that Tyler had fallen out with his supplier or someone else involved in the drugs scene. That was really all he could say at present.

The reporter got out a road map of the British Isles and looked for Kirkcudbright. It took him a while to locate it and when he did it appeared to be a very small place. He'd like to have gone up to Scotland himself and found out what the locals thought about there having been two recent drugs deaths up there, but the story would only be a small part of the bigger piece he was expected to write and there was so little time in which to get it all together. So he rang the paper's correspondent in Scotland and asked him if he could find out any more. 'Don't make a meal of it,' he told him, 'but it'd be good to start off with an immediately topical angle.'

Latymer and Berry were in the bar that evening when a member of the hotel staff came over to Latymer to say there was a message from a Mrs Garleston.

The hospital must have told her he'd been asking after her, thought Latymer, and stood up. 'Is she on the phone? I'll take it now.'

The young man shook his head. 'No. She said could you possibly meet her at her home straightaway. She sounded very upset.'

'Is that all she said?'

'Aye, except that she hoped you could make it and that you'd know what it was about.'

Latymer was frankly puzzled. Was Garleston dead? But if so, why call him? There was nothing he could do. Perhaps there was no one else she could contact immediately. If so she must be feeling pretty desperate. Or was it something else? Was there something that Garleston, on his death bed, was determined he should know about? He looked across at Berry. 'Seems a bit odd to me. I'll see if I can reach her.' He rang the Garlestons' number on his mobile but was unable to get through; possibly the farmhouse lay in one of the areas the signal didn't reach. 'I suppose I'd better go, though I can't say I feel like turning out at this time of night.'

'Do you want me to come with you?' Berry enquired with a marked lack of enthusiasm.

'I'm tempted but there really isn't any point. Whatever it is can't take me long. I'll be back well in time for a nightcap.' As he turned the car on to the coast road a little light snow started to fall.

Fourteen

As he reached the turn-off to the farmhouse some sixth sense kicked in. Why should Fiona Garleston with a husband who was dying, or had just died even, want to see him at such a time? Out in the middle of the countryside on a cold winter night, the notion of an urgent deathbed request now seemed unlikely if not downright foolish. Even though Fiona knew he was soon going back to England, she could have rung him in the morning and arranged a meeting then if it was that vital. Just to the left of the gateway was the ruin of a small building, possibly an old cottage or a derelict barn. He pulled off the track. The ground seemed quite firm and the snow wasn't sticking. He drove the car round to the back out of sight, clicked the remote control to lock it, and set off up the track. He decided against using his torch and kept it his pocket.

Slow as it had been to drive up to the house, it took him a good deal longer on foot. It must be the best part of half a mile, he thought as he trudged on. As he came up to the farmyard gate he wondered first why the outside light wasn't on – all he could see was a dim glow in one of the rooms. There was also something else missing: the dogs. He could see the front door was slightly ajar, surely they would have been barking by now? He moved carefully up to the door staying in the shadow. Something quite definitely wasn't right. He crept silently into the hall and began to make his way up the corridor.

His assailant caught him from behind with an armlock round his neck but he was, to some extent, prepared. He struggled to prise the arm away as his head was banged hard into the granite wall. He felt blood trickling down his cheek. Now thoroughly enraged, he turned on the man and grappled with him. They both fell to the ground, at first with the attacker on top but finally Latymer reversed their positions, got the man's arm across his back, turned his head round and shone the torch directly into his eyes.

Temporarily blinded, his assailant lay still and Latymer had a brief glimpse of the unremarkable face of a man he judged to be in his mid-twenties. 'Who are you?' demanded Latymer, struggling to his knees. 'Who sent you? Why was I asked to come here?' In reply his attacker made a major effort, rolled over and, struggling to his feet, butted Latymer in the midriff and raced down the hallway. Gasping for breath, Latymer held on to the wall to steady himself, then went after him. As he reached the doorway he heard a car door slam, a vehicle start up and dimly saw the outline of a four-by-four hurtling along the track. There was no way he could catch up.

He tried the switch in the hall and to his relief the light came on. The first thing he must do was to see if Fiona Garleston was anywhere in the house either tied up or locked in one of the rooms, though he doubted it. He went through the house, room by room, switching on the lights as he went. There was no sign of her, but in Garleston's study all the drawers in the filing cabinet had been pulled out and files were strewn all over the floor. No ordinary burglar this then, but then he'd never thought it was. Was it possible that she'd already been confined in the attacker's vehicle? Again he thought it unlikely. To make sure he decided to call the hospital but the phone line had been torn out of the wall. There was still no sign of the dogs.

He went outside and dialled the hospital from his mobile and, to his relief, found it worked. The switchboard operator put him through to the relevant ward and the sister in charge confirmed that Mrs Garleston was still in the hospital. She sounded less than pleased when he insisted that he had to speak to her on a matter of the greatest urgency but finally agreed to see if it was possible.

Fiona Garleston had obviously been crying. He guessed what was coming. 'James died about half an hour ago,' she told him. 'Quite peacefully in the end. I'm just making various arrangements then I'm going home.'

'You didn't by any chance ring me earlier did you?'

'No. Why would I? I never moved from James's side.'

'Because a woman rang my hotel. I didn't speak to her myself but she claimed to be you and asked me to come out to your house straightaway. I'm here now. Some bastard tried to kill me and your filing cabinet's been rifled. Though it scarcely seems important in the present circumstances.'

'Oh no!' There was a pause. 'Well, as I said, I was about to come back anyway.'

'I'll stay here until you do. Then I think you'd better come back with me to the hotel and stay there for the night. I don't think whoever it was will try again tonight, but you never know.'

She would, she said, be with him within about half an hour. He then rang Berry, who offered to get a taxi and come over. Latymer was relieved. 'It wouldn't be a bad idea. But

I don't imagine they'll come back again so soon.'

'I'll do that then. Oh, and by the way Tess rang the hotel. She said you'd promised to call her this evening.'

Oh God, he thought, of course I did. He'd fallen again at the first hurdle. He dialled his home number. There was no reply; nor from her mobile. He left a message on both saying he would call her again however late it might be.

Berry and Fiona Garleston arrived almost at the same time. Berry was first and looked round in surprise for the car. 'Don't worry. I trust it's safe,' Latymer told him. 'I just had a funny feeling about the whole thing when I got to the end of the track. It's hidden at the back of that ruin by the gateway. Seems the old instinct isn't quite dead yet.'

As they spoke a taxi came into view. 'The cab driver cursed me coming down the track,' Fiona told them as she got out. 'He had to pull over and said that if he knocked his exhaust or sump off, he'd claim it off me. I said the way I was feeling he could do what he liked.' She looked bone tired.

'I'm sorry you've had to come back to this,' said Latymer, 'but I didn't know what to do for the best. I came out here because at first I thought the phone call was genuine though I was already starting to have doubts before I got as far as the house. Then I realized something was wrong; not least that the dogs weren't around.'

She nodded. 'A friend took them away this morning to look after them. I didn't want to leave them shut outside in this weather.'

They walked into the hall. 'So far as I can see, nothing's been disturbed anywhere else except in your husband's room,' said Latymer. She looked briefly into the living room and kitchen, then surveyed the mess in the study. 'I don't imagine it's possible to tell very easily if anything's been taken,' he commented.

She shook her head. 'Not now. I'll have to go through it all in the morning and I might not know even then. I don't think I ever saw every file James kept here and recently he mostly used his computer. And now he's gone and I'll never know...' Her eyes filled with tears as she turned towards Latymer and saw him clearly in the light for the first time. 'Good God!' A purple bruise was rapidly spreading along the side of Latymer's face although the trickle of blood was now drying. 'Heavens, look at you! Do you think you ought to go to Casualty and get that seen to?'

Latymer felt his face gingerly. 'It's very sore but I don't think it's anything serious. I'm still pretty winded though from when the bastard butted me in the stomach.' He

261

felt tired and suddenly very depressed. 'I must get back to the hotel and Keith agrees with me, I really do think it best you come back with us tonight.'

'Shouldn't we report this to the police?''

'I suppose we should, but as I don't imagine any of us believe this was your average opportunist thief, I think it can wait until morning. Keith and I have an appointment at your local police headquarters tomorrow anyway and we can mention it there as well if you like. We'll lock everything up and leave it as it is. The police will hardly blame you for not getting them out here tonight when you tell them your husband's just died. Also, your phone wire's been cut. You'll need to get on to BT tomorrow.'

She nodded. 'You're probably right. If you're going to Dumfries in the morning, I'll follow you to Kirkcudbright in my own car. If you get in I'll take you down to the end of the drive.' She locked the back door and slumped against it. 'What a mess! As if there isn't more than enough to see to. I hope to God I can get the phone fixed. Apart from anything else I need to make the funeral arrangements.'

Inspector Tom Crozier leafed through the files in front of him without enthusiasm. He felt even less thrilled at the prospect of seeing the two young women and their unwanted escorts at ten o'clock. The last few days had been far from satisfactory. The local reporter had got on to him on behalf of the London journalist almost as soon as he had put the phone down, encouraged by the prospect of earning some extra money and ingratiating himself with a national broadsheet. He'd come straight to the point.

'Doesn't it worry you, Inspector, that there's now been two drugs-related deaths more or less on your patch? Both crew members of the same fishing boat?'

'Yes it does,' Crozier'd responded, brusquely, 'and obviously we're looking into it. But if you want any information on Tyler's death then you'll need to speak to the Carlisle police. They're dealing with that. We're checking out this end.'

'So tell me, is there a particular problem in the ports along the Solway coast? That heroin's easily come by in the area?'

Crozier became impatient. 'I'd say the reverse. OK the first victim was found dead of an overdose in Kirkcudbright, but it looks as if Tyler had to go all the way to Carlisle to get hold of it. Or try to. There's no great mystery about this one.'

The reporter considered this. 'What do you know about the skipper of the boat I understand the two men crewed for?' He'd obviously been doing his homework. 'Name of Douglas. Harry Douglas.'

263

The question hung in the air. 'Not a lot,' Crozier responded. 'And now, if you don't mind, I've other things to do.'

'Have you been looking into his activities at all?' the reporter persisted. 'Up there, rumour has it he's involved in running the stuff.'

'Then if you get any hard information let us know,' replied Crozier and hung up.

Douglas was a sore point with Crozier. The police were fully aware of the rumours surrounding him, but so far had never been able to prove anything. It remained just that: rumour. In the meantime Douglas remained on the list of those to be pulled in when the so-called 'big men' were finally rounded up, a master plan that was still ongoing and at the current rate of progress, Crozier thought sourly, to take until the end of Time.

In fact he'd sent a local constable over to Gatehouse to interview Douglas as soon as he had been told of the link between Douglas and Tyler, following a phone call from one of the pensioners who had been in the pub when the two men had been in. Douglas had been perfectly co-operative, he could hardly be anything else in view of his having met Tyler in front of several witnesses. His young crew member, he told the sergeant, had turned up asking for a sub until they went to sea again and he'd reluctantly agreed and given him £20 up front and money for a taxi back to his home. Pressed for his reaction to the fact that it looked as if Tyler had been a drug addict, Douglas had admitted he'd suspected as much for some time but that it hadn't appeared to affect the lad's capacity to do his job.

'In fact,' he told the sergeant, 'when he turned up asking for money the other night I told him that if it was for what I thought it might be, then the sooner he got himself to a clinic the better and that if he did and got himself clean, he could have his job back afterwards, however long it took. Of course he denied it point-blank. Just asked when we were likely to go back to sea. I told him I'd let him know and the last I saw of him he was going off to ring for a taxi. Never saw him again after that.'

'Couldn't tell whether he was lying or not,' the constable reported back to Crozier. 'If he was, then he was pretty slick with it. He certainly sounded genuine enough.'

The files in front of Crozier on his desk were those for the death of McKinley, a more or less closed case now, and a thin folder filed under 'MisPer' labelled 'Euan Armstrong'. There was a brief statement from Sally Black, McKinley's fiancée, in his file and several notes of visits, telephone calls and copies of letters from Jean in that of Armstrong's. A piece of paper clipped to the inside cover noted that Mrs Armstrong remained convinced her husband was dead and that his body had turned up in Cornwall and been identified as someone else, despite all the evidence to the contrary. A scribbled note from the desk sergeant informed Crozier that Latymer and Berry were both ex-police, and that he assumed they must be private investigators. This set up an immediate prejudice. Crozier had little time for retired members of the Force who turned to such work.

So he was noticeably frosty when at ten o'clock he received what amounted to a small delegation, emphasizing that his time was limited and that he hoped what was being offered was new information, not material that had previously been exhaustively investigated. He then stared at Latymer's battered face.

'I'll explain presently,' Latymer informed him. 'I was the victim of an assault last night. But first, Miss Black was already proposing to come and see you. She has information you need to know.'

Crozier settled back. 'Very well. Let's hear it.'

'It's about Jean's husband, Euan.' Crozier's face took on a set expression. 'Just before he died Andy, my fiancé, told me that when his boat, *Lady of Annan*, was in Cornwall last

August he'd seen the hand of a dead man packed in the ice in the bottom of the boat. And that he was almost certain it was Euan Armstrong because there was a scar on the back of his hand from an injury he remembered Euan doing to himself with a chisel when they were both in woodwork class at school.'

'He did have a scar like that,' added Jean, 'though he never told me how he got it.'

Crozier stared at Sally. 'If that's true, then why the hell didn't McKinley tell the police in Cornwall what he'd seen?'

'He got involved in a fight over it with his skipper, Harry Douglas. They both ended up in hospital.'

'So what stopped him coming to us once he got back home?'

'He thought, or was persuaded to think, he'd imagined it all after being banged on the head as well as having had a lot to drink. When he finally told me, during the night before he died, I told him he *must* tell you, but in the morning he backed off from it. Said he'd just been having bad dreams. I told him I didn't believe him and he said that was up to me. The past was the past and he was looking to the future and starting his new job, then we could get married. A day later, he was found dead of a drugs overdose yet I swear to God he'd never taken drugs in his life.'

'And what was this new job?'

'He didn't say. Only that it was really good money and that he was meeting a couple of people to finalize the details.'

Crozier peered again at the papers on his desk. 'The note from the desk sergeant says you were coming in about Tyler. Where does he fit in?'

'If you've looked into it at all, you must know he was a member of the same crew down in Cornwall with Andy,' declared Jean. 'Sally only told me all this the other night.'

'So what's *your* excuse for not coming here and telling us this earlier?'

'Why should I?' raged Jean. 'You've never taken me seriously: so far as all of you are concerned, Sally was too stupid to know her fiancé was a drug addict, and I was just another abandoned wife trying to track down her wandering man. So we decided the only way we were ever likely to get anywhere was to try and find some kind of proof ourselves and since we were sure Harry Douglas was involved in it all, we thought we'd start with the other two members of the crew.'

'Fortunately I learned what they intended and persuaded them against taking it any further without help,' broke in Berry.

'Let me finish, if you don't mind,' retorted Jean. 'We're quite capable of speaking for

268

ourselves. Yes, well Mr Berry did warn us that we might be running into trouble but when that slimeball Tyler came in, he agreed we should have a go at him.'

'He looked awful bad,' added Sally, 'and he didn't want to talk to us at all. But we kept on asking him things. You know, saying it was pretty weird how we'd both lost our men and didn't he think it funny that Euan had disappeared last August just about the time they sailed for Cornwall? Then Andy dying of a heroin overdose. I asked him outright if anything dodgy happened when they were all down in Cornwall and he choked on his drink, didn't he, Jean?'

'Aye. And when we began talking of the rumours about Harry and how people who worked for him didn't seem to be very lucky, he couldn't wait to get away. Said he felt ill, was going down with 'flu or something, and fairly ran out of the pub. He'd told us was broke and couldn't wait to get back to sea. Next thing is he's found dead in Carlisle.'

'Do you remember what time he left you?' enquired Crozier.

The two women looked at each other. 'About half eight, I reckon,' said Jean.

'I can vouch for that,' Berry added.

Crozier nodded. 'That figures. He was seen in Gatehouse about nine o'clock talking to Douglas in another pub.' He paused.

'I'd like both of you to make statements now. You saw him too, Berry? You too then. And perhaps you could add anything else you think might be relevant. Including everything these two young women told you.' He picked up the phone, called for a sergeant and asked him to take the necessary statements then turned back to Berry. 'Quite a novelty for you, I imagine? To be on the other side of the desk.' Berry didn't rise to the bait, merely stood up and ushered the two women out in front of him.

Crozier motioned Latymer to stay where he was. 'So what happened to you?'

'One of the staff in the Dornoch Arms took a phone message for me purporting to come from a Mrs Garleston, who lives out near Borgue, asking me to come and see her at once. I'd visited her and her husband a couple of days earlier. I was surprised as I knew her husband was terminally ill and had assumed she was at the hospital with him. However, I went. But by the time I reached the house I was feeling uneasy about it. Rightly so as it turned out. The front door was open and when I went in I was attacked by some young thug. I tried to hold on to him but he got away. I had a good look round and it was clear at once that Garleston's study had been ransacked. Then I rang the hospital to be told he'd just died. I spoke to Mrs Garleston herself then, and she said she would be home as soon as she'd made the necessary arrangements, so I waited for her.' He stopped. 'Presumably someone's been up there this morning to see her. It's pretty dreadful for her to have had a break-in while her husband was dying.'

Crozier picked up the phone and barked into it. 'I see,' he said after a little while. 'Keep me up to date on this one.' He put the receiver down.

'It seems there's someone there now. And this message you were given. They were sure it was this woman?'

'As I said, I didn't speak to anyone myself. The manager's son took the call in good faith. He probably wouldn't have recognized Mrs Garleston's voice anyway: she's unlikely to have visited the hotel in recent weeks as she's hardly ever been able to leave her husband.'

'I see.' Crozier sat back in his chair again. 'What I can't understand is your involvement in any of this. In Mrs Armstrong's search for her missing husband or with Mrs Garleston. Were you acting in some capacity for both? What's the connection?'

'It was fortuitous. I just happened to be in Newlyn when the fight took place between McKinley and Douglas. I work as a courier for a tourist firm in the summer, which is why I was there. Equally by chance, my work then brought me up here and I looked up Sean Elliot, a Kirkcudbright skipper I'd met at the same time. I showed him a cutting from the local paper about a body found in the sea shortly after the Scots' boats had left, and a number of people here said it looked just like Armstrong. We showed it to Mrs Armstrong and she was convinced it was her husband. I was reluctantly persuaded to go down to Cornwall with her to check it out since I know the ropes. As to the Garlestons, I contacted James Garleston after logging on to a website he set up to do, among other things, with Gulf War Syndrome. The link between them is that Armstrong was doing some legwork for Garleston, researching a possible pollution story.'

Crozier shook his head, got up and walked across to the window. 'Are you saying that somehow Armstrong's disappearance and Tyler's death are linked to an attempted burglary at Mrs Garleston's house? If so, you've lost me.'

'I think it might be. Indirectly. But it's a long story. It's hard to know where to start.'

Crozier paused. 'What do you *really* believe has happened to Armstrong, Latymer?'

'That it just could be his body that was taken out of the sea in Cornwall and that it had been brought down there from Scotland packed in the ice in Douglas's boat.

And there's something else you should know. Devon and Cornwall police, for perfectly valid reasons, never queried the credentials of the man called David Bentley who identified the body and claimed to be the corpse's brother. Yet when my colleague checked him out later, the firm Bentley was supposed to work for had never heard of him. Nor did the address of the dead man exist either. Now, of course, nothing can ever be proved. The body was cremated.'

'Why should anyone want to get rid of Armstrong?'

'Because he'd fancied himself as a journalist. He took on the work for Garleston, who was dying of leukaemia, because he had visions making his name with some kind of scoop. But whatever he was doing it was patently no job for an amateur.'

'Am I to assume it was to do with drugs and that it got too close to Douglas?'

'Possibly, though there's also another option. You see the research he was doing for Garleston was on something quite different. A possible pollution story which had direct implications for the Ministry of Defence.' And, briefly, he told Crozier about 'Fisherking'.

Crozier heard him out. 'Shit!' he exclaimed when Latymer had finished. 'I need to know that like I need a hole in the head. I make it my business never to meddle with spooks.'

The sergeant detailed to take the statements put his head round the door to inform Crozier that they'd been taken and duly signed, then he put a copy of the *Independent* on the desk. 'Wondered if you'd seen this, sir?'

Crozier took it from him. The trailer on page one informed him that the first of a series on 'The Drugs Scandal' was on page 5. He turned to page 5, which was head-lined 'Sailing into Disaster'. He cast his eye down to the strapline, then showed it to Latymer. 'The Scourge of the Heroin Epidemic in our Fishing Industry stretches from Scotland to Cornwall', it informed readers. 'Does Anybody Really Care?'

He looked across at Latymer. 'Now I'm going to have to deal with this! I'll read the young women's statements and that of your colleague and give the matter some thought. How much longer do you intend staying in Scotland?'

'I'd hoped to go home tomorrow. I've told my wife I would.'

'I'd like to see you again before you do if that's possible. And your colleague.'

'We'll do our best.'

'What are your immediate plans?'

'We need to return the women to their homes, then I promised we'd go over and see Fiona Garleston. It's bad enough for her

274

coping with her husband's death, let alone the rest. She must be very afraid that whoever turned over her house will come back.'

There was a pause. 'Do you think Garleston really was on to something, or was he just another Green troublemaker?'

'I don't know enough about these things to be sure one way or the other. But I'm absolutely certain *he* believed it. And that where this kind of thing's involved, some people prefer any worms there might be to be left firmly unopened in the can.'

In an office in Vauxhall in London the man known as David Bentley was working his way through the morning's post, e-mails and faxes which his secretary had put in front of him. It was a slack day. He yawned and looked out of the window at a flurry of sleet. A barge was making its way downriver towing a lighter. His secretary brought him a cafetière of coffee and, after a minute or so, he pushed down the plunger and poured himself a cup. The daily papers were in a neat pile in the in-tray. He picked up *The Times*, scanned the headline and put it to one side, then gave his usual snort of derision as he cast his eye down the front page of the *Guardian*. Took a gulp of coffee then turned to the *Independent*. He added more sugar to the coffee. He found he needed it in the mornings. He saw the note on the front page and turned to page 5. As he began to read, his hand became rigid on the coffee spoon. He raced through the opening paragraphs then dropped the paper down in front of him.

'Sod it!' he exclaimed. Then reached for the phone.

Fifteen

Crozier wasn't the only one to read the report in the *Independent* that morning with interest. The writer of the drugs series, going through cuttings and files in the office, had taken out a number of incidents he felt were relevant, including several from the *Cornishman*. Among them were the story of the fight at the local carnival and the subsequent discovery of the body in the harbour. A local West Country freelance had sent them in with the scribbled message 'Should I look into this?' on the latter but it had never been followed up. The story in itself hadn't attracted the *Independent*'s journalist but it had encouraged him to ring several contacts in west Cornwall to find out if it was true, as he'd heard, that there was a serious drugs problem in that neck of the woods. The result had been the inference of a possible link between activity in Scotland and that further west.

The intro into the series was predictable: everybody was aware there was a problem, present policy patently wasn't working, which groups of people or communities were most at risk. The next three days' issues promised 'in-depth' research into the use of drugs in fishing communities, in the club scene and in schools, ending with 'expert' views on the best way to tackle the scourge. Under a photograph of Newlyn harbour, today's feature began with an account of a fight between two Scots fishermen in Cornwall in August, a fight some locals had put down to 'the drugs problem'. A brief note added that Penzance was rapidly gaining an unwanted reputation as the drugs capital of the west of England. But the real nugget was the fact that the fight in the summer had been between Harry Douglas and Andy McKinley and that local West Country opinion appeared to have been borne out by the fact that McKinley had later been found dead back home in Scotland of a heroin overdose. Not only that, but a second member of the crew of the same boat had now been found dead, following a brutal attack which the police in Carlisle had no doubt was drugs-related. The body in the harbour was mentioned in passing but there was no mention either of a drugs connection or doubt as to its identity.

There followed a more detailed description of the finding of Tyler, 'kicked to death in a back alley', and an account of an interview by the local freelance (uncredited, much to his annoyance) with skipper Harry Douglas:

> Douglas (42) of Gatehouse of Fleet in Dumfries and Galloway said that he was obviously 'horrified' by the appalling murder of Kevin Tyler, whom he had last spoken to the evening before his death. 'I'm afraid that like all too many young men in the business today he was abusing drugs and recently I'd suspected as much. Indeed I told him that if he was prepared to seek help he would find his job waiting for him, but he denied he was a user.'

Asked about another past crew member, McKinley, Douglas had told the reporter that he'd had no idea that McKinley'd also had a habit. 'Perhaps it was a one-off done out of bravado or as an experiment.' Pressed as to the reason for the fracas between McKinley and himself in Newlyn, Douglas brushed this aside. 'It was the local carnival, it was hot and a lot of us had been drinking all day as there was little else to do. These things happen. The local police didn't bother to take it any further. No, it had absolutely nothing to do with drugs. Just a silly drunken argument.' 'Mr Douglas,' continued the report, 'is a well-known figure in the fishing industry in ports in both

England and Scotland.'

The main story then moved on to several other ports, with particular attention to Peterhead and Aberdeen, with brief interviews with fishermen, police and others on the seemingly unstoppable supply of hard drugs entering the country and whether or not rumours were true that they were sometimes brought in with the catch. Part Two of the series – 'Drugs in Clubs' – would appear the following day.

Scanning it through a second time after Latymer and Berry left, Crozier sighed and awaited the call from his boss asking what the hell was going on and why hadn't he been informed that the death of some lowlife in Carlisle might lead to this kind of unwanted publicity?

Latymer, buying a copy from the nearest newsagent, wondered whether anything might come from someone having finally made a link between the two ends of the country but, other than that, couldn't see how it might help his own particular quest. After dropping Jean and Sally back home, with promises to stay in touch, they returned to the Garlestons' farmhouse. It was comforting to hear the barking of the dogs as Fiona Garleston appeared in the doorway. She invited them in and offered them coffee.

'Sorry it's so cold in here. I've only just got

the stove going again. It's all the more noticeable because we had to keep the house so warm for James, he felt the cold terribly.' She put the kettle on. 'One of our friends is helping make the arrangements for the funeral and my neighbour down the lane has said I can stay with her tonight if I like. James left specific instructions about what should happen after his death as you might imagine. I'm not sure yet whether they'll be doing a post-mortem, although I told them that is what I would prefer in case it might throw any light as to the possible cause of his disease, but I don't think that will happen as he'd been ill for so long and died in hospital. As soon as they say yes or not, it's just a question of getting a date, discussing the service and telling our friends and family. I'm also putting a notice in the *Herald*.'

'I understand you did have a visit from the police this morning,' said Latymer.

'For what it was worth. A nice enough young man with all the routine stuff about opportunist thieves, though he admitted it was unusual that the burglar had gone for the filing cabinet, rather than the TV, video or computer. I told him it had happened once before and that perhaps he should look it up on the files.' She turned to Latymer. 'I don't think he really took it in that someone had impersonated me in order to get you

281

out here and then attacked you. It hardly squares with the theory of a passing thief.'

Latymer agreed. 'I gave Chief Inspector Crozier my side of the story in Dumfries this morning. You never know your luck – they may actually put two and two together and make four.'

'What do you make of all this, Mr Berry?' enquired Fiona. 'Do you think we're all mad?'

He smiled. 'I think something's gone very wrong indeed but it's like fighting your way through fog. You keep thinking you've come across something solid, then it melts away in front of your eyes. You won't have seen today's papers, but there's a story in the *Independent* on drugs in the fishing industry, directly linking the Solway ports with Cornwall. Personally I'm sure there's a very strong drugs connection but agree with John that there seems to be something else behind almost everything that's happened. But whether it has to do with a cover-up of pollution, I simply don't know.'

'This must all seem irrelevant to you anyway,' added Latymer. 'Your whole world must be upside down.'

'I'm sort of numb at the moment. It'll all hit me later on when the funeral's over and that's it. Except that it *must not* be "it". I owe it to James that the fight goes on. I mustn't give up. I'm sure if it was you, your wife would feel the same.' I wouldn't bet on it, thought Latymer. She came over and put her hand on Latymer's arm. 'Please will you help me? Surely between us we can find out if James was right in what he suspected? That the depleted uranium and radioactive particles in the sea and air round here are causing people to become ill and that the Ministry of Defence is well aware of it. James spoke of you right towards the end. "Tell him it's an appalling scandal and that they'll go to any lengths to stop the truth getting out. But it must. They must be fearful of what might happen if it did, first the Solway shells, and the possibility that they then might finally have to deal with the pollution from Sellafield." '

She paused. 'I've given you most of the stuff he wanted you to have but could you possibly have a quick look at what's left and see if there's anything that might be useful? I know you must have to go back home but if you find anything of interest you can take it with you and post the information on the website.'

'I'll see what I can do but I can't promise anything. I'm soon going to be caught up again in my spring and summer job and we really do have to go back tomorrow. Keith has his business to run and I ... well, I have other problems that need to be dealt with.' Then he remembered something. 'There is one thing. Were you able to ask James if Armstrong had met up with his mysterious contact back in August? There's no note of it in the stuff you've already given me, but such information could be crucial. I've been through it all again and again but there's nothing there. I suppose it just might be among the papers you've given me now.'

'You see, if he did leave a note of any kind it might be possible to try and track down who it was,' added Berry, 'that is, if the meet was genuine. If he was being set up, then that's something else entirely. It could even have led directly to his death.'

'I did intend to ask James, but then he was in so much distress I simply couldn't bring myself to do it. Then I quite simply forgot. If there was such a meeting, then all I can say is that James never told me about it. He drove me to exasperation. He knew he had all my support for everything he did, was prepared to help him to the best of my ability, but he also had old-fashioned notions that it would be better I didn't know absolutely everything in case I was put at risk. Though surely, if Euan had come up with something really important James would have found a better way of safeguarding it than simply putting it into a file?

'Proving James was right won't bring him back.' Her voice shook. 'But it would greatly comfort me. You only met him when he was so very sick. He'd been such a vital, energetic man. He climbed, swam, sailed, had never been ill before in his life. He was reduced to the wreck you saw simply because he was a soldier and served his country in a war which finally turned out to have done so little. Saddam Hussein is still in Iraq, entrenched stronger than ever. We "saved Kuwait for democracy", what democracy? And nearly five hundred of our own people have died of a disease our government denies exists.' Her eyes filled with tears again. 'I wish you weren't going back. At least, not yet.'

'I really can't stay,' he told her, gently. 'Once we've seen the police again tomorrow we must be off.'

'So there's nothing much more you can do?'

'I can't see how at present. But if I change my mind, I'll let you know.'

'As I said, I'll keep the website going for a while. You never know. You might find you can't let it rest.'

Latymer felt there was little left to say. 'I'm sorry I won't be here for the funeral. Your husband was a very courageous man.'

'It'll be very simple. There's a place called the Mote of Mark near Rockcliffe, some kind of ancient fortification. James loved it up there. It's a steep climb with a wonderful view. I feel that's where he should be, so I intend sprinkling his ashes on the very top once the weather makes it possible.'

Douglas didn't see the *Independent* piece until lunchtime, when he went over to the pub for a drink. 'See you're starring in the papers,' commented the landlord as he pulled a pint of light. 'There's a copy on the end of the bar if you haven't seen it. Jimmy from over the road brought it in for me.'

He took the paper over to a corner and opened it on the relevant page. He'd spoken to the freelance only with reluctance, assuming that he was after a story for one of the local papers. In fact he was almost sure the reporter had told him so. Instead of which he found himself splashed across the pages of a national daily. He read through the piece twice. He was not slow to realize the implication of a direct link being made between Newlyn and the Solway: not only that, but that the inference he was it.

He'd never believed in trusting to luck. He relied on careful planning and organization, the utmost discretion, providing a reliable service, keeping a healthy distance between himself and those for whom he acted and never taking any unnecessary risks. Until last August. Which is why he had at first refused to have anything to do with the man who'd appeared on the quay that night when he was checking his boat ready for

286

going to sea in the morning. It was well after midnight and he was about to go back home and snatch a few hours sleep when the dark figure loomed up in front of him. At first he assumed it to be one of the crew on some last minute business, but when the man leaned over and looked down into the boat he realized it was a stranger.

'Your name Douglas?' the visitor called down, softly.

He was immediately suspicious. He'd managed matters so well that he'd rarely been sought out in person either by addicts or petty dealers, but he couldn't imagine who else would be looking for him at such an hour. 'Why? What's it to you?'

Without waiting for a reply, the man jumped down on to the deck. 'I've got to talk to you. Out of sight.'

Douglas felt round for something he might use as a weapon should the necessity arise, and picked up a hefty spanner he'd been using earlier. 'Go into the cabin then and this'd better be good. I want some sleep.' He went to put the light on but his visitor stopped him.

'Leave it dark.' Then he came straight to the point. He had something which needed to be disposed of. Now.

Douglas heard him out with incredulity. 'You're either mad or think I came down with the last shower of rain. If you're telling the truth, which I doubt, do you seriously expect me to take such a risk?' He tightened his grip around the spanner. 'Piss off out of my boat.' The man made no effort to move. It was as if Douglas hadn't uttered. 'I want you to take it out to sea and get rid of it a long way from here.'

From his visitor's confidence and air of authority, Douglas assumed he must be one of the 'big men', the shadowy figures, who ran the operation with which he had long been connected. He certainly hadn't come across him before but this was hardly surprising. The agreement on both sides had always been that direct contact be kept to a minimum. But he felt he should at least be offered some proof that he was dealing with the right people.

'Who are you?' he demanded. 'Who else is in on this? And why me?'

'Never mind who I am. Just believe me when I tell you that unless you do as I say – exactly as I say – I'll provide absolute proof of your activities to the police, and if you refuse, or discuss what's passed between us in any way, you won't live to see court let alone serve your sentence. And don't think that because of your death other heads will roll. They won't. Right then. I'm going for some assistance, I'll be back within the hour.'

The following week had been the worst of

Douglas's life, culminating in his ending up in hospital following the fight in Cornwall. He was on edge for days after he'd got back home, waiting for some reaction from his employers, but it never came. At least local publicity about the fight had been minimal. A month later, having been given his usual instructions, he'd undertaken a successful run with a temporary crew member in McKinley's place. He'd been well paid for it and no reference had been made by any of his contacts to the night visitor and his appalling request. It seemed to be all over.

But some time later, rumours began to circulate that a dead man found floating off Newlyn harbour was identical in appearance to an Annan fisherman, Euan Armstrong, who had been missing since the middle of August. This had shaken him somewhat until it turned out that the body had been that of a man from London who'd been identified by a relation. He wondered what the Londoner had been doing up in Scotland, then decided he was glad he didn't know. The man who died and whose body he'd been asked to dispose of could have been murdered for a number of reasons. He might have been a grass or a member of another drugs outfit with whom his own was involved in some kind of turf war.

But the rumours persisted. Nosy people

started asking questions, locals dropped loaded hints. Some kind of ex-cop arrived playing at detectives. And Andy McKinley was found dead of a drug overdose. He knew, better than anyone, that Andy had never taken drugs. Finally Kevin Tyler had turned up on his doorstep and it came home to him just how much he'd put himself at risk by using him to assist with the disposal, even though at the time he'd no other option. To be fair, Kevin had behaved himself right up until he'd come knocking on the door desperate for help, pleading for heroin on credit and hinting at what he might do if he didn't get it.

After which, of course, he had to go, and without waiting for any authority from above or consulting anyone else, Douglas had made the necessary arrangements. He trusted his employers would realize why it had been necessary, even commend him for dealing with the matter so swiftly and efficiently. That is, if they ever enquired into it.

He swallowed down his drink and left the pub without a word and let himself into his house, his mind in turmoil. He'd naturally assumed there might be some brief local interest once Kevin's body had been identified but, after all, it was only the death of yet another addict and it had taken place sufficiently far from home. He reckoned he could handle any subsequent enquiries. But this blaze of publicity ... The 'big men' wouldn't like that. They wouldn't like it at all. Then the telephone rang.

Latymer had a brief look through the rest of the papers that afternoon, but there was little of interest. But putting all Garleston's careful research together, it was beginning to look as if he'd painstakingly pieced together sufficient information to make out a case for an independent inquiry into the possibility that the thousands of depleted uranium shells lying in the silt did pose a real hazard to health. 'At least a case sufficiently convincing to prove an embarrassment to the Ministry of Defence,' he commented to Berry, wearily.

'Among the files is one of letters here from him to MPs. Some of the replies do show interest, but hardly great concern and, as we know, Garleston was racing against time. He'd also gathered a good deal of material from international sources. There's a report from an official at some outfit called the Military Toxic Project in the States alleging that communities living around similar US sites show verifiable increased cancer rates. It concludes by saying that the proper health studies needed have never been done. Nor here. That was what Garleston was getting Armstrong to do, try and track down every case of cancer and leukaemia he possibly could, either personally or via the website, since he was told no official statistics were available. Because the relevant authorities continue to assert that there's no hazard and that such cases were of no statistical significance. But how can they square that if there aren't any statistics?'

He stood up and stretched. 'It's hopeless. We can't possibly do any more. I'll take the stuff back with me as I promised but I can't see what more I can do.'

'So you will *definitely* be home tomorrow?' Latymer had rung Tess as soon as he and Berry had returned to the hotel. 'What time?'

'I really can't say. The weather's pretty bad again and it'll be no joke driving down. I'll keep you posted on the way.'

'You're quite sure about coming back?' she persisted. Then she paused. 'If you let me down again, John, it really will be all over. I've thought about it a lot since we last spoke and I can't stand any more of this.'

As they set off next morning to see Crozier before heading for home, Latymer felt just about as low as he could remember. His frenetic involvement in the events of the last months had ended, so far as he could see, in almost complete failure. Worse, he had involved others, not least Keith who now sat beside him happily looking forward to seeing his wife and picking up the threads of his business again. 'Don't be so down,' he'd said the previous evening over dinner. 'We never could win them all even when we had every kind of back-up and nothing else to do.' Again he envied Keith his marriage. And he thought of Fiona Garleston and Jean Armstrong. They had little in common in background, education or lifestyle but they shared a single-minded determination to see justice done.

Fiona Garleston. He'd been shaken by the attraction he felt for her, something quite different from that he'd ever felt for Tess. No, he mustn't even begin to consider the possibility that his marriage to Tess had been a mistake.

Crozier saw them at once and this time was more forthcoming. 'I still doubt I can convince my colleagues here that it was Armstrong who was fished out of the sea in Cornwall, but at least they're coming round to the possibility that a body might have been hidden in the ice on Douglas's boat. So I got back to the Cornish police to see what they thought of the notion.'

'And what did they think of it?' enquired Berry.

'Not a lot. Surely I wasn't going to dig up the story yet again. It had been gone into at exhaustive length and the case was closed.

So I tried a different tack and said that might well be the case, but suppose it had been this other man, Graham Bentley, whose body had been hidden in the ice? What then? But I was assured there was no point in any further speculation because the man had died of natural causes. My query as to the possibility of asking the pathologist to consider the possibility that the body had been frozen fell on deaf ears. However, I had two minor successes. I finally persuaded my opposite number to ask the pathologist if he recalled any mark or scar on the back of one of the hands. I also asked for the name, telephone number and employer of the person who identified the body.

'They were pretty reluctant but in the end they gave it to me.' Crozier paused. 'You're right, Berry. I rang up this "David Bentley". The first number, the answerphone or whatever it was, had been discontinued. The response of the outfit in Brussels was the same as it was to you. There was no one of that name at that number and there never had been.' He fiddled with the papers in front of him and turned to Latymer. 'Obviously I've thought of the possibility you and I have considered but I mean it when I say I do everything possible to avoid meddling with spooks. Even if it was the case, I'm not sure it's all that relevant. This has to be about drugs.' Latymer said nothing.

'Presumably Tyler's death gives you more scope now for getting to Douglas and hopefully those higher up the chain,' commented Berry. 'If he is in it up to his neck, he must be worried about what his bosses might do after they've seen the stuff in the papers. Will they leave him alone for a while until it all calms down? Or shop him with an anonymous tip-off? He must even wonder if they might dispose of him too, like they did McKinley and Tyler.'

'McKinley possibly,' said Crozier. 'Even I'm now beginning to think his death was too much of a coincidence and convenience. But not necessarily Tyler. It's an all too common story, an addict being beaten up, even killed, because he owed his dealer money. Douglas's alibi checks out, of course. On the evening of Tyler's death he took his wife out for a meal in Dumfries, he's a credit card receipt to prove it, then went home and had a last drink on his own in the local pub. That checks out too. His wife could be lying about what happened next but the neighbours say both his car and the old pickup he uses for gear were outside the house all night. No one in Kirkcudbright recalls seeing Tyler out on the relevant evening. His mother thought he was in bed, she didn't realize he wasn't there until the morning. But she wasn't too worried. She assumed he'd been drinking with a mate and crashed out somewhere else.'

'So what next?'

Crozier shrugged. 'It's up to my superiors. They finally sent men up to Douglas's house yesterday and turned his house over anyway. Personally I thought it a waste of time but it seems they felt they should be seen to be doing something after all the publicity. There was nothing, of course. Either there or on his boat. Until he makes a major mistake, he may well continue to get away with it. His home phone's tapped but he probably realizes that and anyway it's pretty pointless now with mobiles. For all we know he's got half a dozen, all pay as you go and all with different names. His poor wife was in a state, I don't think she's any real idea of what's going on.'

'He wasn't there himself then?'

'Apparently he took a call from some fish processors who wanted to see him. It checked out OK, except for the fact that the constable who rang them was told they'd already had a call from the police about Douglas earlier on. Whoever it was, it wasn't anyone from here but then one hand doesn't seem to know what the other's doing these days. It could be us, the Drug Squad or even Customs and Excise.' He stood up. 'So that's everything up to date.' The interview was obviously at an end. 'I'm grateful to you both for your help.'

He moved towards the door. 'Are you really going to be satisfied with spending the rest of your life taking coachloads of tourists around the countryside, Latymer? I can't imagine it. Though I can see the attractions of Berry's bookshop.'

'I don't know. I have to do something, retirement doesn't suit me.'

They shook hands as the phone rang. 'Hang on a minute,' said Crozier. 'I'll just take this then see you to your car. Yes?' he said, into the receiver. 'Well, put him through.' He motioned to them both to stay where they were. 'You did? I see. He does? Well, that is interesting. He's sure of that? Look, I'll get a couple of copies of statements faxed to you so you can see for yourselves. No, I'm not sure either, but it raises interesting possibilities, you must admit. Many thanks. I'll be in touch.' He carefully replaced the receiver on its cradle.

'That was a call from the police in Cornwall. When asked, the pathologist did recall noticing a mark or scar on the back of the dead man's hand. It hadn't seemed relevant since it was obviously an old one. Something else he'd noticed at the time, too, but which he only mentioned after the inquest, was that from the state of the hands he would have guessed that the man had been used to a fair amount of hard, physical work which is strange if Graham Bentley came from such an obviously upmarket family. But as it turned out he'd no settled employment, he might well have done manual work from time to time to help make ends meet. So it doesn't prove anything. But, yes, there was a scar.' He turned back to his desk. 'I need to make a few more calls. Do you think you could hang on a bit longer?'

Sixteen

In fact Douglas received two phone calls on the morning the story appeared in the press. The first was both chilling and mystifying. He had a vague feeling he'd heard the voice before but couldn't recall where. The message, however, was clear and concise: that he had broken his side of the bargain. Dialling 1471, unsurprisingly, proved fruitless. His mouth felt dry. When the phone rang again almost immediately, he hesitated for a while before picking it up but as the ringing went on and on he finally did so, merely answering, 'Hello.'

'Where were you? On the lav?'

Douglas felt a sense of relief as he recognized the familiar tones of his one regular contacts with the big men. 'Did someone else your end just try to get me? A minute or two ago?'

'Not that I know of. Why?'

'There was a call. Probably someone trying to be funny. So what it is you're after?' The caller told him. Anyone listening in on the call would merely have heard an employee of a firm in Ayr discussing fish stocks and prices and suggesting a meeting at the end of the morning along the coast at Girvan, roughly halfway between Ayr and Gatehouse, to discuss future requirements in more detail than was practicable over the phone. A police trace on the caller did indeed prove it came from a well-known fish processing plant. An enquiry to the manager of the firm brought a response to the effect that any one of a number of people could have made it, since there was regular contact between the firm and skippers of a variety of vessels, beamers, trawlers and scallopers among them.

'What is this?' the manager demanded, 'don't you people talk to each other or something? I took a call a couple of hours ago from the police asking if we had dealings with Harry Douglas.' The constable detailed to make the call mumbled an apology and rang off.

Aware now that he might be under some kind of surveillance, Douglas constantly checked his mirror to see if he was being followed as he drove over to Girvan. But after a while he relaxed. It was impossible for a car to pursue him along that particular road without his noticing, as there was so little traffic in either direction. He drove into the town, made a point of very obviously parking his car in the car park of a hotel as was usual when such a meeting took place, went in through the front door and bought a drink at the bar, downed it quickly, visited the gents and left discreetly by a back entrance. There was no one about. He then walked down to the place specified for the meeting, again ensuring there was no one behind him. The rain of the morning had turned to sleet and a cold wind blew in from the Irish Sea.

His caller, who he knew only as 'Eddie', was waiting for him. Without saying a word, Eddie turned and led the way into a small, dingy pub nearby. There were no other customers and the landlord was reading the racing page to the accompaniment of pounding music from two loudspeakers. 'Everything's bloody well off because of the bloody weather, it'll have to be the dogs,' he commented in the way of a greeting. Eddie motioned Douglas into a seat at the back of the room and bought two drinks, which he brought over and placed on the shabby table. The landlord was once again engrossed in his newspaper, his foot tapping to the monotonous beat of the tape.

Eddie put down the drinks and came straight to the point. 'What the hell do you think you've been doing freelancing? I take it you are responsible for that lad's death in Carlisle.'

Douglas agreed that to be the case. 'What

was the alternative? He'd become a liability to the whole operation. He'd begun threatening me. I couldn't guarantee he'd keep his mouth shut any longer. What else was I to do?'

'Why did you employ him if you knew he was an addict?'

'It didn't affect his work, so long as he got his supplies, and it gave me a hold over him, which I'd put to good use. I couldn't risk waiting for you to clear it. There was no time to lose and someone had to make a decision. But there's nothing to link me with it. Nothing at all.'

'But you've got your name in the papers, man!'

'Only because I was Tyler's skipper. There's nothing anyone can prove about the other stuff. Yes, of course I'd rather it hadn't happened. But it'll soon pass. You know what the papers are like these days. Everyone goes mad on something for a week, ten days later it's just fish and chip wrappers.'

'You'd better be right,' grunted Eddie. 'But if you ever do anything like that again or act on your own without clearing it with us first, man, you're finished! My orders are to make sure you're under no illusion about that. The only reason you aren't out now is because you've done well for us over the years. But everyone's expendable, including you. Got that?'

'So what do you want me to do now?'

'Absolutely nothing at this end for some time. For the immediate future the operation will concentrate on the West Country: Plymouth, Brixham and Cornwall. It's where the money is at the moment anyway, they can't get enough of the stuff and the authorities are overstretched.' He paused. 'Do you think you're being watched?'

Douglas shrugged as if the possibility was unlikely. 'I suppose I might be. As could any of us. But no one followed me here today, of that I'm sure. I'd have known on that road.'

Eddie nodded. 'How soon can you put to sea again?'

'Just as soon as the weather improves. The forecast shows a definite improvement. Give me two days. But I'm short of crew and I'm having trouble locally – after Andy McKinley, then Tyler. Now the man who replaced Andy McKinley isn't too sure he'll sign on again. Says I'm unlucky.' He began to feel on firmer ground. 'It's bloody rich you blaming me for Tyler's death, telling me I'm putting the operation at risk. What about Andy? That had to be down to you. We all know he didn't do drugs.'

Eddie looked completely mystified. 'Who's Andy?'

'The guy who'd crewed for me for years up until last summer. The one you lot shot full of a fatal dose of heroin just before

Christmas.'

Eddie stared. 'No,' he said, 'we did no such thing. I've never even heard of the man. We've no interest in your crew, or who works for you, that's your business – or was until Tyler's death – so long as they don't ask questions. That raises something else. What was all that in the paper about a fight in Newlyn? It didn't register at first since you weren't even doing a job for us at the time. It's one of the ports we want you to go to next time.'

Douglas stared at him. 'For Christ's sake, *now* what are you playing at? Or don't they tell you anything? The fight with McKinley was over the fact that he'd just discovered I'd a dead man in the ice in the boat. The dead man you people made me take to sea and ordered me to dispose of. I wasn't told who he was and I didn't want to know.'

Eddie looked at him with open incredulity. 'Have you completely lost your marbles?'

'Don't mess about with me,' returned Douglas. 'Your hard man threatened me with God knows what if I didn't obey your orders to the letter, so I did what I was told. He delivered the body, I took it out with me buried under the ice. But things didn't go to plan.' He stopped. 'But you must know all this. And that the weather turned too bad to risk putting him overboard as all the crew had to be up on deck and would've have

304

known about it. I was only finally able to get rid of it because McKinley was kept in hospital. I sent the third crew member down below and told him to stay there until he was wanted – then, when I was sure he was asleep, I took the boat out into the Bay and dumped the body overboard. Tyler helped me, you see, because I knew I'd a hold over him. Rob, the other crew member, did surface when he heard the splash but easily accepted it when I told him we'd run into some old gear floating out in the bay and I'd had to stop and disentangle us.

'But as for Andy, so far as I know he never said a word about it afterwards. He was far too scared. And it must have been quite something to arrange for someone to turn up in Cornwall and identify the body as that of a London tourist. But don't try and kid me it wasn't you who wanted rid of Andy.'

Eddie stood up. 'Is this some kind of a joke? If it is, I'm not laughing.' He finished his drink. 'D'you think my mother knitted me or something?' He hustled Douglas out into the street then lunged at him, grabbing the lapels of his jacket. 'I don't know what your game is, but we gave you no such orders. No one came asking you to dispose of a body. It had nothing to do with us.'

Douglas wrenched himself free. He felt as if he was staring into an abyss. 'So who did?' he managed, at last. Then, 'Where does this leave me?'

Finally Eddie calmed down and at least appeared to believe him. 'It looks like you were stitched up by some other set-up. Why did you never say anything to us?'

'Because I was sure it *was* you. So what was there to say? I did as I was asked, admittedly not as well as it might have been done. Since nothing was ever said about it, I assumed you were reasonably satisfied and I put it behind me.'

Eddie regarded him. 'I must report back. We'll have to put the word out to find out just who did do it. Sounds like someone wanting to get back at us. In the meantime you'd best go to sea as planned. In case you are being watched, make your movements really obvious. So put in to Newlyn, then do the same in Looe or Plymouth. If you are being watched, those doing it will be wasting their time. But this is your last chance. God, I'm getting soaked. I'm off. Remember, do exactly as you've been told.' He pulled up his collar and trudged off into the rain.

Before leaving Girvan, Douglas had a drink in the hotel, from where he rang round possible contacts in an attempt to find two more crew members. An hour later, he'd managed to find only one, a young man who had recently come off the boats and was living with his family in

Ardrossan, but who agreed to make the trip on condition he was given a higher percentage share of the profit than was usually the case. But that still left him one short.

He arrived home, bad tempered and tired, to be greeted as he pulled up at his gate by an excited neighbour telling him that the police had been at his house almost ever since he'd left. He found his wife in tears, his home looking as if a bomb had hit it. Drawers had been pulled out and their contents tipped on to the floor, shelves cleared, mattresses and bedding stripped off beds, carpets, even floorboards, taken up.

'Oh Harry,' his wife wept, 'they said they were looking for drugs. They kept on and on about it. I told them there were no drugs here and that boy Tyler's death had nothing to do with you. And that it isn't your fault if one of your crew takes drugs. But they wouldn't listen.'

Douglas regarded his wrecked home. 'I suppose I'd better go over and see if they searched the boat as well. Not that they'd find anything there either.'

His wife gave him a searching look. 'For God's sake, Harry, will you tell me what it is you've got yourself into? I've never asked, never pestered you, partly because I haven't wanted to know. But if you really are in deep trouble, then surely I should be told?'

'What is there to tell? I make us as good a

living from the fishing as is possible in these hard times.'

'But there's more to it, isn't there?' she persisted. 'You know what people were saying about Andy's death. And now Kevin. Next thing we have the police here. What must the neighbours think?'

For a moment he considered finally taking her into his confidence, but his deep-seated conviction that women were incapable of holding their tongues, even a woman as loyal as his wife, was too strong. 'I've no time to listen to gossip,' he told her. 'As well as going down to see if the boat's still OK, I'm still one crew short. There's a guy coming down from Ardrossan but that still only makes three.'

His wife brightened up at that. 'Oh, I'd forgotten with all this,' she said, looking around at the mess. 'A young fellow rang this morning to say he'd heard you needed crew. I wrote his name and phone number down. It's as well I put it in my handbag or I'd never have found it again. Here you are. He didn't sound as if he came from round here, he sounded English.'

The name Bob Taylor meant nothing, but the number was local. He called it and Taylor answered the phone himself. He'd never been part of a regular crew, he told Douglas, going to sea only as and when it suited him, and only hitherto from West

Country ports, mainly Plymouth. But he'd been visiting friends in Scotland and was short of cash. Asked how he'd learned he needed a man, Taylor replied that he'd been over in Kirkcudbright with a mate from Dumfries and mentioned that he was looking for a berth. 'Someone said you were a couple of men short and gave me your number.'

'Can you leave the day after tomorrow?' asked Douglas. 'That is, if the weather's OK.'

'Sure thing. What time?'

'Around midday. My boat's the *Lady of Annan*. I'll meet you at eleven tomorrow morning in the Dornoch Arms and fill you in.'

He put down the receiver. At least he'd sorted something. He briefly considered informing Eddie as to what had happened, then decided against it. It could only lead to more grief – the less his employers knew at present the better. As he drove around to Kirkcudbright, he was so deep in thought that he nearly hit a tractor on a tight bend. He'd been as shocked as Eddie to discover last summer's night visitor had not been part of 'the firm'. If that really was true, then who the hell was he? Eddie must be right. The only possible explanation was that his visitor was from a rival outfit. It would be quite a scam to get a skipper attached to one organization to do the dirty work of another, a real coup in fact. If that proved to be the case, there was going to be trouble. Almost certainly violence. He was only too pleased to be going back to sea. He was best off out of it.

He wasn't too worried about the police raid. They had absolutely no proof of anything and he'd never risked keeping anything in the house. But it was time he considered retirement. He was getting too old for all this. He'd made a good extra living out of the business, much of it carefully salted away in nice clean equity bonds under another name. The rest was in a handy bank account in the Isle of Man and his house was paid for. It was definitely time to give up. He'd do this one trip as promised, since there could be no possible risk as he wouldn't be doing anything in the least dodgy. That was the whole point of the trip. Then he'd finally pack it in. He yawned. It had been a very long day.

Crozier had excused himself briefly after taking the call from Penzance police, leaving Latymer and Berry in his office. 'I simply can't hang about here long,' said Latymer. 'It's Sod's Law, of course. Something turns up just as we have to go home.'

Berry looked at his watch. 'It's still only half ten. If we did stay a bit longer you'd still be back home by tonight since we're sharing the driving.'

Crozier returned almost at once. 'Seems we've had a tip-off. Douglas's going back to sea tomorrow morning. Not one of our usual contacts, but he told us everything in great detail. I'm beginning to believe Douglas's own lot will be happer if he's safely locked up or he's found himself in the middle of a bust-up between two rival outfits. We could take a chance and bring him in, I suppose, but I honestly think it a waste of time. There's no harm in going down to see him again to give him the idea we really are on to something.' He turned to Latymer. 'You were actually there, you've followed this story right from the start. Can you spare the time to come with me? Berry, too, of course.'

I've no option, thought Latymer. 'I suppose so, having got this far. But there's no way we can stay on longer than this morning.'

A call to Douglas's home elicited the information that Douglas was down on the boat preparing to go to sea the next day. When they arrived, he was standing on the quay talking to a young man who was carrying a large canvas bag. Douglas saw them coming and turned to him. 'I'll stow that for you, Rob. Go back and wait for me in the pub. This won't take long.' The young man did as he was told, looking curiously at the visitors as he left.

'Can you tell me what the hell this is about?' demanded Douglas as soon as he was out of earshot. 'First you have the nerve to search my house while I'm away, and my boat, now you're down here hassling me again. What is it this time?'

'With regard to the search, we were reliably informed that there were Class A drugs on your premises,' lied Crozier, blandly. 'Therefore we acted on the information.'

'And found nothing.'

'And found nothing,' Crozier agreed.

'So what now? Unlike you, I don't sit around while a fat salary's paid into my bank account every month. I have to go out on my own and earn my living the hard way. Harder than anything you can imagine. I've already lost days and days through bad weather and one way or another I intend leaving tomorrow. If you want to stop me, you'll have to lock me up.' He looked past Crozier at Latymer and Berry. 'And what the hell are they doing here?' He turned to Berry. 'Thinking of knocking up a few crime books in your spare time? Oh no, I forgot, you're up here book buying.'

'Both Mr Latymer and Mr Berry are ex-police and have been helping us with our enquiries,' Crozier informed him. 'Mr Latymer was a witness to your fight in Newlyn last summer and has been pursuing an investigation of his own.'

'Newlyn?' Douglas spat into the water. 'There were never any charges. Now, if you don't mind, I'll get on.'

'Did you know that a body was found off Newlyn shortly after you left?' continued Crozier.

For a moment Douglas froze, then relaxed. 'I heard something about it. What's that to me?'

'You tell me. Before he died, your crew member – Andy McKinley, the other half of the fight in Newlyn – told his girlfriend he'd seen a body in the ice in your boat. And that was the reason for the fight. And that it was the body they later found floating outside the harbour.'

Douglas shook his head in exasperation. 'Then Andy was out of his skull on drugs. He must have been. I told the guy from the newspaper that I didn't know Andy ever did drugs, but if he was going round saying that sort of thing then I was wrong. And he did die of an overdose.'

'McKinley told his fiancée the body was that of Euan Armstrong.'

This time Douglas laughed out loud. 'You're away in a dream! *Euan Armstrong* ... isn't he the guy whose wife's been kicking up a fuss after he dumped her back in the

313

summer? I hardly knew the man, he didn't come over here very often. Jeannie Armstrong was born here, though I can't remember when I last saw her.' He turned to Latymer. 'D'you fancy Jeannie then? Is that why you keep chasing up here?' He turned to Crozier. 'Police ever track him down? I thought not. You're pathetic, the lot of you. So Andy tells Sally there was a man hidden in the ice in the boat. She then tells Jeannie Armstrong – who's mad as hell because her husband's left her and gone missing – that it was him. If you really think there's any truth in this crazy tale, why haven't you gone down to Cornwall or wherever and dug this fellow up to take a look?'

'The body was cremated,' said Latymer. 'And identified as someone else. But the pathologist says there was a scar on one of the hands exactly like one Armstrong had.'

Douglas obviously felt he was on safe ground. 'But no one can prove that now, can they? You can't stand Andy in a witness box because he's dead. And who's going to believe a story told to a young woman by a boyfriend on heroin? Give me one good reason why I should want to kill Euan Armstrong. I had no dealings with him.'

'Possibly because he knew something he shouldn't,' said Crozier.

'You don't give up, do you?'

'Not until I get the result I want.'

'Well, don't hold your breath. For your information, I've decided this will be my last trip. After I've sold my catch I'm going to come back here, sell my annual quota for as much as I can get for it, then apply to decommission the boat. And retire. I fancy a place in the sun somewhere.'

'So that's that,' said Latymer as they walked back to the cars. 'We weren't much help, were we? But I'll go to my grave believing it was Armstrong they cremated, and in an odd way to some extent I believe Douglas. Armstrong posed no direct threat either to him or his operation. It makes far more sense that he was got rid of to stop him getting any further with the work he was doing for Garleston. After all, Garleston himself would soon be no threat.'

'You can't expect me to go along with all that,' responded Crozier.

'Do you believe Douglas when he says he's going to give up the fishing?' enquired Berry.

'Why not?' responded Crozier. 'It must be getting too hot even for him. If he stops everything now, he might well get away with it. He's right. We've absolutely no real proof.'

'We sympathize,' said Berry, 'we really do. We've both been in your position. But why

315

are hard drugs so rife among young fishermen in particular?'

'It used to be booze,' said Crozier. 'They'd
drink themselves to a standstill as soon as
they were paid off. It was a way of finding
release. Think about it. Most people in work
set off every morning and it never even
crosses their mind they might be dead
before going-home time. With us, well, it's
slightly different, there's always a chance we
might not make it if something comes up
and circumstances go against us, but it's
hardly an everyday occurrence even in the
Force. But these boys never ever know.
Every time they put to sea, often these
days in something little better than a rust
bucket, they know it could be for the last
time. It's happened to their mates, they've
seen their friends' wives become widows,
young women with families left without a
partner. When you have to live with that,
telling you doing drugs will kill you means
nothing at all!'

Seventeen

'Cheer up,' said Berry as he drove them down towards the Border.

Latymer looked out across the bleak countryside. 'What am I supposed to be cheerful about? I've wasted months of my time and a good bit of yours to little purpose. Even if the police now believe Douglas had a body in the boat and that it was Armstrong, Douglas is right. They can't possibly prove it. The drugs business will go on, with or without him, Garleston's dead and the likelihood of any action being taken as a result of his research is just about nil. Jean Armstrong's got nowhere, there's not even any way she can convince anyone that she's a widow.'

'Well, we couldn't win them all even when we were in a far better position to do so,' commented Berry. 'And I don't think it's been a waste of time. In fact it's given me a taste for it all again. No, not going back to the police, but the investigative side. Who knows? We might have a crack at something else one day.'

Latymer gave a derisory laugh. 'I doubt that very much. I'm not at all sure what I'm going home to as it is.' He lent forward and pressed the button on the tape recorder. The car was filled with the sound of the tape Jean Armstrong had given him and Fiona Garleston had liked so much. He'd played about half of it, then wound it back to listen again to the song she'd said made her feel life could get better.

'What the hell's that?' demanded Berry. 'I didn't know you went in for mad Scottish dance music?'

'It's called *Delirium*.'

'I'm not surprised.'

'And it's not really dance music. Give it a chance. You'll find it grows on you.'

That same morning in a room in an anonymous motel not far from Carlisle, 'David Bentley' was waiting with growing impatience for his expected visitor. When he finally arrived, Bentley asked Reception to send him up straightaway and when the knock came on the door he opened it, motioning his visitor in without a greeting. 'You took your time.'

The man shrugged. 'You didn't give us much notice and we do actually have other things to do.' He looked at the opened bottle of whisky on a side table and added, 'I could do with a drink.'

318

'Help yourself then. They didn't give me a name.'

'Maxwell. Peter Maxwell. I take it you're Bentley.'

'It'll do.'

Maxwell sat down on one of the two chairs in the room. 'Now, perhaps you'd be so good as to tell me what all this is about and why it couldn't have been discussed over the phone.'

'I'd have thought that was obvious even to you.' Bentley went over to the table and poured himself a drink. 'You saw the stuff in the *Independent*. What a cock-up!'

'Hang on a minute,' countered Maxwell. 'What are you saying? Surely you can't believe the death of the druggy in Carlisle was anything to do with us? It's not us who cocked things up, we could have handled the whole thing ourselves far better back in August. And before we go any further, I'll tell you now that I personally wouldn't have gone to anything like such lengths to shut Armstrong up. There were other ways of getting him off our backs. Planting drugs on him and a subsequent prison sentence come immediately to mind. But oh no, you had to send one of your own goons up here to organize his removal, "assisted" by us. But as it turned out, our man was given no option but to do as he was told.'

'We sent up one of our best and most

experienced freelances and his orders were to do whatever was necessary. Garleston wasn't going to be a problem for much longer. But Armstrong was roaming round putting all kinds of stuff up on the net from cyber cafés. There was no other way of stopping him.'

Maxwell banged down his drink. 'I'm not convinced. But if we're to take it you really believed the only option was to kill Armstrong, why the hell did your man go to such elaborate lengths to get rid of the body? Our guy couldn't work it out. All he need have done was throw him in the Solway when the tide was going out.'

'He did what he did because he thought that if the body was washed up close to home a lot of people would start asking questions. Not least Garleston.'

'If he had been disposed of up here, and we'd been fully informed as to what was going on, our man could have come forward and "confessed" how he and Armstrong had been drinking hard all day – the landlord of the last pub they went in would have supported him on that. How Armstrong had been determined to walk along the beach on his own to clear his head, when there was a stiff onshore breeze and the tide was coming in, even though he was pissed out of his mind and behaving like an idiot because his wife had left him. End of story.'

Bentley was derisive. 'And you believe everyone would have accepted that? It's amateur night.'

'Instead of which,' continued Maxwell, ignoring the interruption, 'your man came up with the fatuous notion of persuading Douglas to take the body away and dump it out at sea.'

'There was nothing fatuous about it. Had he done exactly as he was told and the body gone over the side somewhere in the middle of the Irish Sea, there is every likelihood that it never would have been found and everyone would simply believe Armstrong had gone off with another woman. Most people still think that anyway.'

'But Douglas didn't dump him out at sea, did he? It all went wrong and what did he do? Tip him into the water just outside a busy harbour. Not only that, it turned out one of the crew realized something funny was going on and threatened to blow the whole lot. Started a fight in fact which got into the paper. It was a crazy risk to take. And all the time we were kept completely in the dark. I understand you had to go down there yourself to "identify" the body.'

'Which I did to everyone's satisfaction. It's known as damage limitation. The body was cremated as Graham Bentley. And there's no way anything can ever be proved to the contrary. As to McKinley, the other man

321

involved in the fight, that was seen to after we'd been warned there might be a problem. We'd kept a contact up there afterwards and although McKinley seems to have kept quiet about everything our man told us he'd been seen in local pubs looking rough and drinking heavily. Shortly afterwards we were informed that an ex-cop turned investigator, John Latymer, had turned up asking questions – he'd actually been in Newlyn at the same time as Douglas and McKinley. It could be that McKinley had learned of Latymer's interest and was proposing to tell him his suspicions. In the state he was in, it's quite possible. We simply couldn't take the risk.'

'And again you acted without telling us. Tell me something else, what made your man pick on Douglas for the job?'

'Because we had it on good authority that he's up to his neck in running drugs. And that gave us a lever. It would've been safe enough if he'd simply followed orders.' He paused. 'I take it you're aware of his activities? Or is that something else going on under your nose you don't know about.'

'Of course we know! So do the regular police. And Customs and Excise, and Uncle Tom Cobleigh and all, no doubt. Customs and the Drug Squad have been leaving him be, hoping he'd lead them to bigger fish. Then some hack writes yet another series on drugs, more or less fingers Douglas, and another idiot, this time in police headquarters in Dumfries, sends the plods in to search his house thus more or less confirming the story and drawing attention to the whole thing yet again.'

Bentley leaned back in his chair. 'I don't like your attitude, Maxwell.'

'And I don't like yours,' countered Maxwell, now really angry. 'I don't have to take this from you. I'm not one of your substandard freelances. If you've come all this way and dragged me down to see you merely to trade insults, then I'm going. I've no more time to waste.' He got up as if to make for the door.

'As to this man, Latymer,' commented Bentley as if Maxwell had never spoken. 'Poking around asking questions. How about him? You're not very clever when you try and do things yourselves, are you? Sending off some thicko to saw through his brake pipes ... well, I ask you! All it succeeding in doing was convincing him he really was on to something.'

'We had to do something once the MoD police, the Mod Plod, had found him wandering around close to the firing ranges. I was told they'd informed you.' Maxwell looked at Bentley and shook his head in disbelief. 'You've no one but yourselves to blame for this spate of publicity. What could have been managed quietly and discreetly locally and never gone any further is now completely out of hand. You've managed to involve half the police forces both sides of the Border, Customs and Excise, the Mod Plod, us, a couple of retired cops and two hysterical women. I've been waiting for questions in the Edinburgh Parliament.'

Bentley sighed. 'All right, all right, calm down. I admit it could have been handled better. Which is why I wanted to discuss with you what to do about Douglas. If he is ever brought in for running drugs, not to mention murder if the police could somehow convince the CPS he was involved in Tyler's death, he could make lots of trouble and even more questions would be asked. He must go.'

Maxwell looked doubtful. 'You may consider us little better than peasants up here but my view is that unless this whole business is allowed to die a natural death – that means no more intervention – it will eventually occur to anyone with a handful of wits that some cover-up's been going on. If absolutely nothing more is done, then there's every chance that any remaining anxiety over nuclear pollution from the Solway will have died with Garleston. But no doubt you think you know best. So what had you in mind?'

Bentley told him.

'I still don't like it. And if it goes wrong, don't expect any sympathy from us. All this has done nothing to promote a better relationship between our respective organizations. Now, if your expenses will run to it, could we have some coffee before I go?'

'Is there much more of this?' enquired Berry after about ten minutes of the *Delirium* tape. As they crossed the Border into Cumbria it had started to snow again.

Latymer laughed. 'I'm not sure. I've never played it to the end.' He lent forward and switched it off. 'I take it you don't like it?'

'Dead right. Haven't you got anything else? I never move without a dozen or so tapes.' He stared ahead into the snow. 'Look, there's a services coming up in a mile. Shall we stop for something to eat?'

'Why not, we're making good time. I could do with some soup and a sandwich, then we can press on.'

'And they're bound to have some cheap tapes. I'll buy a couple.' He turned to his companion. 'You've got that thoughtful look again.'

'I think I've finally worked out what might have happened. I'll tell you after we've had something to eat.'

Douglas met Bob Taylor in the pub in Kirkcudbright as planned. He turned out to be a pleasant, soft-spoken young Englishman. Douglas reckoned his age as about twenty-five. He explained to the skipper that he had only ever fished part time, but had usually been able to get work when he wanted it as he was good with engines.

I must be having some good luck at last, thought Douglas. 'You are?' he commented. 'Then perhaps you'd check over a couple of things for me. I'd rather we left later than I'd planned, than run into trouble after we've put out.'

'No problem,' responded Taylor. 'I'll be only too happy to have a look.' Douglas explained his concerns as they walked down to the quay together shortly afterwards. 'I know it really needs some work doing,' he told Taylor, 'but you know how it is. Either there isn't the time or, if there is, then there isn't the money.' When they reached the boat, Taylor lowered himself down to where the engine was housed while Douglas waited on deck for young Rob and the other new crew member.

'There's one or two things I'd like to adjust,' Taylor called out a little later. 'I reckon it'll only take me an hour. Can you afford to wait that long?'

'Do whatever you think necessary,' Douglas told him. 'We can wait.'

A little over an hour later they were moving down the Solway towards the open sea.

'You're right, you really could do with a complete overhaul of that engine,' Taylor told Douglas. 'It's well past its sell-by date.'

Douglas nodded. 'I'm only too well aware of that. But all I want for now is to keep it going. I'm thinking of packing all this in very shortly. Hopefully it will see me out.'

'Not enough profit any more?' queried Taylor.

'You could say that.'

'So,' said Berry as they joined the M6 once again, 'let's have it.'

'I do now believe that Armstrong was disposed of because he got too near to disclosing that the depleted uranium in the Solway was a genuine health risk. News of what he was doing might even have gone as far as the government and could have proved very embarrassing. There was a good bit of publicity at the time about Gulf War Syndrome and depleted uranium shells in Kosovo and the Gulf.'

'Are you seriously suggesting this was state murder? Surely not!'

'I don't think anyone in government specifically ordered MI5 or whoever to get rid of Armstrong. It would've been more a remark on the lines of "Who will rid me of this meddlesome priest?" Do you remember the Hilda Murrell murder?'

'The old rose grower who was murdered

327

before she gave evidence at that nuclear power station inquiry? They never did solve it, did they, and there were lots of conspiracy theories at the time. What did you think?'

'I don't know. What I do know is that it turned out later that a whole host of dodgy people were carrying out surveillance on the protestors for the security services, starting with a private agency which was a class act (staffed by ex-MI5 and Special Branch people), through to a fellow running an agency who took on more than he could cope with, right down to a convicted paedophile running a Nazi memorabilia shop. It could have been anyone from any of the agencies who actually cocked it up and killed her, then the professionals moved in for the cover-up. I believe this could have been something similar. A freelance was given the job to avoid any direct link and he got it wrong.'

'You're never ever going to convince anyone of that,' responded Berry.

'No, I'm not, am I?'

In the end they made good time and even after stopping again for a short break and dropping Berry back in Bristol, Latymer reached home just before eleven. There were no lights on in the front of the house, so he let himself in as quietly as possible in case Tess had gone to bed early. He was appalled to find he rather hoped she had and that they wouldn't need to talk much until the morning. But as soon as he came in through the door, she appeared from out of the kitchen which was at the back of the house.

'So you actually got here,' she said, flatly.

'I told you I'd come back as soon as I could.'

He waited for her to ask him what he had been doing, how it had all gone. Instead she merely enquired if he wanted anything to eat or drink. He replied that he'd eaten at a motorway services on his way back, but that he'd like a mug of tea. 'And a large Scotch.' She made no reply but went back into the kitchen and plugged in the kettle as he went into the sitting room and poured himself a drink. He sat in silence as the kettle boiled. She made the tea, then brought him a cup.

'Don't you want to know what's happened?' he asked her.

'I'm not sure that I do,' she said. 'But anyway, no doubt it can wait until tomorrow.'

He felt bleak. So many fences to mend and in no time he'd be back working again. He closed his eyes for a moment and as a result saw the long ribbon of the motorway again coming towards him. Would the remains of Armstrong's memo to himself on the tape have made any difference to the outcome? A track from *Delirium* kept running through his head in an endless loop. He'd wanted to convince Tess why it had been so important to him, that you can't retire from injustice – now he wondered if it was worth the effort. He thought of Fiona Garleston, what she had gone through and must still be going through.

'Are you coming to bed?' There was no hint of a warm invitation in Tess's voice.

He swallowed his whisky, drank down his tea and followed her upstairs. He got into bed but she made no move towards him. He turned on his side, and went out like a light.

Three days later, at approximately four thirty in the morning, Falmouth Coastguard scrambled rescue helicopter R 193 from RNAS Culdrose following a Mayday from the fishing vessel *Lady of Annan*. She was, they learned, some forty miles off Land's End and taking in water following some kind of minor explosion in the engine room. Every effort was being made to keep the boat afloat. The skipper and one of the crew members were down below trying to discover what had happened while the other two men manned the pumps. By the time the helicopter reached the stricken vessel the crew were already taking to the life raft. Of the skipper, Harry Douglas, there was no sign. Later, Bob Taylor, who had been below with him, was to tell the subsequent inquiry that he had been certain the skipper was following behind him when he scrambled out on to the deck and they had launched the life raft. 'The last thing he said was for us to get off while we could.'

A last ditch attempt by the winchman from the rescue helicopter, lowered on to the steeply sloping deck, had failed to find the skipper. 'He must somehow have been trapped below,' the winchman told the local paper. 'We might have been able to save him had we got there sooner, but we got there as fast as we could. A couple of minutes after I was lifted off, the boat simply rolled over on her side and sank. We can only assume her skipper went down with her.'

At this point a local fishing vessel had arrived on the scene, having also heard the Mayday. Its crew rescued the men from the life raft and, after waving off the helicopter, took the surviving fisherman into Newlyn to the Seamen's Mission. Falmouth coastguard praised the rescue services and expressed relief that the weather that morning had been reasonably calm, with good visibility and light winds, as otherwise there might well have been more fatalities. A local reporter, visiting the Mission where the 'shattered crew' were recovering from their ordeal, asked them what happened. All three agreed that they'd heard what sounded like a small, muffled explosion from the engine and that the skipper had at once gone down to investigate.

Bob Taylor (aged 25), who had only joined the crew of the vessel a few days earlier, told our reporter that following the explosion he had at once followed skipper Harry Douglas, down below 'since he'd asked me to check out the engine before we left port. I warned him then that I thought it was in pretty poor shape, but he said he reckoned it would be OK, at least for this trip.' It is understood that Douglas, from Gatehouse of Fleet, Dumfries and Galloway, leaves a widow and a grown-up daughter.

The name had rung a bell with the reporter and he'd checked through the files to discover that Douglas had been involved in a fight at the Newlyn Fish Festival the previous August. But on mentioning the fact to his editor, he was told there was no point in dredging the matter up. Douglas's family would have enough to contend with. The editor did, however, take the opportunity of writing a short editorial to the effect that there were too many such mishaps at sea these days. In this case there had only been one fatality, but that was one too many. It was impossible at this stage to hazard a guess as to what had gone wrong, but there was no doubt that in the present economic climate, the temptation in the fishing industry to cut corners and hope for the best was all too prevalent.

After being checked over by the port doctor and having a good night's rest, the three survivors went off to the railway station to make their way home. Rob Campbell and Jamie Duncan took the Glasgow train, Bob Taylor that to London. 'I think I'll spend a few days with my sister,' he told them. 'I feel like Jonah. It was my first trip for such a long time and look what happened!' His train was nearly empty and there was no one else sitting anywhere near him as it left Penzance. He took out his mobile phone and dialled directly through to his boss. 'Just to let you know, it's all been taken care of,' he said. Then settled down with a paperback.

Eighteen

Crozier received the news of the sinking of
Lady of Annan with furious incredulity. 'I
don't believe I'm hearing this,' he raged at
his colleagues. 'At last we were actually getting somewhere. Customs and Excise were
to watch him every step of the way when in
port. And he was planning to make this his
last trip. What the hell happened?'

'They could hardly have prevented his
boat from sinking,' remonstrated a sergeant.
'It seems there was some fault with the
engine. It was just bad luck.'

Crozier shook his head. 'I don't think so.
And how come everyone else gets off safely
except him? Get me Customs and Excise.'

The official at Customs and Excise was
equally mystified. 'We were working on a
joint operation with the Drugs Squad down
there. There was also a possibility of sending
in a fishery protection vessel if it looked as if
he'd made a pick-up en route.'

'Surely it can't be coincidence?'

'A turf war, I'd say,' the official responded.
'Some other outfit wanted rid of him.' He

paused. 'Unless, of course, he'd become too much of a liability to his own lot. The stuff in the papers can't have helped. It's a bastard! It's thrown the whole operation out of sync.'

Crozier replaced the receiver. Whoever organized the sinking of *Lady of Annan* knew exactly what they were about. And why didn't Douglas escape like the rest? According to what he'd been told, the other man who was down below with him said that once the two of them had realized nothing more could be done, Douglas told him to abandon ship and he'd thought Douglas was right behind him. But if so, Douglas would have had time to join the others on the life raft. It was interesting that two of the crew were new both to Douglas and the area. Could one or other of them have been working for a rival drugs firm and somehow sabotaged the boat?

It would be useful if Douglas's body was found. Signs of violence would offer an explanation as to why he'd gone down with his ship, but the Cornish authorities reckoned it extremely unlikely that it would be washed ashore. The vessel had gone down at a point where several tides meet and the currents are strong. Added to which, the tides, which were at springs in both the Channel and the Atlantic, were outgoing at the time. But even if, by some faint chance, the body was washed up somewhere it was unlikely it would have much to tell once the congers and other sea scavengers had got at it.

The headline in one Scottish daily said it all: 'Crew of Three Saved but Skipper Drowns'. The Secretary of the Seamen's Mission in Newlyn, it reported, had immediately got in touch with the relevant authorities in Scotland before the names of the survivors and the missing skipper were released to the press. A second paper headed its story, 'Yet Another Fishing Tragedy'.

A policeman, accompanied by a local minister, had gone round to break the news to Mrs Douglas before she learned of it in the media. 'I can't take it in,' she told them. 'This was to have been his last trip. The night before he sailed he told me he was planning to give up the fishing.' Her eyes filled with tears. 'What am I going to do? Harry's always seen to everything. Dealt with the bank, paid the bills ... and I didn't have to work, he's always wanted me to stay home and keep house.'

Gentle questioning elicited the information that there was a married daughter in Dundee and the minister immediately called her to explain what had happened. 'Your daughter says she'll be here as soon as possible,' he told the widow. 'In the meantime I'll stay with you a wee while. Then perhaps one of your neighbours could come in until she gets here.'

'What about the body?' she asked. 'Is there any chance he might be found?'

'I've been told to tell you that it's very unlikely,' replied the policeman. 'I know how hurtful that must be.'

She shook her head. 'I can't understand it. What could have been wrong with the boat? And why did the rest of the crew escape but not Harry? Was he injured? Did they just leave him to drown?'

'We simply don't know,' said the policeman. 'There'll be an inquiry. Perhaps that'll tell us something.'

He left the minister with her then phoned Crozier. 'She was obviously pretty shaken up,' he told him. 'I find it hard to believe she knew what was really going on. I didn't feel able to press it in the circumstances.'

There would, of course, be an inquiry into the sinking, but although there was little now to be gained, Crozier made a few enquiries of his own. The remaining member of Douglas's original crew, nineteen-year-old Robert, was as helpful as possible but had little or nothing to add. Everything had seemed OK when they set out, he said, though one of the two new crew members – the Englishman – had checked out the engine before they set off and had told Douglas it needed an overhaul. But both he and Douglas had considered it up to the trip. Everything had gone according to plan and the weather quite good. They'd spent two or three days fishing and were making for Newlyn to sell their catch in the local fish market before going out again. The crew had been up on deck and Douglas at the wheel in the wheelhouse when they'd heard a muffled bang.

'Not very loud, not like a real explosion. Then she started to lose way. Harry and Bob Taylor went straight down below and the next thing we knew *Lady* was taking in water, loads of water, and they couldn't get the pumps to work properly. Harry shouted out for me to radio a Mayday to Falmouth coastguards, which I did. But it got worse and worse until she was fairly wallowing in the sea.

'Harry told us to launch the life raft and prepare to abandon ship, and Jamie and I got it out and over the side. Then Bob came running up to join us, saying Harry was behind him, just as the helicopter arrived. But there was no sign of Harry. The winchman went down on to the deck but he couldn't stay to find out why as *Lady* was about to go. They got him back up in the nick of time. A couple of minutes later she rolled over and sank. They would have taken us up in the chopper too but then a Newlyn beamer arrived. She stayed around for a while to see if there was any sign of Harry but there was nothing. I can only think he must've got trapped down below somehow. That's all I can tell you.' Nothing, he declared, would now induce him to return to fishing. 'First Andy dies, then Kevin. Now Harry and we've lost the whole bloody boat. Someone, somewhere, is trying to tell me something. I've had enough.'

Jamie Duncan, safe back home in Ardrossan, was equally puzzled as to what had happened. A sudden engine failure might have been sufficient for them to have lost all power and start to drift, but not actually *sink*. Like Robert, he'd expected Harry to jump down into the life raft behind Bob Taylor. 'Bob never said he'd been injured or anything. It's a mystery.'

It was not the only one. All Crozier's efforts to discover the whereabouts of Bob Taylor met with failure. There was no reply from the local telephone number he had given Douglas's wife, and no one seemed to have heard of him or come across him before. It was, as he told Latymer over the telephone, as if he'd never existed.

'It certainly looks as if someone was determined this was to be Douglas's last voyage,' Latymer agreed. 'And in the circumstances, I imagine there'd be no shortage of takers.'

'Dead right,' said Crozier. 'It has to be the drugs connection. Who else would have the resources to organize it so tidly?' There was a long silence on the other end of the phone. Crozier took the point. 'No,' he declared. 'That's a road I'm just not prepared to go down.'

Easter was fast approaching and with it Latymer's first literary tour, for which he felt little enthusiasm. He'd recently had a letter from Jean Armstrong. 'So Harry got away with it in the end,' she'd written. 'I reckon we'll now never know what really happened.' But life was moving on. She had finished her IT course and was now in the early stages of a relationship with her ex-tutor. She was young, bright and attractive and he sincerely hoped something would come of it. Yes, he was pleased for Jean Armstrong; that she'd moved on sufficiently to start again. But as for his own relationship, something real and vital had gone out of it, something he was beginning to believe could never be recovered. Tess spent a good deal of time either visiting her daughter, who was experiencing a sickly pregnancy, or making long telephone calls to her. She was planning a series of visits to coincide with his trips away. Possibly, he thought, it might have brought them together more if the coming baby had been a mutual grandchild.

Appearances were kept up. They went shopping together, out for meals and spent time in the village pub. Tess asked for his help in the garden when she needed it and they discussed a possible holiday later in the year. But between them lay the apparently unbridgeable chasm of his recent activities, 'his crazy obsession' as Tess described it. He had given her a brief account of what had happened the day after he returned, but she'd made little comment and when he tried to raise the matter again, told him she didn't want to discuss it any further. Coming into the hall one day when she was on the phone to her daughter, he heard her saying how relieved she was that the literary tours were soon to start again. 'At least it's kept him busy. I'll never know what got into him and I don't want to!'

In Vauxhall, 'David Bentley' finally closed the file on the problem that had arisen with regard to the possible effects on public health of the depleted uranium shells in the bottom of the Solway Firth. Coincidentally, there had been another flurry of interest in the subject of depleted uranium and the use of such shells in conflict in the weeks immediately preceding Douglas's death, interest which had nothing to do with Garleston or Scotland as it concerned the aftermath of war in the Gulf and Kosovo. But bigger stories soon swept it out of the media. The fact that relations between his own organization and Special Branch in Scotland were at an all time low worried him very little. The removal of Douglas had finally ended the business. It had been noted that the 'fisherking' website was still in existence but most of the material now on it was increasingly to do with general environmental issues. There was little that was new. He made a note that it be checked from time to time, however, just in case, but with the death of Garleston there was no longer any driving force. He felt sufficiently satisfied therefore to take out to lunch one of his best operatives, a young man who showed great initiative, along with his personal assistant who had played the role of 'Mrs Bentley' at Armstrong's cremation.

Latymer had indeed been busy but not with preparation for the summer tours. Back home and with more time to think, he had gone through all Garleston's files again as well as the material stored on the computer discs. He was certain now that no note or report remained of Armstrong's fateful meeting, but finally seen as a whole the amount of material he and Garleston had amassed between them provided chilling reading. Latymer had found the information and statistics on radiation and pollution hard to grasp and so took the data along to an expert acquaintance who lectured in such subjects at Bristol University and who kindly put it into more accessible tables for him along with relevant explanations understandable to the layman. 'You know you might really be on to something there,' he'd said. So Latymer wrote to Fiona Garleston asking her to give him a contact number where he might safely talk to her in the event that her telephone was tapped.

She rang him a couple of days later from the home of a friend in Cumbria. 'She's married to a parson, so I'm assuming it's safe enough,' she told him, with a laugh.

He was delighted to hear her voice. 'I've gone through it really carefully and no, I can't prove anything beyond all shadow of doubt, but with help I've knocked it into some kind of shape. The weird stuff about lobsters and shrimps and so forth now makes sense and my friend has also sorted out the local information your husband and Armstrong collated on cancers and leukaemia and so on, set them out in tables regarding age, type, spread, etc and compared them with the national average. There's a definite discrepancy. I'm sorry it took so long, but I had to have expert help.'

'You're a star,' she responded, 'a real star. How can I ever thank you?'

'Don't get too excited,' he warned. 'I imagine there's a long way to go before you can really get anywhere, but on the basis of all this it might be possible to find a friendly SMP or MP prepared to raise the matter in Edinburgh or London.' He would, he told her, be sending her the information by post, recorded delivery, from Berry's bookshop. 'He'll put it in with a couple of books just in case anyone's inquisitive. I simply haven't got the time to put it on the website myself.'

She thanked him again. 'I'll put it all on as soon as I get it. It might prompt others to add to it. For the first time since James's death, I feel positive and alive again. It's the best memorial he could have. Oh, and I've come to a decision. Not only am I going to keep the website going, I'm opening it out to other similar issues like GM crops, pesticide pollution and so on.' There was a short silence then she added, 'Is there any chance of seeing you again soon, John? I'd like that.'

'So would I,' he replied, 'very much. I'll see what I can do.'

In the early hours of the morning the day before leaving for his first tour, Latymer woke, his mind racing. He and Tess had made love the evening before, an occurrence now sufficiently rare for him to hope it might presage better things, but in the event he felt that at root it had done nothing to improve their relationship. In front of him stretched the wretched literary tours. He wondered how he could ever have thought them sufficiently interesting to take on. He tried not to think of what Berry had said about acquiring a taste for investigation again. It was tempting, too tempting. Carefully, so as not to disturb Tess, he got out of bed and went into his study.

Such a string of deaths. Euan Armstrong, eager to make his mark as a journalist, longing for a scoop, murdered by some less than obvious means, then taken hundreds of miles from home before being cremated as somebody else. Andy McKinley, an ordinary decent young fellow, shortly to be married, who'd seen something he shouldn't and chillingly paid the price for it. As had the misfit, Kevin Tyler. Which brought him to Douglas himself. Latymer had little doubt as to the sort of people who had seen off Douglas, though he could only hazard a guess at which branch of the security services had been involved. Nor would he ever know whether 'Bob Taylor' had been one of their own or a freelance.

So that was that. He looked at his watch. He should go back to bed, but he'd rarely felt more wakeful. He made himself a cup of tea, put the *Delirium* tape on the recorder at the point he'd switched it off in the car, turned it down low and logged on to the fisherking website. He felt a glow of satisfaction as he saw that Fiona had put all his information on to it.

He was so absorbed that it was some time before he realized the taped music had come to an end and he could hear a man's voice. Startled, he turned round but there was nobody there. It had come from the tape. He wound it back a little and switched the machine on again.

The man's voice was Scots and he was obviously in the middle of a sentence. '...so if he's not bullshitting it sounds as if it's even worse than we thought. Got no hard facts or proof to give me this time but we've arranged to meet again on Saturday, this time in a pub in Castle Douglas, and he'll have some notes of secret tests made on the silt, along with unpublished health statistics. He also says he might well bring a colleague along who can tell me more. Am putting this memo on tape to remind myself exactly what he did say. Will leave telling Garleston until I've got the rest, he's been fussing round like an old woman. Might well contact papers first via internet then tell him after. Why not? I need the break and the money.' There was a pause, then Armstrong added, 'Date August 20.'

Latymer played it again. It was clear what had happened. Jean had told him the tape had been recorded from a CD 'to use in the car'. She'd obviously come across the tape after Armstrong's disappearance, a tape which looked new and had no label on either side and simply re-used one side of it and so had recorded the music over Armstrong's memo to himself. Given the chaotic state of Jean's flat it was hardly surprising that it had happened. Presumably she'd never played it all the way through since she had the CD of it and her car, she'd told him, was off the road. He wondered what else might have been on it and lost, but it proved beyond a shadow of doubt that Armstrong had met up with his supposed expert contact and arranged to do so again. He'd thought he was being given confidential information by a sympathizer instead of which he was naively telling his enemies exactly what he knew. He'd walked straight into a trap.

He would ring Berry first thing in the morning. After only a brief pause for thought, he returned to the website, logged on and began to write.

Those of you who regularly log on to this site will know of the death of James Garleston, the brave man who set it up and who was convinced that he, and others like him, had contracted their illnesses through their service in the Gulf War. The whole purpose of this site originally was to collate as much information as possible on the subject of contamination caused by the use of depleted uranium shells during that conflict. It was then he discovered that depleted uranium was not just a hazard in the Middle East, and later in Kosovo, but could be a matter of concern closer to home, due to the existence of the thousands of shells containing the same substance which lie at the bottom of the Solway Firth. The tables already posted on the site have been compiled using his data.

But what you have not been told previously is that it's likely this knowledge has led to the deaths of a number of other people, not least that of fisherman-turned-journalist Euan Armstrong. On James Garleston's instructions he was researching into both the amount of pollution in the Solway and the number of known cases of different kinds of leukaemia and other cancers in the surrounding area. It is now known that Armstrong met a contact he thought was from the MoD base on the 20 August 2000 who gave him some information and promised to bring further proof to a second meeting in the town of Castle Douglas several days later. It would seem that Armstrong kept the appointment and then went on, with the contact and another man, to Kirkcudbright. After which he was never seen alive again.

Some days later, the body of a man answering his description, a 'dead ringer' for him in fact, was found off the Cornish coast – and identified and cremated under another name. If anyone knows anything that might be useful concerning this matter, please leave the information on the website.'

He smiled, then added the pseudonym 'Kinmont Willie'.

He was reading the paragraphs through again, just to check them, when he realized that it was rapidly getting light. He yawned and rubbed his eyes. He became aware suddenly that he was no longer alone and turned to find Tess staring over his shoulder at the computer screen, a look of bleak disbelief on her face.